OTTO PENZLER PRESENTS
AMERICAN MYSTERY CLASSICS

THE EIGHT OF SWORDS

JOHN DICKSON CARR (1906-1977) was one of the greatest writers of the American Golden Age mystery, and the only American author to be included in England's legendary Detection Club during his lifetime. Though he was born and died in the United States, Carr began his writing career while living in England, where he remained for nearly twenty years. Under his own name and various pseudonyms, he wrote more than seventy novels and numerous short stories, and is best known today for his locked-room mysteries.

DOUGLAS G. GREENE is an American historian, editor, and author. Until 2017, he was the co-owner and editor of mystery publisher Crippen & Landru. His biography of John Dickson Carr, titled *The Man Who Explained Miracles*, was nominated for the Edgar Award.

T0017988

THE EIGHT OF SWORDS

JOHN DICKSON CARR

Introduction by
DOUGLAS G. GREENE

AMERICAN MYSTERY CLASSICS

Penzler Publishers
New York

Published in 2021 by Penzler Publishers
58 Warren Street, New York, NY 10007
penzlerpublishers.com

Distributed by W. W. Norton

Cover image: Andy Ross
Cover design: Mauricio Diaz

Paperback ISBN 978-1-61316-256-9
Hardcover ISBN 978-1-61316-257-6

Library of Congress Control Number: 2021916281

Printed in the United States of America

9 8 7 6 5 4 3 2 1

THE EIGHT
OF SWORDS

INTRODUCTION

> Each new development seemed to lead the case in
> a different direction, and each opened up like a
> magician's casket to show only another box inside
> the last.

Thus John Dickson Carr described his plotting in *The Eight
of Swords*, and in other novels. He saw the detective novel as "the
Grandest Game in the World"; it was a challenge between writer
and reader, in which the writer attempted to mislead the reader
and surprise him or her at the conclusion. Each time the reader
thought the mystery had been revealed, Carr would introduce
more complexities.

When *The Eight of Swords* was written, Carr and his wife
Clarice had recently moved to England. He had been born in
Uniontown, Pennsylvania, in 1906, and the insular nature of
that coal-mining community made him long for what he called
"Adventure of the Grand Manner." He read swashbuckling
historical novels by Alexandre Dumas and adventure fiction by
Robert Louis Stevenson and, above all, detective stories by A.

Conan Doyle and G. K. Chesterton and the almost forgotten Thomas W. Hanshew.

As a lad in high school, he wrote historical romances and sensational detective stories, and continued in preparatory school and at Haverford College. He spent time in France in 1927, ostensibly to study at the Sorbonne, "this being," he said, "probably the only thing in Paris I did not do." On his return, he wrote for *The Haverfordian* a novella called *Grand Guignol*, featuring Monsieur Henri Bencolin of the French police. He later enlarged and revised the story into a full-length detective novel entitled *It Walks by Night*.

In 1930, Carr moved to Columbia Heights in Brooklyn, and when he wasn't writing more detective novels spent his time concocting bathtub gin during the final, raucous days of prohibition. With the earnings from his writing, he took ocean voyages, on one of which he met a pretty young woman from Wales named Clarice Cleaves. The shipboard romance resulted in marriage in 1932 and a move to England early in 1933, where the Carrs would live until the end of the decade.

After writing three more novels featuring Henri Bencolin (two set in France and one in London), Carr invented new detectives, Sir Henry Merrivale, who would feature in novels published as by "Carter Dickson," and Dr. Gideon Fell, published under Carr's own name.

In the first Fell novel, *Hag's Nook*, Fell is described as a "lexicographer," though he never does any dictionary making. He is in fact a historian, author of *The Drinking Customs of England from the Earliest Times*, and he is a connoisseur of English beer— he objects to the word "ale."

Fell is modeled on Carr's literary idol, G. K. Chesterton. Not only his huge shambling appearance but also his speech patterns are drawn from Chesterton. Like Chesterton's great Father Brown, Fell speaks in paradoxes. "Everything is right," says a Chief Constable. "Yes," Fell replies; "that's what makes it wrong, you see." He solves mysteries not by physical evidence or police procedure but by what he calls "wool-gathering." Fell has immense curiosity about all sorts of unusual things. In his first case, *Hag's Nook*, he lectures about cryptograms, and the novel features an ancient family curse repeated in the present.

The early Dr. Fell novels are filled with anglophilic warmth:

> There is something spectral (Carr wrote in *Hag's Nook*) about the deep and drowsy beauty of the English countryside, in the lush dark green grass, the evergreens, the great church spire and the meandering white road . . . . A feeling that the earth is old and enchanted . . . . The bells at twilight seem to be bells across the centuries; there is a great stillness through which ghosts step, and Robin Hood has not strayed from it even yet.

Dr. Fell's first cases feature incongruous events—the second Fell novel, *The Mad Hatter Mystery*, begins with the mystery of a joker who steals hats of prominent citizens and places them in ridiculous places—a cab-horse or a lamp-post or atop Nelson's statue in Trafalgar Square. And his third case, *The Eight of Swords*, begins with the report of a Bishop sliding down a bannister.

Dorothy L. Sayers gave *The Mad Hatter Mystery* what Carr later called "a whopping, magnificent review" in London's *Sunday Times*:

> [Carr shows] extravagances in character and plot, and the sensitiveness to symbolism, to historical association, to the shapes and colours of material things, to the crazy terror of the incongruous. Mr. Carr can lead us away from the small, artificial, brightly-lit stage of the ordinary detective plot into the menace of outer darkness. He can create atmosphere with an adjective, and make a picture from a wet iron railing, a dusty table, a gas-lamp blurred by the fog. He can alarm with an illusion or delight with a rollicking absurdity . . . . In short, he can write—not merely in the negative sense of observing the rules of syntax, but in the sense that every sentence gives a thrill of positive pleasure.

Carr told an interviewer that Sayers' review meant that he was "established overnight."

Which leads us to *The Eight of Swords*, the book that followed immediately after *The Mad Hatter Mystery*. John and Clarice with their new daughter Julia had moved to a small community outside Bristol, and the extravaganza which is *The Eight of Swords* reflects his joy of a new marriage and of living in England—though in a more comic way than in *Hag's Nook*. The focal character, Hugh Donovan, is a Carr stand-in. Like Carr when he lived in Paris, Hugh had been sent overseas to study, which he neglected to do. Like Carr when he lived in Columbia Heights, Hugh knew how to measure out the ingredients of home-made gin. Carr even makes fun of his romantic idealization of England. Hugh imagines himself "leaning on his ash stick in the twilight . . . looking with sad eyes at the brook, and musing on the villainy of those who drink alcohol-and-water in the cities, and then come out and seduce poor girls all over the countryside."

But as he muses, he comes upon Henry Morgan, who is another stand-in for Carr. Morgan writes Carrian detective novels, and he agrees with Carr in disliking mystery stories that try to be realistic. Morgan immediately invites Hugh for a drink. Back in the United States, Prohibition was still in effect and Carr was pleased that in England he could imbibe freely. And in *The Eight of Swords*, most of the characters do just that.

Newly married, Carr thought he understood how women should treat their men. Patricia Standish is based on Carr's new wife Clarice Cleaves Carr. At this point in his life, Carr believed that the main role of a loyal wife was to gaze fondly and admiringly at her husband. Clarice may have played that role early on but, as time progressed, she became the strength of the marriage.

But within all this, Carr created a crafty mystery, and I am not revealing too much in challenging readers to open the magician's book, think about the tarot card (Eight of Swords), and to come to the solution before Dr. Fell.

—DOUGLAS G. GREENE

THE EIGHT
OF SWORDS

CHAPTER I

Extraordinary Behavior of a Bishop

CHIEF INSPECTOR Hadley had been almost cheerful when he reached his office that morning. For one thing, the diabolical August heat wave had broken last night. After two weeks of brass skies and streets that shimmered crookedly before the eye, rain had come down in a deluge. He had been in the middle of composing his memoirs, a painful labor, at his home in East Croydon; fuming, and guiltily afraid that some of it must sound like braggadocio. The rain restored him somewhat, and also his sense of values. He could reflect that the new police reform bothered him not at all. In a month he would retire for good. Figuratively, he could take off his collar—only figuratively, for he was not the sort of person who takes off collars; besides, Mrs. Hadley had social ambitions—and in a month more the manuscript should be in the hands of Standish & Burke.

So the rain cooled him, while he noted in his methodical way that it began at eleven o'clock, and went more comfortably to bed. Though the following morning was warm, it was not too warm; and he reached Scotland Yard in at least the open frame of mind of the Briton willing to give things a sporting chance, if they don't make too much of it.

When he saw what was on his desk, he swore in astonishment. Then, after he had got the assistant commissioner on the phone, he was still more heated.

"I know it isn't a job for the Yard, Hadley," said that dignitary. "But I hoped you could suggest something; I don't quite know what to make of it myself. Standish has been appealing to me—"

"But what I want to know, sir," said the chief inspector, "is what *is* the business, anyway? There are some notes on my desk about a bishop and a 'poltergeist,' whatever that is—"

There was a grunt from the other end of the telephone.

"I don't know myself exactly what it's about," admitted the assistant commissioner. "Except that it concerns the Bishop of Mappleham. Quite a big pot, I understand. He's been taking a vacation at Colonel Standish's place in Gloucestershire; overworked himself, they tell me, in a strenuous anti-crime campaign or something of the sort . . ."

"Well, sir?"

"Well, Standish has grave doubts about him. He says he caught the bishop sliding down the banisters."

"Sliding down the banisters?"

There was a faint chuckle. The other said musingly: "I should like to have seen that performance. Standish is firmly convinced he's—um—off his rocker, so to speak. This was only the day after the poltergeist had got busy—"

"Would you mind telling me the facts from the beginning, sir?" suggested Hadley, wiping his forehead and giving the telephone a vindictive glare. "It hardly seems to concern us if a clergyman goes mad and slides down the banisters in Gloucestershire."

"I'll let the bishop speak for himself, later on. He's coming to see you this morning, you know. . . . Briefly, what I understand is this. At The Grange—that's Standish's country place—they have a room which is supposed to be haunted off and on by a poltergeist. Poltergeist: German for 'racketting spirit'; I got that out of the encyclopedia. It's the sort of ghost that throws china about, and makes the chairs dance, and what not. D'you follow me?"

"O Lord!" said Hadley. "Yes, sir."

"The poltergeist hadn't been active for a number of years. Well, it happened the night before last that the Reverend Primley, the vicar of a parish somewhere nearby, had been dining at the Grange—"

"Another clergyman? Yes, sir. Go on."

"—and he missed the last bus home. It was Standish's chauffeur's night off, so they put up the vicar at The Grange. They'd forgotten all about the poltergeist, and he was accidentally accommodated in the haunted room. Then, about one o'clock in the morning, the ghost got busy. It knocked a couple of pictures off the wall, and made the poker walk about, and I don't know what all. Finally, while the vicar was praying away for dear life, a bottle of ink came sailing off the table and biffed him in the eye.

"At this the vicar set up a howl that alarmed the whole household. Standish came charging in with a gun, and the rest of them after him. It was red ink, so at first they thought murder had been done. Then, at the height of the hullabaloo, they looked out of the window, and there they saw him standing on the flat leads of the roof in his nightshirt—"

"Saw *who?*"

"The bishop. In his nightshirt," explained the assistant commissioner. "They could see him in the moonlight."

"Yes, sir," said Hadley obediently. "What was he doing there?"

"Why, he said that he had seen a crook in the geranium beds."

Hadley sat back and studied the telephone. The Hon. George Bellchester had never been precisely the person he would have chosen as assistant commissioner of the metropolitan police; though an able official, he took his duties with some lightness, and above all he had an exceedingly muddy way of recounting facts. Hadley cleared his throat and waited.

"Are you by any chance pulling my leg, sir?" he inquired.

"Eh? Good God, no!—Listen. I may have mentioned that the Bishop of Mappleham claimed to have made an exhaustive study of crime and criminals, though I can't say I ever encountered him in his investigations. I believe he wrote a book about it. Anyhow he swore he had seen this man walking past the geranium beds. He said the man was heading down the hill in the direction of the Guest House, which is occupied by a studious old coot named Depping. . . ."

"What man?"

"This crook. I haven't heard his name mentioned, but the bishop says he is a well-known criminal. He—the bishop—had been awakened by a noise, which was probably the racket in the poltergeist's room, *he* says. He went to the window, and there was the man on the lawn. He turned his head, and the bishop says he could see him clearly in the moonlight. The bishop climbed out of the window on to the roof—"

"Why?"

"I don't know," said Bellchester, rather testily. "He did it, anyway. The crook ran away. But the bishop is convinced that a dangerous criminal is lurking about The Grange for the purpose of mischief. He seems to be rather a formidable person, Hadley. He insisted on Standish's telephoning me and our doing something about it. Standish, on the other hand, is pretty well convinced that the bishop has gone potty. Especially, you see, when the bishop assaulted one of the housemaids—"

"*What?*" shouted Hadley.

"Fact. Standish saw it himself, and so did the butler, and Standish's son." Bellchester seemed to be relishing the story. He was one of those people who can talk comfortably and at any length over the telephone, sitting back at his ease. Hadley was not. He liked talking face to face, and protracted phone sessions made him fidget. But the assistant commissioner showed no disposition to let him off. "It happened in this way," he pursued. "It seems that this scholarly old fellow Depping—the one who occupies the Guest House—has a daughter or a niece or something, living in France. And Standish has a son. Result: matrimony contemplated. Young Standish had just come back from a flying visit to Paris, whence he and the girl decided to make a match of it. So he was breaking the news to his father in the library, asking blessings and the rest of it. He was painting an eloquent picture of the Bishop of Mappleham uniting them in holy matrimony at the altar, and orange blossoms and so on, when they heard wild screams coming from the hall.

"They rushed out. And there was the Bishop, top-hat and gaiters, holding one of the housemaids across a table—"

Hadley made expostulating noises. He was a good family man, and, besides, he thought somebody might be listening in on the wire.

"Oh, it's not quite so bad as that," Bellchester reassured him. "Though it's puzzling enough. He seemed to have got hold of the girl by the back hair and was trying to pull it out, making most unepiscopal threats. That's all Standish told me; and he was excited, anyhow. I gather the Bishop thought the poor girl was wearing a wig. In any event, he made Standish promises to 'phone me and arrange an interview for him with one of our people."

"He's coming here, sir?"

"Yes. Do me a favor, will you, Hadley, and see him? That will probably pacify His Reverence. I want to oblige Standish, and it never does any harm to keep on the good side of the clergy. By the way, Standish is the silent partner in that publishing firm you're writing your memoirs for; did you know it?"

Hadley tapped the mouthpiece thoughtfully. "Um," he said. "No. No, I didn't know that. Burke is the only one I've met. Well—"

"Good man," said Bellchester approvingly. "You see him, then. Good luck."

He rang off. Hadley folded his hands with a patient and gloomy air. He muttered "Poltergeist!" several times, and indulged in some reflections on the evil days which had befallen the Metropolitan Police when the Chief Inspector of the Criminal Investigation Department was required to listen to the maunderings of every loony bishop who went about sliding down bannisters, attacking housemaids, and firing ink-bottles at vicars.

Presently his sense of humor struggled into being again. A grin appeared under his clipped gray moustache, and he fell to whistling as he sorted out his morning's mail. He also reflected, in as sentimental a fashion as his nature would permit, on his thirty-five years in the Force; on all the villainy and nonsense he had seen in this little bare room, with its brown dis-tempered walls and windows that overlooked the sedate Em-bankment. Each morning he placidly shaved himself in East Croydon, kissed his wife, cast a troubled eye over the newspaper (which always hinted at sinister things, either from Germany or the climate) as the train bore him to Victoria; and took up afresh his duties in murders or lost dogs. Around him was the ordered hum of this clearing-house for both. Around him—

"Come in," he said, in reply to a knock at the door.

A constable, obviously perturbed, coughed.

"There's a gentleman here, sir," he observed, rather in the manner of one making a deduction. "There's a gentleman here." He laid a card on Hadley's desk.

"Um," said the Chief Inspector, who was reading a report. "What's he want?"

"I think you had better see him, sir."

Hadley glanced at the card, which said:

> Dr. Sigismund Von Hornswoggle
> Vienna

"I think you'd better see him," the other insisted. "He's mak-ing a row, sir, and psychoanalyzing everybody he can lay hold of. Sergeant Betts has hidden himself in the record room, and swears he won't come out until somebody takes the gentleman away."

"Look here," said the exasperated Hadley, and creaked round in his swivel-chair. "Is everybody trying to play a game on me this morning? What the hell do you mean, making a row? Why don't you chuck him out?"

"Well, sir, the fact is," said the other, "that—well, I think we know him. You see . . ."

The constable was not a small man, but he was shoved aside by a much larger one; certainly one of five times his girth. The doorway was filled by an enormously stout figure in a black cape and glistening top hat. But the chief inspector's first impression of him was concerned with whiskers. He wore, almost to his cheekbones, the most luxuriant set of black whiskers Hadley had ever seen. His eyebrows were also of the same variety, and seemed to take up half his forehead. Small eyes twinkled behind eyeglasses on a broad black ribbon. His red face beamed, and he swept off his hat in a great bow.

"Goot morning!" he thundered in a rumbling voice, and beamed again. "Haf I der honor of speaking to das chief inspector, yah? *Du bist der hauptmann, meinherr, nicht wahr?* Yah, yah, yah. So."

He came over at his rolling gait and set out a chair with great nicety, propping his cane against its side.

"I vill myself sit down," he announced. "So."

He sat down, beamed, folded his hands, and inquired: "Vot do you dream about?"

Then Hadley got his breath. "*Fell—*" he said. "Gideon Fell . . . What in the name of God," continued Hadley, slapping the desk at each word, "do you mean by putting on that crazy get-up and coming into my office in it? I thought you were in America. Did anybody see you come in?"

"Eh? My goot friend—!" protested the other in an injured tone, "surely you haf yourself mistaken, yah? I am Herr Doktor Sigismund von Hornswoggle. . . ."

"Take it *off*," said Hadley firmly.

"Oh, well," said the other, dropping his accent in a voice of resignation. "So you penetrated my disguise, did you? The chap in New York told me I was perfect in the art. I had a sovereign bet that I could deceive you. Well, aren't you going to shake hands, Hadley? Here I am back, after three months in America—"

"There's a lavatory at the end of the hall," said the chief inspector inexorably. "Go out and take off those whiskers or I'll have you locked up. What do you want to do: make a guy of me in my last month of office?"

"Oh, well," grunted Dr. Fell.

He reappeared in a few minutes, his old self again, with his double chins, his bandit's moustache, and his great mop of gray-streaked hair. His face had grown even redder with the friction of washing off spirit gum. Chuckling, he propped his hands on his stick and beamed at Hadley over his eyeglasses. His headgear had changed to the usual shovel hat.

"Still," he observed, "I flatter myself that I deceived your subordinates. It takes time, of course, to become perfect. And I have my diploma from the William J. Pinkerton School of Disguise. It's what they call a mail-order course. Heh-heh-heh. You pay five dollars down, and they send you your first lesson; and so on. Heh-heh-heh."

"You're a hopeless old sinner," said Hadley, relenting, "but, all the same, I'm devilish glad to see you back. Did you enjoy yourself in America?"

Dr. Fell sighed with reminiscent pleasure, blinking at a corner of the ceiling. Then he rumbled and hammered the ferrule of his cane on the floor.

"He pasted the old apple!" murmured Dr. Fell ecstatically. "*Il a frappé l' oignon!* Ha, woof!—kill the umpire! I say, Hadley, how would you construe into Latin the following text: 'He poled the tomato into the left-field bleachers for a circuit clout?'

I've been debating it all the way across the ocean. 'Poled' and 'tomato' I can manage, but how Virgil would have said 'left-field bleachers' rather stumps me."

"What's all that?"

"It would appear," said Dr. Fell, "to be the dialect of a province called Brooklyn. My friends from the publishing house took me there, thank God, when we were supposed to be attending literary teas. You can't imagine," said the doctor, with unholy glee, "how many literary teas we contrived to miss, or, better still, how many literary people I avoided meeting. Heh-heh. Let me show you my scrap-book."

From beside his chair he took up a brief-case, and produced a volume of cuttings which he spread out proudly on the chief inspector's desk.

"I may mention, to explain some of these headlines," he pursued, "that I was known to the newspapers as 'Gid'—"

"Gid?" said Hadley, blankly.

"It is short, snappy, and fits into a headline," explained Dr. Fell, with the air of one who quotes. "Look at these examples, now."

He opened the book at random. Hadley's eye was caught by the announcement: "Gid Judges Beauty Contest at Long Beach." The accompanying photograph showed Dr. Fell, with cloak, shovel hat, and a beam like a burnished apple on his face, towering among a group of amorous young ladies in almost nonexistent bathing costumes. "Gid Opens New Fire-Station in Bronx; Created Honorary Fire Chief," proclaimed another. This cutting was decorated with two snapshots. One showed Dr. Fell wearing a complicated headgear on which was printed the word *Chief,* and holding up an axe as though he were going to brain somebody. The other pictured him in the act of sliding down a silver-plated pole from the second floor of the fire station; a very impressive sight. It bore the caption: "Did He Fell Or Was He Pushed?"

Hadley was aghast.

"Do you mean to say you actually did all these things?" he demanded.

"Certainly. I told you I had a good time," the other reminded him complacently. "Here is an account of my speech to the convention of the Loyal and Benevolent Order of Mountain Goats. I seem to have spoken very well, though my recollection is hazy. I was also made an Honorary Something of the Order; but I am not sure what my title is, because it was late in the evening and the President couldn't pronounce it with any degree of certainty. Why? Don't you approve?"

"I wouldn't have done all that," said Hadley fervently, "for"— he searched his mind for a suitable inducement—"for a thousand pounds! Close the book; I don't want to read any more. . . . What are your plans now?"

Dr. Fell frowned.

"I don't know. My wife hasn't returned from visiting her in-laws yet; I had a wire when the boat docked this morning. I'm rather at a loose end. Still, I happened to run into an old friend of mine at Southampton—a Colonel Standish. He's a member of Standish & Burke, my publishers; though it's only a financial interest, and Burke handles the business for him. *Eh?* What did you say?"

"Nothing," answered Hadley. There was a gleam in his eye nevertheless.

A long sniff rumbled in the doctor's nose. "I don't know what's the matter with him, Hadley. It seems he'd come down to the boat to meet the son of a friend of his—a fine young fellow, by the way, and the son of the Bishop of Map-pleham. I got to know him pretty well before they locked him up in the brig—"

"Locked him up in the brig?" said Hadley, sitting back in his chair. "Well, well! What was the trouble? Did he go mad too?"

A reminiscent chuckle ran over the bulges of Dr. Fell's waist-coat. With his cane he poked at the edge of Hadley's desk.

"Tut, tut, Hadley. What do you mean, mad? It was only a matter of a pair of lady's—hum—well, undergarments of some description. . . ."

"He assaulted the lady, I suppose?"

"I say, Hadley, I wish you wouldn't interrupt. No; good Lord, no! He pinched 'em out of her cabin. Then he and a few other stout-hearted fellows ran 'em up the mast in place of the house flag. They didn't discover it until next morning when a passing ship wirelessed congratulations to the captain. Then, d'ye see, there was a row. This young fellow is a wonder with his fists, by the way. He laid out the first officer and two stewards before they subdued him, and—"

"That's enough," said the chief inspector. "What were you saying about Standish?"

"Why, he seems to have something on his mind. He invited me down to his place in Gloucester for the week-end, and said he had a story to tell me. But the odd part of it was the way he treated young Donovan—that's the bishop's son. He shook his hand sadly, and looked at him in a sympathetic, pitying man-ner; and told him not to lose heart . . . Incidentally, they're both downstairs in Standish's car now, waiting for me. Eh? What's the matter with you now?"

Hadley leaned forward.

"Listen!" he said. . . .

CHAPTER II

"Shot through the Head—"

IN THE short little thoroughfare called Derby Street, which runs off Whitehall to Scotland Yard, Mr. Hugh Answell Donovan sat in the front seat of the car and surreptitiously swallowed another aspirin. The absence of water made him gag, and taste the full vileness of the pill before he could get it down. He pushed his hat over his eyes, shuddered, and stared gloomily at the wind screen.

His dreary outlook was not merely physical; though that was bad enough. His farewell party in New York had become a long, curving bender which did not cease until they put him in the brig when the *Aquatic* was two days out of Southampton. He was a little better now. Food did not turn green before his eyes, and his stomach had ceased to come together like a collapsing telescope at the sight of it. His hand had begun to regain its steadiness, nor was his conscience crawling through him with such cold feet as before. But there was a worse thing to destroy the pleasure he would have felt at seeing London after a year's absence.

All he had left, he reflected, was his sense of humor, and he had better use it.

Donovan, an amiable and easy-going young man with a dark face, and one of the neatest middleweight battlers who ever came out of Dublin University, tried to say, "Ha ha" to the dashboard. He only gurgled, for he was thinking of his first meeting with his father.

In some ways, of course, the old man was a stout fellow, even if he did happen to be a bishop. He was old-fashioned, which meant that within reasonable limits he believed in a young man sowing an oat or two by the way. But the old man's hobby had been betrayed, and his son shivered to think of the result.

A year's leave had been granted him on the only condition it would ever have been allowed: to study criminology. At the time he had considered it an inspiration. "Dad," he said, straightforwardly and frankly, "Dad, I want to be a detective." And the formidable old boy had beamed. Moodily his son recalled this now. Several times during his stay in America, he had seen photographs in which he had been struck by the really remarkable resemblance of his father to the late William Jennings Bryan. People who had known both of them personally said that the likeness was even more striking than the photographs indicated. There was the same square massive face and broad mouth; the same heavy brow, the long hair curling down behind; the curved nose, fluffy eyebrows, and sharp dark eyes; the same shoulders and decisive stride. Then there was the voice. That the Bishop of Mappleham had the finest voice in the Church of England was never doubted; it was resonant, Bryanesque, and effective as a pipe organ. Altogether, a commanding figure.

His son swallowed another aspirin, automatically.

If the bishop had a weakness, it was his hobby. A great criminologist had been lost to the world when Hugh Donovan, Sr., took up holy orders. His information was enormous; he could recite you the details of every atrocity in the last hundred years; he knew all the latest scientific devices for both the advancement and prevention of crime; he had investigated the police departments of Paris, Berlin, Madrid, Rome, Brussels, Vienna, and Leningrad, driving the officials thereof to the verge of insanity; and, finally, he had lectured all about it in the United States. It was possibly his warm reception in America which had induced him to grant his son permission to study criminology at Columbia University. . . .

"Gaa," muttered Hugh Junior, and goggled at the dashboard. He had registered there in a burst of ambition, and bought a variety of indigestible books with German titles. Afterwards he had gone no nearer West 116th Street than the apartment of a little blonde who lived uptown on the Drive.

He was now, he perceived, sunk. The old man would be down on him roaring for all the grisly details, and he didn't know one tobacco ash from another. To cap it all, there were mysterious events on foot already. His father had not been at the pier to meet the *Aquatic* that morning. Instead there had appeared a certain Colonel Standish, whom he vaguely remembered having met somewhere before. . . .

He glanced sideways at the colonel, who was fidgeting in the seat beside him, and wondered what ailed the man. Ordinarily the colonel must have been an easy and amiable sort; fleshy and port-wine-colored, with a puffing manner and clipped hair. But he had been acting very strangely. He shifted about. He rolled round a squinted brown eye, and removed it hastily. He had taken to thumping his fist on the steering-wheel, as though he had some sort of internal agony; and several times he accidentally thumped the button of the horn, which let out a squawk that made Donovan jump.

They had driven up from Southampton with a jovial old codger named Fell; and, like a nightmare, Donovan found himself being driven straight to Scotland Yard. There was dirty work here, somewhere. He had a horrible suspicion that his old man, energetic as always, was going to send him before some sort of tribunal for an examination. The thing became worse because not a word had been said to him about his father, or what was afoot, or—

"Damme, sir," said Colonel Standish, suddenly and energetically. "Damme, damme, damme, damme!"

"Eh?" said Donovan, "I beg your pardon?"

The colonel cleared his throat. His nostrils were working as though at a sudden resolve.

"Young fella," he said in a gruff voice. "Got to tell you. Only right I should. Eh?"

"Yes, sir?"

"It's about your father. Got to tell you what's in store for you, and warn you."

"Oh, my God," said Donovan inaudibly. He slouched down in his seat.

"Happened this way, you see. Poor fellow'd been overworking, and I asked him down to my place for a rest. We'd a comfortable little party: my son—don't think you've met him—my wife, and daughter; hum. Then there was Burke, my partner, and Morgan, the writer fella, and Depping who lives in the Guest House. His daughter and my son—hurrumph, ne' mind. Listen. It started the very first night. The very first night," said the colonel, lowering his voice, "it started."

"What started?" said Donovan, still fearing the worst.

"We'd Lady Langwych to dinner. *You* know; dem'd suffragette gel used to break all the windows, eh? She was anxious to meet the bishop and talk social reform with him." The colonel was breathing noisily and tapping Donovan's arm. "We were all standing in the hall, hey, downstairs, and talking to Lady Langwych—she'd just got there. All on our best behavior, hey. I remember my wife said: 'The Bishop of Mappleham will be delighted to see you, Lady Langwych.' Old gel said, 'Heh-heh.' My daughter said, 'Damme, yes indeed, damme. When he knows you're here, Lady Langwych, I'm sure he'll be down in a hurry.' Then, all of a sudden—*whr-r-r-ree!*" goggled the colonel, sweeping out his arm and making a whistling noise like a six-inch shell, "down he came on the bannisters—*whr-r-ree!*—one whole flight of stairs—like a demn'd gaitered avalanche."

Donovan was not sure he had heard right.

"Who did?" he demanded.

"Your father, poor fellow. Like a demn'd gaitered avalanche, 'pon my oath!"

The colonel stared, and then chuckled. "Old gel carried it off, too, by Jove! Got to admire her. Your father landed slap at her feet—bing! Like that. Old gel put up her eyeglass and just said it was dashed kind of him to be so prompt. But then was when I began to grow suspicious."

Peering round him to make sure there was nobody there, the colonel assumed an expostulating tone. "I took him aside, and said, 'Look here, old fellow, demmit, this is Liberty Hall, but after all—demmit!' Eh? Then I asked him tactfully whether he was feeling well, and whether I hadn't better have the doctor in, eh? By Jove, he went off the deep end! Swore it was an accident. Said he'd been leaning over the bannisters to look at somebody without being seen; and lost his balance, and had to hang on to save himself from falling. Well, I said, who was he staring at? And he said it was Hilda, one of the housemaids—"

"Great suffering snakes!" said Donovan, pressing his hands to a head that had begun to ache again. "*My* old man said—"

"He's seeing crooks all over the place, poor fella," grunted the colonel. "Fact is, he thought Hilda was a woman called Piccadilly Jane, a crook, and had a dark wig on. Then he saw the other crook on the lawn. That was the night somebody up and biffed the vicar in the eye with the inkpot. Poor devil. Shouldn't be at all surprised if he thought the vicar was Jack the Ripper in disguise, demmit."

"This is getting to be a little too much for me," said Donovan, beginning to feel ill. "Look here, sir, do you mean that my governor has gone off his onion? Is that it?"

Standish drew a deep breath.

"Didn't like to say it," he grumbled, "but hanged if I see any other explanation. And what makes it worse is that *I'm* the chief constable of the county. When I wouldn't listen to him, he made me get him an appointment to see the chaps at Scotland Yard, and—*s-hhh-sh!*"

He broke off suddenly and stared over his shoulder. Following the direction of his glance, Donovan was startled to see what he had been fearing for a long time: a tall, portly figure marching in from Whitehall, with a grim and preoccupied stride as though it were trying to step on every crack in the pavement. Even the top hat had an Onward-Christian-Soldiers look about it. Now and again, out of the massive lined face, sharp eyes would swing left and right, and the Bishop of Mappleham seemed to be muttering to himself. His son noticed this; and also that the bishop looked paler than usual. Even in his incredulous perplexity, a stab of pity went through Donovan. After all, the old man was a stout fellow. He had been warned against overwork. It might be expected, sooner or later, that if a man of such colossal energy didn't constrain himself, he would be in danger of a nervous breakdown.

"You see?" said the colonel, in a hoarse barrack-room whisper. "Talking to himself now. Sawbones told me that was one of the first signs, damme. A pity, ain't it? Off his rocker, poor fella. Humor him; be sure to humor him."

Colonel Standish had been under the impression that he was speaking in a whisper. Actually he had been trumpeting down the street, but the bishop did not seem to hear. He saw his son, and stopped. His heavy face lighted up with one of his famous Bryanesque smiles, which were a part of the man's very genuine charm. But the smile had a note of grimness. He hurried over to shake Donovan's hand.

"My boy!" he said. The magnificent voice, which in his younger days could make people believe anything, flowed into Derby Street in its hypnotic fashion. Even Standish was impressed. "I'm delighted to see you back. I should, of course, have been down to meet the boat, but weighty matters demanded my attention. You are looking well, Hugh; very well."

This startling pronouncement added to Donovan's uneasiness. It showed how preoccupied the old man must be.

"Hullo, Dad," he said, and pulled his hat further down.

"You will be able, with your new training," pursued the bishop impressively, "to assist me on a matter of momentous import, which, due to the failure of others to comprehend my plans,"—he looked heavily at the colonel and tightened his broad mouth—"they have not as yet fully appreciated. Good morning, Standish."

"Oh, ah. Er—good morning," said the colonel nervously.

The bishop studied him. There was a curious gleam in his eye.

"Standish, I regret to say it to such an old friend, but you are a fool. Duty compels me to say so. I have blundered. I admit it freely. But . . ." He swept his arm about slowly, and there was a roll and thrill in his voice, "stormy waters could not shake me, nor tempests keep me from my path. The humblest man, when clad in the armor of a righteous cause, is more powerful than all the hosts of error."

His son restrained an impulse to cheer. When the old man got to talking in this fashion, he could stampede an audience of mummies. It was not so much what he said; it was the hypnotism of voice and bearing, orchestrated together, with the mesmeric eye and the latent persuasive kindliness.

"Often said so myself," agreed the colonel. "But look here, old fellow; I mean to say, demmit!—why did you cut along from The Grange last night without telling us where you were going? Almost had a search party out after you. Wife frantic, and all that."

"To prove my case, sir," the bishop said grimly. "And I am pleased to say that I have proved it; and that I have information to lay before Scotland Yard. I travelled to my home for a brief visit, to consult my files. . . ."

He folded his arms.

"Be prepared, Standish. I am going to place a bomb under you."

"Oh, my *God*!" said the colonel. "Easy, old fellow. Come, now; I mean to say, we were at school together—"

"Kindly stop misunderstanding me," interposed the bishop, whose face had assumed a sinister expression. "You were never a man of outstanding intelligence, but at least you can understand this. If I were to tell you—"

"Excuse me, sir," said a voice. A large policeman was addressing Colonel Standish. Young Donovan, who was in no mood to be accosted by policemen that day, backed away. "Excuse me," repeated the law. "You are Colonel Standish?"

"Um," said the colonel doubtfully. "Um. Yes. What is it?"

"Will you step up to the chief inspector's office, sir? The chief inspector understands you were waiting down here. . . ."

"The chief inspector? What does he want?"

"Couldn't say, sir."

The bishop narrowed his eyes. "I venture to predict," he said, "that something has happened. Come along; we'll all go. It's quite all right, constable. I myself have an appointment with Chief Inspector Hadley."

Young Donovan manifested a strong reluctance to go, but he could not stand up under his father's eye. The constable led them down Derby Street, into the courtyard where the dark-blue police cars stand under the arches, and into the echoing brick building which had the general appearance and smell of a schoolhouse.

In Hadley's unpretentious room on the second floor, the morning sunlight was full of dust motes, and a noise of traffic floated up from the Embankment through the open windows. Behind a flat-topped desk, Donovan saw a compact man, quietly dressed, with cool watchful eyes, a clipped moustache, and hair the color of dull steel. His hands were folded placidly, but there was an unpleasant twist to his mouth as he looked at them. The receiver of the telephone had been detached from its hook and stood on the desk at his elbow. In a chair near by, Dr. Fell was scowling and poking at the carpet with his stick.

The bishop cleared his throat.

"Mr. Hadley?" he inquired. "Allow me to introduce myself. I am—"

"Colonel Standish?" said Hadley, looking at that fussed gentleman. "There is a phone message for you. I took down its contents, but perhaps you had better speak to the inspector yourself. . . ."

"Eh? Inspector?" demanded the colonel. "What inspector?"

"Your county official, under you. You are acquainted with a Mr. Septimus Depping?"

"Old Depping? Good Lord, yes. What about him? He lives in the Guest House on my property. He—"

"He has been murdered," said Hadley. "They found him shot through the head this morning. Here's the telephone."

CHAPTER III

The Eight of Swords

FOR A moment the colonel only stared at him. His broad-checked sport suit looked wildly out of place in that dingy office. "Oh, look here—!" he protested. "Depping? Can't be Depping, demmit. Depping wouldn't *get* murdered. Lay you a fiver he'd never think of getting murdered. I say—"

Hadley pushed out a chair for him. Growling, the other stamped over to it and took up the telephone. He had the air of one who was determined to quash this nonsense at the beginning.

"Hallo, hallo, hallo . . . Eh? Murch? How are you? Oh, but I mean to say, what's all this rot? . . . But how do you know?"

A pause.

"Well, maybe he was cleaning his gun and it went off," Standish cut in with an air of inspiration. "Knew a fella who did that once. Fella in the Fifty-Ninth. Blew his foot off . . .

"No, demmit. I see that. He couldn't 've done it if there's no gun. . . . Right, right. You take charge, Murch. Be down this afternoon. Always something, dash it! Right, right. 'Bye."

He hung up the receiver and regarded it gloomily. "I say, look here! I forgot to ask him—!"

"I have all the facts," interposed Hadley, "if you will explain them to me. Please sit down. These gentlemen . . . ?"

Introductions were performed. The Bishop of Mapple-ham, who had seated himself with solid grimness on the other side of Hadley's desk, regarded Standish almost in satisfaction. He seemed genuinely concerned, but he could not help mentioning it.

"Much," he said, "much as I regret the passing of any human being, I must point out that I gave warning of this. It does not in any sense allay the blame, or mitigate the deep damnation of his taking-off. Yet—"

Standish got out a handkerchief and mopped his forehead. "Dash it," he said querulously, "how was I to know the poor devil would get himself done in? Something's wrong. You don't know the fella. Why, he even had a share in my firm!"

Hadley, Donovan noticed, was looking from one to the other of them with an irritated expression. But he addressed the bishop deferentially.

"I must thank you, my lord," he interposed, "for your prompt action and assistance in this matter. When we have heard the facts of the Depping murder, I should be pleased if you would explain further—"

"But, confound it, he slid down the bannisters!" protested Standish in an injured tone. "Smack down the bannisters, like a demn'd gaitered avalanche, demmit, and landed in front of Lady Langwych!"

The bishop froze. He swelled. He looked at Standish as once he had looked at a minor deacon who slipped on the altar steps with the collection plate and sent a shower of coppers over the occupants of the first three pews.

"Those circumstances, sir," he said coldly, "I have already explained, to the satisfaction of any normal-witted person. In an unlucky moment I overbalanced myself, and in order to avoid the consequences attendant upon a disastrous fall, I was compelled to clutch at the bannister and thus—er—expedite my descent somewhat. That was all."

The colonel resented these slurs on his intelligence.

"Well, then, why did you chuck ink bottles at the vicar?" he demanded heatedly. "By Jove, I may not be a bishop, but, damme, I never biffed a vicar in the eye in my life! If you call that a sign of intelli—"

Bluish tints were appearing round the bishop's nostrils. He sat bolt upright, breathing hard, and looked round the circle. His eye rested on Dr. Fell, who was making curious noises behind the hand he had pressed over his mouth.

"You spoke, sir?" inquired His Lordship.

"No, my lord, I didn't," rumbled Dr. Fell guardedly. "*Whoosh! Whee! Gurrunk!* N-noo." He clapped on his hand again; but he was shaking all over, and there was a moisture in his eyes.

"I am glad to hear it, sir. But you thought something, perhaps?"

"Well, then," said the doctor frankly, "why *did* you chuck ink-bottles at the vicar?"

"Gentlemen!" roared Hadley, hammering on his desk. He controlled himself with an effort, and set all the papers straight before him to regain his equanimity. "Perhaps," he went on, "I had better outline the facts as I heard them from Inspector Murch, and you, colonel, can supply the blanks. . . . First, however: What do you know of this Mr. Depping?"

"Very good sort, old Depping is," Standish replied defensively. "Related to some good friends of mine in India. Turned up one day five or six years ago; visited me; heard I'd the Guest House vacant; liked it; rented it, and been there since. . . . Stiffish sort of fella. Fastidious, d'ye see? All books and what not; over my head. Even carried a special cook with him—liked the fancy dishes." the colonel chuckled. "But you had to know him, damme!"

"What do you mean by that?"

Standish assumed a confidential air. "Why, like this. Didn't know the fella ever drank much; only liked half a bottle of Burgundy—fastidious—bah. But I dropped in on him one night, unexpectedly. There was the old boy without his pince-nez, sitting in his study with his feet up on the desk, and three-quarters of a bottle of whisky gone—whistle-drunk. Ha. Queerest thing I ever saw. I said, 'Er, damme.' He said, 'Heh-heh.' Then he started to sing and roar, and . . . Look here," said the colonel uneasily. "I don't want to say anything against him, eh? But I think he was a secret drinker, and went on those sprees about every two months. Why not? Did him good, *I* say. Made him human. Why, before I was married I did it myself. Hum." Standish coughed. "Hey, what's the harm, if nobody sees you? He was anxious for nobody to see him. Dignity. After I'd barged in on him, he made that valet of his sit in the hall outside his study door, every night, damme!—every night, in case somebody dropped in and he wasn't ready."

Hadley frowned.

"Did it every occur to you, colonel, that he had something on his mind?"

"Eh? Something on his mind? Tosh, tosh! Nonsense. What would he have on his mind? He was a widower—he'd got pots of money—"

"Go on, please. What else did you know about him?"

Standish fidgeted. "Not much. He didn't—mix, d'ye see? Fell in with Burke, my partner, and invested a dashed sight with us. Said he'd always wanted to read for a publisher, and, by Jove, he did! He took all the heavy stuff nobody else would touch. You know—somebody's treatise on something, that took seven years to write, or what not; bundle about six inches thick, all interlined so you can't read it, and author sending you letters every other day. Bah."

"Had he any relatives?"

Standish's red face was complacent, and then grew uneasy. "I say, this will knock the stuffing out of . . . H'm, yes. He'd a daughter. Dem'd fine gel. None of your hussies, d'ye see, that knock you off the road in a two-seater, d'ye see?" said the colonel viciously. "Fine gel, even if she does live in France. Used to worry Depping no end, what she might be up to. He'd kept her in a convent, though, till she was of age, so maybe she liked France, but God knows why. Ha. I said, 'Right, right; time she was married.' And the gel and my son—" He brooded. "There's always something,—eh?"

Hadley's eyes moved about the group. They rested on the bishop, who seemed about to speak; so Hadley went on quickly:

"Then you never knew of an enemy he might have had? I mean, somebody not in your circle, whom you had never met?"

"Good Lord, No!"

"I asked that," Hadley went on, "because of the circumstances surrounding his death. According to Inspector Murch, who has the testimony of his valet and cook, this is what happened. . . ."

He rustled his papers. "His valet, Raymond Storer, says that he came back to the Guest House about seven o'clock, after having been out to tea—"

"Had it with us," grunted the colonel. "We were all pretty bucked about the news: his daughter and my son, I mean. He'd got a letter from her the day before, and he and I talked it over night before last. So he came up to tea yesterday and told the whole crowd."

"Did he seem in good spirits?"

"Good Lord, yes. Tickled pink."

Hadley's eyes narrowed. "Did anything occur, then, while he was with you that—upset him?"

Standish had taken out a cigar, and he was lighting it when an uneasy thought seemed to strike him. He screwed round his neck and looked somewhat malevolently at the bishop.

"Hey . . . Look here, I've thought of something!" His boiled eye protruded. "He did seem down in the dumps when he left, by Jove. And that was just after *you* took him aside and spoke to him. Eh?"

The bishop folded his hands over his umbrella. His heavy jaw had a curious expression of seeming to move about with repressed satisfaction.

"Quite so, my friend," he replied. "I shall tell the chief inspector about it when he has finished outlining the facts. . . . Pray go on, sir."

"The valet testified," Hadley went on, after a slight pause, "that he seemed disturbed when he arrived back at the Guest

House. He ordered his dinner to be sent to him in the study. And he did not, as seems to have been usual, dress for dinner.

"His dinner was taken up to him about half past eight, when he seemed to have been even more restless. He told the valet that he had work to do, and would be at home to nobody that night. Last night, you remember, was the end of the heat wave. The storm broke late in the evening—"

"Damme, and *what* a storm!" grunted the colonel. "Henry Morgan got caught in it, and had to walk three miles to—"

Hadley's temper was wearing thin. "If you don't mind, colonel," he said, "it will be rather necessary for you to know these things. . . . Shortly after the storm broke, it blew down a wire or something of the sort, and all the lights went out. The valet, who was on the ground floor closing all the windows, rummaged about until he found some candles. He was about to go upstairs with them when there was a knock at the outer door.

"The wind blew out his candle when he opened the door, but when he had got it lighted again, he saw that the caller was nobody he had ever seen before . . ."

"You have a description of the man, Mr. Hadley?" the bishop put in crisply.

"Not a very good one. He was medium-sized, youngish, dark hair and moustache, loud clothes, and spoke with an American accent."

An expression of grim triumph drew the bishop's neck in folds over his collar. He nodded. "Pray go on, Mr. Hadley."

"The valet was about to shut the door, saying that Mr. Depping could see no one, when the man put his foot in the door. He said"—Hadley glanced at his notes—"he said, 'He'll see *me*. Ask him.' Inspector Murch was not very clear about this. The man seems to have pointed to some sort of speaking tube."

"Right," said the colonel. "You know. You whistle in 'em, demmit. Then you talk. Depping only used two rooms to live in: study and bedroom. He'd got a speaking tube running up to the study. It was beside the outer door."

"Very well . . . The man was insistent, so Storer spoke to Mr. Depping upstairs. Mr. Depping finally said, 'All right; send him up,' though the man would give no name. But Depping told the valet to be close at hand, in case he should be needed. Storer suggested that he had better go and see to fixing the lights, whereupon Depping said not to mind the lights; that he had plenty of candles in the study, and they would suffice.

"However, Storer woke up the cook, a man named Achille Georges, and sent him out in the rain with a flashlight—under great protest—to find out whether or not the wires had come down. Meantime he was going about shutting the upstairs windows, and he heard Depping and his guest talking in the study. He couldn't hear anything that was said, but they seemed on amiable enough terms. Presently the cook returned, swearing no wire was down. They had a look at the fuse box, and discovered that there had only been a short circuit of some sort, and that plugging in new fuses restored the lights. . . ."

For the first time Dr. Fell, who had been sitting abstractedly filling a pipe, rolled up his big head and stared at the chief inspector. His eyes had a curiously cross-eyed look. A long sniff rumbled in his nose.

"I say, Hadley," he muttered, "that's very interesting. It's the first interesting detail you've mentioned so far. Go on, go on."

Hadley grunted. He looked speculatively at the doctor, and went on:

"By that time it was nearly midnight, and Storer wanted to get to bed. He knocked on the study door, told Depping the lights were repaired, and asked whether he could retire. Depping said, 'Yes, yes,' rather impatiently. So he turned in. There was still a terrific thunderstorm going on, and it kept him awake. . . . On reflection, this morning, he thinks he heard the sound of a shot about a quarter past twelve; he noticed it at the time, but he thought it must be a part of a thunderclap, and didn't investigate. Inspector Murch says the police surgeon reports a quarter past twelve to be about the time of death.

"The next morning, when Storer went downstairs, he saw over the transom that the lights were still burning in the study. He knocked at the door for some time, and got no answer; the door was locked on the inside. So he got a chair, climbed up, and looked through the transom.

"Depping was lying forward across his reading desk, with the back of his head shot open directly against the bald spot. Finally Storer plucked up enough nerve to push the transom back, crawl through, and get into the room. Depping had been dead for many hours, and there was no weapon to be found."

Young Donovan found his morning-after head rapidly disappearing. This cool, unhurried, gruesome recital roused his wits and his imagination. That wild talk of sliding down bannisters now seemed a part of yesterday night's tippling; it was the first time he had caught the scent of a man hunt, and he was beginning to understand its fascination. There was a silence. With a return of uneasiness he found the bishop's complacent paternal eye fixed upon him.

"This, Mr. Hadley," said the bishop, "is most interesting. And instructive." He waved his hand towards his son. "My son, Mr. Hadley, is a student of criminology like myself. Hem. I shall see presently what good his studies have done him." He became businesslike, and considered. "There are several suggestive points, I fancy. For example—"

"But, demmit!—" protested the colonel, mopping his forehead, "I say—!"

"—for example," the bishop continued coldly, "you say the door of the study was locked on the inside. Did the murderer escape through a window?"

"No. Through another door. There is an upstairs balcony running along the side of the house, and a door opens out on it. This door—which Storer says is generally locked—was partly open." Hadley regarded him without sarcasm, and very patiently. "Now, then. If you will explain your own part in the matter . . . ?"

The bishop nodded, and smiled at Standish in a kindly fashion.

"With pleasure. Fortunately, Mr. Hadley, I can tell you the name of the man who called on Mr. Depping last night. As a matter of fact, I can show you a photograph of him."

While the colonel stared, he took from his inside pocket a sheet of glazed paper, carefully annotated in a small hand, and bearing two photographs, which he handed across to Hadley. Now that he was vindicated, the bishop's sense of humor seemed to reassert itself.

"His name is Louis Spinelli. In case the name fails to stir your memory, Mr. Hadley, there are a few notes on him at the bottom of the sheet."

"Spinelli—" repeated Hadley. His eyes narrowed. "Spinelli—got it! Blackmail. That's the chap. One of Mayfree's mob, who tried to get into England last year—"

"The only one," the bishop corrected, "who *did* get into England. This man, Mr. Hadley, is too intelligent to try to walk into this country in his own name in character. Allow me to explain."

This, young Donovan reflected, as he had always reflected, was weird language to hear from a bishop of the Church of England. And the odd part of it was that the old boy carried it off. He talked in this vein as easily as he would have spoken from a pulpit. His son had never quite got used to it.

"At the Police Museum in Centre Street, which is similar to your Black Museum here, their exhibits are classified to represent various *types* of crime, Mr. Hadley. The commissioner gave me permission to bring back a great deal of interesting lore. This man Spinelli was originally a blackmailer, a lone hand; singled out for notice because of a curious peculiarity he had, which caught him before long.

"He is a young Italian-American, about thirty years old, of decent parents and excellent education. I am told that his manners are good, and that he could pass almost anywhere but for one incredible weakness. He cannot resist the temptation to wear the loudest and most conspicuous attire procurable, in addition to rings and jewelry of all kinds. Look at what you can see of it in that photograph. When he was about twenty-three, they caught him and sent him to Sing Sing for ten years."

The bishop paused. His heavy-lidded eyes moved round the group.

"He was out of prison in three. Nobody knows exactly how it was contrived. According to what I can gather, he realized it was unsafe to play alone. He joined up with Mayfree, who was all-powerful at the time, and nobody could touch him. Then—"

Dr. Fell snorted.

"Look here," he protested, "by God and Bacchus, I hope this little affair isn't going to turn into a dull and stodgy piece of gang-history. Hurrumph. Ha. If there's anything I dislike, it's to see the classic outline of a murder case involved in any such monotonous red tape. I was just becoming interested in that question of the lights . . ."

The bishop shook his head.

"You needn't be afraid of that, my dear sir. You may take my word for it that Spinelli is back on his old lone-hand blackmail tactics. Mayfree's organization is broken up. Nobody knows why, and I know it puzzled the commissioner. It began to decline in power some time ago. The leaders tried to leave the country: some to Italy, some to England, some to Germany. They were refused entrance. But, in some fashion, Spinelli got in . . ."

"We'll soon see to that," snapped Hadley, and spoke briefly into the telephone. He looked at the bishop, and went on rather curtly: "You must know, sir, that this is pure guesswork on your part. I take it you never saw Spinelli face to face?"

"As it happens," said the bishop calmly, "I saw him face to face twice. Once in the police line-up at Centre Street, where nothing was proved against him; that was how I happened to hear the details of his case. And again last night. He was coming out of a public house not far from The Grange. Before that I had seen him at a distance, and in the moonlight, under—hum—somewhat unusual circumstances, in the park of The Grange." The bishop coughed. "It was his clothes which started my memory working, and I thought his face was familiar. But last night I saw him as close as I see you now."

"By Gad!" said the colonel, staring at him with a new expression now. "So that was why you cut away this morning, hey?"

"I do not believe that my story would have been listened to with great respect by the chief constable," the bishop answered frostily. "There, gentlemen, is one of the things I have discovered. The question is—"

Hadley tapped his knuckles moodily on the desk. He glanced at the telephone, which refused to ring.

"The question is," he said, "that we shall have to look into this very carefully, but I think somebody is under a misapprehension. This business of American gangsters shooting scholarly country gentlemen in the wilds of Gloucestershire . . . Pah. Confound it. All the same—"

"I do not think," the bishop said deliberately, "that Louis Spinelli did shoot him. This is no time for going into my reasons. But I should like to ask, Mr. Hadley, what you intend to do."

Hadley was blunt. "It's all up to Colonel Standish. He's the chief constable of his county. If he wishes to call in the Yard, he can do so. If he wishes to handle it himself, it's all the same to me. What do you say, colonel?"

"Personally," observed the bishop in a reflective voice, "I should be most happy to lend the police any assistance in my humble power in this unfortunate business." He pulled out all the stops in the organ of his voice. The massive face swelled, and there was a hypnotic gleam in his eye.

"Got it!" exclaimed Standish, with an air of inspiration. He was tactless. He went on: "Got it, by Jove! There's our man—Fell. Look here, demmit. You promised to come down to The Grange and spend a few days, didn't you? I say, old man. You wouldn't let a demnition foreigner come and blow the daylight out of a friend of mine, hey? Hey?" he turned to the bishop. "This is Fell, you know. Fella who caught Cripps and Loganray and the fake preacher what's-his-name. Look here, what about it?"

Dr. Fell, who had got his pipe lighted at last, rumbled and scowled and poked at the floor with his stick.

"For a long time," he said querulously, "I have protested against these utterly commonplace cases. There's no picturesque or bizarre feature about this thing at all. Where's your drama? Where's—"

Hadley regarded him with a sort of dry and bitter satisfaction.

"Yes. Yes, I know. You are in your element," he agreed, "with the sort of fantastic lunacy of a case which doesn't come our way once in a dozen years, ordinarily. People shot with a crossbow bolt at the Tower of London, or thrown off the balcony of a haunted prison. All right! But what about the featureless, prosaic case that *we* get week in and out, and that's the hardest to solve? Try your hand at one of them. I don't think you'll make so much fun of the police after that. . . . Excuse me, gentlemen. This is merely a little private matter."

He hesitated, and then growled.

"Unfortunately, I've got to tell you something else. There is one small point Inspector Murch mentioned which isn't exactly commonplace. It may mean nothing at all, or even be a possession of Depping's; but it certainly isn't commonplace."

"There are several points," said Dr. Fell, "which aren't commonplace, if you must drive me into saying it. H'mf. Ha. No. Well?"

Hadley rubbed his chin uneasily "Near Depping's hand," he went on, glancing down his notes, "there was a card . . . Yes, that's what I said: a card. It was about the size and shape of a

playing card, according to this, with a design beautifully painted in water colour. The design consisted of eight figures which
looked like swords, set in the form of a star, and a symbol like
water running through the middle of it. There you are. Now go
ahead and construct your romance." He threw the notes down
on his desk.

Dr. Fell's hand stopped with the pipe halfway to his mouth.
He puffed a long breath, wheezily, through his moustache, and
his eyes grew fixed.

"Eight swords—" he said. "Eight swords: two on the water
level, three above, and three below . . . Oh, Lord! Oh, Bacchus!
Oh my ancient hat! Look here, Hadley, this won't do."

He continued to stare at the chief inspector.

"Oh, all right," said Hadley irritably. "You're in your element
again. A secret society, I imagine? The Black Hand, or something like it? A sign of vengeance?—Bah!"

"No," said the doctor slowly, "nothing of the sort. I wish it
were a simple as that. This is as mediaeval, and devilish, and
imaginative, as . . . Yes, by all means. I shall certainly go down
to Gloucestershire. It must be a strange place. And I shall spare
no pains to meet a murderer who knows about the eight of
swords."

He got up, flinging his cape over his shoulder like a bandit,
and stumped to the window, where he stood for a moment staring down at the traffic on the Embankment; with his white-
plumed mane of hair ruffled, and the glasses coming askew on
his nose.

CHAPTER IV

"Look for the Buttonhook"

HUGH DONOVAN saw The Grange for the first time late that afternoon. He had lunched with the bishop, Dr. Fell, and Colonel Standish at Groom's in Fleet Street while they discussed plans. The bishop was affable. When he learned that the stout man in the cloak and shovel hat, who had blinked on everybody with such good humor in Hadley's office, was the celebrated schoolmaster whose amiable eye had singled out half-a-dozen of the shrewdest murderers ever to appear at Madam Tussaud's, then the bishop unbent. He was disposed to make his conversation that of one criminologist to another. But he seemed shocked at the doctor's lack of knowledge, and even lack of interest, with regard to modern criminals and up-to-date scientific methods.

Fortunately, he did not try to draw his son into the discussion. And the latter realized, with silent profanity, that he had missed the best opportunity ever put before him to save his face. If he had known on the boat who Dr. Fell was, he could have explained his difficulties to the old codger, and the old codger would have helped him. You had only to listen to Dr. Fell's rumblings and chucklings, and his roaring pronouncements on the world in general, to be aware that nothing would have pleased him more than a game of this sort. Even now it was not too late. And besides, Hugh Donovan reflected, there was a consolation. Undoubtedly he would be admitted to the shrine now, under the most excellent of false pretenses, and see the high priests making their magic in a real case. He had always wanted to do so. Hitherto the bishop would have instructed him to go and roll his hoop, or some other undignified pastime, while papa had a shot at it. But now he theoretically knew all about ballistics, microphotography, chemical analysis, toxicology, and other depressing studies with figures in them. From the one or two glances he had taken at his textbooks, he had been mystified and annoyed. It was a fake. Instead of giving you something juicy in the way of hints about catching axe-killers, all they seemed to do was babble on about something being four-point-two and one-half plus x more than eleven nought-nought-point-two over y hieroglyphic. It was worst than chemistry.

Morosely he listened to the bishop expounding theories to Dr. Fell, and sipped Groom's excellent beer. All the alluring-sounding things were fakes, anyway: like chemistry. He remembered as a boy being fascinated by the toy chemical outfits in the shops. When they bought him one for Christmas, he had been delighted first off to see instructions for making gunpowder. That, he thought, was the stuff. Your mixture produced a fine black compound, very sinister-looking and satisfying. But it was a failure. He put a mound of it under his father's favorite easy-chair, attached a paper wick, lighted it, and awaited results. All it did was flare out like a flashlight-powder, and scorch the bishop's ankles; though his leap showed his athletic training of old. However, Hugh had to admit, better results were obtained with his manufacture of chlorine gas. By a liberal use of ingredients, he had contrived to paralyse the old man for fully five minutes. But, all in all, he was disappointed, and it had been the same with criminology. He much preferred detective work as set forth in the novels of his favorite author: that distinguished and popular writer of detective stories, Mr. Henry Morgan.

He frowned. This reminded him. If he remembered correctly, Morgan's novels were published by the firm of Standish & Burke. He must ask the colonel who Morgan was, and what he was like, "The *nom de plume* Henry Morgan," his blurbs always announced, in tones of hushed reverence, "conceals the identity of a figure internationally known in the world of letters and politics, who has turned his genius and his knowledge of police procedure to the writing of the *roman policier.*" Donovan was impressed. He pictured the original as a satanic individual in evening clothes, with forked whiskers and piercing eyes, who was always frustrating somebody's plot to pinch the plans of the latest electromagnetic gun.

But he did not dare question Standish now, not only because the colonel seemed moody and distraught at the lunch table, but because he did not want to attract his father's attention at all. The Bishop of Mappleham was busy with Dr. Fell.

So they left London in Standish's car early in the afternoon, and the bishop was still explaining how his efforts had been misdirected by unfortunate circumstances. How (he freely admitted) he had been mistaken in thinking that Hilda Doffit, a housemaid, was the notorious and light-fingered Piccadilly Jane; and had been led thereby into several equivocal positions. Then, on the night he genuinely did see Louis Spinelli in the geranium beds, his conduct had been misinterpreted by Colonel Standish, due to somebody's idiotic prank at playing ghost on the Reverend George Primley.

This prank, it must be confessed, roused the interest and approval of Hugh Donovan. He looked forward to meeting the person, whoever it might be, who had taken advantage of a poltergeist's notoriously rowdy habits to throw ink at the vicar. But it seemed evident that Colonel Standish was not yet satisfied, and had his own secret doubts about the bishop's conduct.

They made good time through the countryside, and at four o'clock they had turned off the London road at a village called Bridge Eight. It was a hot, still afternoon. The road wound through dips and hollows, overhung by maple trees; and bees from the hedgerows were always sailing in through the wind screen and driving Standish wild. Towards the west Donovan could see the smoky red roofs of the suburbs round Bristol; but this was rural scenery of the thatched-roof and cowbell variety. Here were rolling meadows, frothing yellow with buttercups, and occupied by cows that looked as stolid as a nudist colony. Here were rocky commons, and unexpected brooks, and dark coppices massed on the hillsides. And, as usual when he ventured into the country, Donovan began to get good resolutions. He breathed deeply. He removed his hat and let the sunlight burn his hair to an uncomfortable state. This was health.

He could look back on New York with a mild pity. What asses people were! To be shut into a hot apartment, with twenty different radio programs roaring in your ear; with every light shaking to the thunder of parties on each floor; with children yelling along Christopher Street, and papers blown in gritty over-hot winds, and the rumble of the Sixth Avenue L rising monotonously over the clatter of traffic. Sad. Very sad. Already he could picture his poor friends staggering in and out of cordial shops; wasting their substance by depositing nickels in the slot machines, pulling the lever, and getting only a row of lemons for their pains. Tonight, round Sheridan Square, one poor friend would be measuring out gin drops, with the fierce concentration of a scientist, into a glass jug containing half-a-gallon of alcohol and half-a-gallon of water. Others would be thirstily waiting to drink it, poor devils. Then they would forget to eat dinner, and make love to somebody else's girl, and get a bust in the eye. Sad.

Whereas *he* . . . The bishop was saying something about Thomas Aquinas, and his son eyed him benevolently as the car sped on. Whereas *he* . . .

There should be no more of that. He would rise with the thrush (at whatever hour that exemplary bird does begin raising hell outside your window). He would go for long walks before breakfast. He would decipher inscriptions on gravestones, and meditate on the fallen tower, like those fellows who write the pleasant essays, and who never have any base impulse to go and get plastered at the nearest pub.

And he would listen to quaint bits of philosophy from rustics—those fellows who always tell the local legends to the writers. "Aye," he could hear an old graybeard saying, "aye, it were twenty year come Michaelmas that poor Sally Fevverley drownded herself in yon creek, and on moonlight nights . . ." Excellent. He could already see himself leaning on his ash stick in the twilight as the story was told, looking with sad eyes at the brook, and musing on the villainy of those who drink alcohol-and-water in cities, and then come out and seduce poor girls all over the countryside, and make them drown themselves in brooks. He had worked himself into a high state of virtue, when he was suddenly roused by a hail from the roadside.

"What ho!" cried a voice. "What *ho!*"

He roused himself, putting on his hat again to shield his eyes from the sun, as the car slowed down. They had come through a cluster of houses, the largest of which was a white-washed stone pub bearing the sign of the Bull, and turned to the left up a long low hill. Midway up on the right was a little square-towered church, a miniature of great age, with flowers round it and the gravestones built up close to its porch. At the crest of the hill the road ran straight for a quarter of a mile; and, far away to the left, Donovan could see acre upon acre of parkland, enclosed along the road by a low stone wall. In the middle of the park lay a vast, low stone house, with its eastern windows glowing against the gold sky.

But the hail had come from closer at hand. On the opposite side of the road, just past the top of the hill, stood a timbered house of the sort that used to be called black-and-white. Its frontage was enclosed by a box hedge as high as a tall man's head. An iron gate in the hedge bore a name plate in small, severe black letters, HANGOVER HOUSE. Leaning on this gate, and gesturing at them with a pipe, stood the lounging man who had called out.

"What ho!" he repeated. "What *ho!*"

Donovan noticed that his father closed disapproving jaws, but the colonel uttered a grunt of pleasure or relief and swung the car towards the gate. The amiable figure proved to be a lean young man, not many years older than Donovan himself, with a long face, a square jaw, a humorous eye, and tortoise-shell glasses pulled down on a long nose. He was dressed in a loud blazer, soiled gray trousers, and a khaki shirt open at the neck. With one hand he shook the ashes out of his dead pipe, and the other held a glass containing what looked very much like a cocktail.

The colonel stopped the car. "Don't go on saying, 'What ho,' demmit," he complained. "We can't stay. We're in a hurry. What do you want?"

"Come on in," invited the other hospitably. "Have a cocktail. I know it's early, but have one anyway. Besides, there's news." He turned his head over his shoulder, and called, "Madeleine!"

At the sight of the amber-brown contents of that glass, Donovan's feelings underwent a sudden convulsion. On the lawn beyond the hedge he could see an enormous beach umbrella propped up over a table bearing materials which reminded him forcibly of New York. And, unless his eyes were deceiving him, the sides of that great nickelled cocktail-shaker were pale with moisture. A nostalgia swept over him. He was aware that ice for drinks was an almost unknown commodity in rural England. At the young man's hail, a girl's head appeared round the edge of the umbrella and gave everybody a beaming smile.

Getting up from a deck chair, she hurried to the gate. She was a dark-eyed, bouncing little piece of the sort known as a Japanese brunette; and that she was sturdy and admirably fashioned was rendered obvious by the fact that she wore beach pyjamas and one of those short silk coats with the flowers on them. She hung over the gate, inspected them all pleasantly, raised her eyebrows, and said, "Hullo!" as though she were very pleased with herself for thinking of it.

Colonel Standish coughed when he saw the pyjamas, looked at the bishop, and went on hastily:

"Don't think everybody knows everybody. Hum. This is Dr. Fell—detective fella, you know; heard me speak of him, hey?—come down from Scotland Yard. And Mr. Donovan, the bishop's son. . . . I want you to meet," he said, rather proudly, "Henry Morgan, the writin' fella. And Mrs. Morgan."

Donovan stared as the introductions were acknowledged. Not even his formidable father could keep him quiet now.

"Excuse me," he said, "*you* are Henry Morgan?"

Morgan wryly scratched the tip of his ear. "Um," he said in an embarrassed way. "I was afraid of that. Madeleine wins another bob. You see, the bet is that if you say that to me, I pay her a shilling. If, on the other hand, you look at her and make some remark about 'The Old, Bold Mate of Henry Morgan,' then I win it. However . . ."

"Hoora!" gurgled Madeleine delightedly. "I win. Pay me." She regarded Dr. Fell and said with candor: "I like you." Then she looked at Donovan and added with equal impartiality: "I like you too."

Dr. Fell, who was chuckling in the tonneau, lifted his stick in a salute. "Thank you, my dear. And I'm naturally pleased to meet you both. You see—"

"Hold on a bit!" Donovan interrupted with pardonable rudeness. "*You* are the creator of John Zed, diplomatist-detective?"

"Um."

Another question, which could not be kept down despite his father's eye, boiled to the surface. He pointed to the glass in the other's hand and demanded: "Martinis?"

Morgan brightened eagerly.

"And how!" agreed the creator of John Zed, diplomatist-detective. "Have one?"

"Hugh!" interposed the bishop in a voice that could quell the most rebellious chapter, dean and all. "We do not wish to take up your time, Mr. Morgan. Doubtless all of us have more important matters to which we can attend." He paused, and his furry brows drew together. "I hope I shall not be misunderstood, my friend, if I add that in the solemn presence of death your attitude seems to me to be somewhat reprehensibly irreverent. Start the car, Standish."

"Sorry, sir," said Morgan, looking at him meekly over his spectacles. "I mean to say—sorry. Not for a moment would I in my irreverence stay your headlong rush to get at the corpse. All I wanted to tell you was—"

"Don't you mind *him*, bishop," said Madeleine warmly. "Don't you mind him. You can slide down *our* bannisters as much as you like, and nobody shall stop you. There! I'll even get a big cushion for you to land on, though I expect," she added, scrutinizing him with a thoughtful air, "you won't need it much, will you?"

"Angel sweetheart," said Morgan dispassionately, "shut your trap. What I was about to say was—"

"Madeleine gurgled. "But he won't, will he?" she protested, swinging on the gate. "And what's more, I wouldn't be mean like you, when you said *you'd* put the goldfish bowl there instead of a cushion. I mean, that isn't nice, is it?"

"Dawn of my existence," said her husband querulously, "all this is beside the point. Whether nature in her abundance has equipped His Reverence with a lower dorsal frontage sufficiently spacious to withstand the shocks of sliding down bannisters all over England, is not only beside the point, but savors of indelicacy." He looked at Standish, and his face suddenly clouded. He moved the loose spectacles up and down his nose, uneasily. "Look here, sir. We don't—well, the bishop is right. We don't take this very seriously, I admit. If it weren't for what Betty would feel about it, I shouldn't be very much cut up about it. I know; *de mortuis,* and all that. But after all, sir—old Depping *was* rather a blister, wasn't he?"

Standish punched at the steering-wheel, hesitantly.

"Oh, I say!" he protested . . .

"Right," said Morgan in a colorless voice. "I know it's none of my business. All I wanted to tell you was that I was to look out for you when you arrived and tell you that Inspector Murch has gone home for something to eat; he said to tell you he would be back directly . . . He allowed me to prowl about the Guest House with him, and we found a couple of things . . ."

"And may I ask, young man," said the bishop, stung, "on what authority you did that?"

"Well, sir, I suppose it was rather like your own. There wasn't much to be seen there. But we did find the gun. I should say *a* gun, though there isn't much doubt it's the one. The autopsy hasn't been performed, but the doctor said it was a thirty-eight bullet. The gun is a thirty-eight Smith & Wesson revolver . . . You will find it," said Morgan, in the negligent manner which would have been employed by John Zed, diplomatist-detective, "in the right-hand drawer of Depping's desk."

"Eh?" demanded Standish. "In Depping's *desk?* What the devil is it doing there?"

"It's Depping's gun," said Morgan; "we found it there." He noticed that he had a cocktail in his hand, and drank it off. Then he balanced the glass on the edge of the gate, thrust his hands deep into the pockets of the red-and-white blazer, and tried to assume a mysterious profundity like John Zed's. But it was difficult. For the first time Donovan saw the excitability of his nature. He could imagine him striding up and down the lawn with a cocktail in one hand, shifting his spectacles up and down his nose, and hurling out theories to a beaming wife. He said:

"There's no doubt it was his gun, sir. His name on a little silver plate on the grip. And his firearms license was in the same drawer, and the numbers tallied . . . By the way, two shots had been recently fired."

Dr. Fell bent forward abruptly. He made a queer figure against the hot green landscape, in his black cloak and shovel hat.

"Two shots?" he repeated. "So far as we have heard, there was only one. Where was the other bullet?"

"That's the point, sir. We couldn't discover it. Both Murch and I are willing to swear it isn't lodged in the room anywhere. Next—"

"I am afraid we are wasting a great deal of time," the bishop interposed. "All this information can be obtained officially from Inspector Murch. Shall we proceed, Standish?"

There were times, Donovan thought, when his old man was lacking in ordinary courtesy. Still, these constant references to sliding down bannisters must be wearing on his temper; and Madeleine Morgan seemed to be pondering some new remark about cushions. Dr. Fell rumbled something angrily, glaring at the bishop, but Standish was under the influence of that cold ecclesiastical eye, and obediently pressed his starter.

"Right," said Morgan amiably. "Break away as soon as you can," he suggested to Donovan, "and come down and try one of our Martinis. . . ." He leaned over the gate as the car backed round. He looked at the bishop. And then up rose Old John Zed himself, to speak in a tone of thunder across the road. "I don't know what deductions you will make, Your Reverence," said Old John Zed, "but I'll give you a tip. *Look for the buttonhook.*"

The car slewed round slightly as it sped on. Standish goggled.

"Eh?" he inquired. "What was that he said, hey? What button-hook? What's a demnition button-hook got to do with it?"

"Nothing whatever," said the bishop. "It is merely some of

that insolent young man's nonsense. How sensible people can read such balderdash by a young man who knows nothing of criminology, is more than—"

"Oh, look here!" warmly protested the colonel, whose favorite reading was the saga of John Zed. "*Murder on the Woolsack*, eleventh printing comprising 79,000 copies. *Who Shot the Prime Minister?* sixteenth printing comprising—well, I don't remember, but a dem'd lot, demmit. Burke told me. Besides," added Standish, using a clinching argument, "my wife likes him."

Dr. Fell, who had been cocking a thoughtful eye at the house along the left, seemed to repress a chuckle. He cast a surreptitious glance at the bishop, and observed dreamily:

"I say, you are in a most unfortunate position, I fear. The impression seems to be widespread that your conduct is at times, humf, a trifle erratic. Heh. Heh-heh-heh. Sir, I should be careful; very careful. It would be unfortunate, for instance, if other lapses occurred."

"I don't think I understand."

"Well, the colonel and I would be compelled to put you under restraint. It would exclude you from the case. It might get into the newspapers. Listen, Your Grace . . ." Dr. Fell's red face was very bland, and his eyes opened wide. "Let me warn you to walk very softly. Attend to those who want to speak, and what they say; and brush nothing aside as unimportant. Eh?"

Dr. Fell, it was obvious, had been struck with an idea which he continued to ponder while the car turned through the lodge gates of The Grange. The iron gates were shut, and at the porter's lodge a large policeman was trying to maintain a Jovian unconsciousness of the little group of idlers that had gathered outside. He opened the gates at Standish's hail.

"Tell you what," said Standish, "I'll drive on up to the house and tell 'em to make ready for you and get your luggage out. You fellows go along to the Guest House and look about. Join you shortly. The bishop knows where it is."

The bishop assented with great eagerness. He asked the policeman, sharply, whether anything had been touched, looked round him with satisfaction, and then sniffed the air like a hunter as he strode off across the lawn. The three of them, his son reflected, must have made a queer picture. Up beyond them, at the end of a shallow slope, the gables of the low, severely plain house were silhouetted on the yellow sky. Except for a border of elms on either side of the driveway curving up to it, all the ornamental trees were massed behind The Grange in an estate that must have covered eight thousand acres. The Grange was restored Tudor in design, full of tall windows, bearded in ivy, and built on three sides of a rectangle with the open side towards the road. It had almost the stolid aspect of a public building; and must, Donovan reflected, take an enormous income to keep up. Standish could certainly be no army man retired on half-pay.

The Guest House lay on the southern fringe of the park, in the clearing of a coppice which gave it a deserted, mournful, and rather ominous appearance. It was in a hollow of somewhat marshy ground, with a great ilex tree growing behind it, so that it seemed much smaller than it was. If The Grange itself was of plain design, some domestic architect seemed to have spread himself to make this place an unholy mongrel from all styles of building, and to give it as many geegaws as a super-mighty pipe organ in a super-mighty cinema theatre. It looked as though you could play it. Upon a squat stone house rose scrolls, tablets, stops, and fretwork. Every window—including those of the cellar—was protected by a pot-bellied grille in the French fashion. It was encircled by an upper and lower balcony, with fancy iron railings. Midway along the upper balcony Donovan could see on the west side of the square the door by which the murderer must have escaped. It still stood ajar, and a flight of stairs near it led down to the lower balcony. The very bad taste of the house had a sinister look. Despite the sunlight, it was gloomy in the coppice, and the stickiness of last night's rain had not disappeared.

The bishop was leading them up a brick walk, which divided at the house and encircled it, when he stopped suddenly. At the side of the walk that ran round the west end, they could see the figure of a man kneeling and staring at something on the ground.

The bishop almost said, "Aha!" He strode forward. The kneeling figure raised its head with a jerk.

"But they're my shoes!" it protested. "Look here, confound it. They're *my* shoes!"

CHAPTER V

Somebody's Footprint

"Good afternoon, Morley," said the bishop imperturbably. "Gentlemen, allow me to present Morley Standish, Colonel Standish's son. . . . What's this about your shoes?"

Morley Standish got up, brushing the knees of his trousers. He was earnest, stocky, and thirty-five; a younger, somewhat more intelligent-looking edition of his father. You could see how he had been molded by that association. He had a heavy, not-unhandsome face, and one of those moustaches recently associated with serious purpose by Herr Hitler. Though he wore a loose sport coat, it was of sombre color, and a black tie apparently from some vague idea of doing the correct thing by the late father of his fiancée. You could almost take it as a symbol of him: correct, O.T.C., hesitantly religious; yet wanting to unbend, and with a streak of impetuousness allied with humor.

"I seem to have blurted out something," he said, after a pause. Donovan could not tell whether it was anger or humor in his eyes. He looked from one to the other of them. "Ever have that experience? Someone startles you by coming on you unexpectedly, and you crack out with the thing that's in your mind?"

The half-smile faded off his face.

"Murch told me, sir, that you and my father knew all about this business. It's pretty bad. I've wired Betty the news, before she should see it in a paper. And I'll attend to all the arrangements. But Murch said you'd probably call in Scotland Yard, and we mustn't touch the body until then. If these gentlemen"—he looked at Donovan and Dr. Fell—"are from the Yard, I hope they'll make a quick examination and let the undertaker carry on."

The bishop nodded. He clearly thought very highly of the practical Morley Standish. "This," he said, "is Dr. Fell, whom my—hum—my good friend the chief inspector sent down to assist us. Our investigation should make excellent headway with him. . . ."

He nodded with some stiffness towards the doctor, who blinked amiably upon Standish. "And this is my son, Hugh, of whom you have heard me speak. You are in charge, doctor. Shall we go into the house? You will find Mr. Standish an admirable person to tell us the facts."

"Quite," said Dr. Fell. He jerked a thumb towards the house. "This valet fellow—is he there now?"

Standish had been looking at him with a correct concealment of surprise which thus made itself evident. He had clearly expected Donovan to be a young police official of some description, and he was jarred a little to see Dr. Fell was the man in charge.

"Yes," he said. "Would you care to go in? The cook, Achille, refused to stay. He says there are ghosts in the house. But Storer will stay as long as he is needed."

"No hurry," said Dr. Fell easily. He indicated the few steps which led up to the side entrance of the veranda. "Sit down, Mr. Standish. Make yourself comfortable. Smoke?"

"Surely," observed the bishop, "if we went inside—"

"Rubbish," said Dr. Fell. He settled matters by lowering himself with some difficult on an ornamental bench opposite. Morley Standish, with an expression of great gravity, sat down on the steps and produced a pipe. For a time Dr. Fell was silent, poking at the brick wall with his stick, and wheezing with the labor of having sat down. Then he said with an off-hand air:

"Who do you think killed Depping, Mr. Standish?"

At this unorthodox beginning the bishop folded his arms and looked resigned. It was curiously as though Dr. Fell were on trial, sitting there big and abstracted, with the birds bickering in the trees behind him. Morley Standish looked at him with slightly closed eyes.

"Why," he said, "I don't suppose there's much doubt of that, is there? The chap who came to visit him—the one with the American accent—?" He frowned inquiringly.

"Spinelli," put in the bishop complacently.

"For God's sake," said Dr. Fell, turning to glare, "shut up, will you? I happen to be in charge here."

Morley Standish jumped. There was a puzzled and somewhat shocked expression on his face. But he answered bitterly:

"You know his name, do you? Well, that reminds me. Bishop Donovan was right. If we'd had the sense to listen to him when he first told us about the fellow, *this* mightn't have happened. With all my father's good points—" He hesitated. "Never mind. We could have prevented it."

"I wonder," said Dr. Fell. "What traces of him have you found today? I gather Spinelli hasn't been tracked down?"

"Not so far as I know. But I haven't seen Murch since noon."

"H'mf. Now, Mr. Standish, if Spinelli killed your prospective father-in-law, why do you suppose he did it? What connection was there between a studious, harmless old gentleman like Depping, and an American blackmailer with a police record?"

Standish got his pipe lighted, and twitched the match away before he answered. His heavy face had grown more stolid. "I say, Mr.—what was it—oh—Dr. Fell, why ask me? I don't know any more than—well, my father, say. Why ask me?"

"Did you and Miss Depping ever discuss him, for instance?"

"Ah," said Standish. He looked straight at the doctor. "That's rather a personal question, you know. Still, it's easily answered. Betty—Miss Depping—scarcely knew her father at all. And she doesn't remember her mother. From the age of seven or eight she was in a convent at Trieste. Then she was put in one of those super-strict French boarding schools. When she was eighteen she—well, hang it, she's got spirit, and she couldn't stand it; so she broke out and ran away. . . ." First Morley Standish's correct face looked somewhat embarrassed, and then he grinned. "Ran away, by Jove! Damned good, eh?" he demanded, and brushed at his Hitler moustache, and slapped his leg. "Then the old ba— Mr. Depping permitted her to live with a hired companion (one of those courtesy aunts) in Paris. All this time she only saw him at long intervals. But she wrote to him at some address in London. About five years ago, when she was twenty, he suddenly turned up and said he'd retired from business. The funny part of it was that though he was always worrying about her, and what mischief she might be up to, he never asked her to live with him—" In full flight Standish checked himself. "I say, you needn't repeat all this, need you? That is, I know more about it than my father, I admit, but . . ."

"Suggestive," said the bishop, drawing down the corners of his mouth. "Very suggestive, doctor. I recall a similar case at Riga in 1876; another in Constantinople in 1895; and still a third in—hum—in St. Louis in 1909."

"You do get about, don't you?" inquired Dr. Fell admiringly. He studied Morley Standish. "What business was Depping in?"

"Oh, something in the City, I believe."

"Um. It's a curious thing," grunted Dr. Fell, scowling, "that whenever a man wants to give somebody a character of sound and colorless respectability, he says that he's something in the City. Why did Depping have a bad character hereabouts?"

Standish's manner became defensive and uncomfortable in a way that was reminiscent of his father.

"Bad character?" he repeated. "What do you mean?"

There was a pause. Dr. Fell only shook his head deprecatingly and continued to look at Standish in a benevolent fashion. For a still longer time he kept on staring, his massive head on one side.

"Er," said Morley Standish, and cleared his throat, "I mean, what makes you think he did have a bad character?"

He spoke with a certain weak truculence, and the doctor nodded.

"Well, one person, at least, appears to think he is a blister, and even your staunch parent didn't contradict it. Besides, you know, you yourself referred to him as an 'old ba—.' Eh?"

"What I say is this," replied Morley, hurriedly and defensively. "What I say is this. While it would have been more dignified, and all that, all the same you've got to look at it from an impersonal point of view. The only reason why anybody thought it was funny, or else disliked it, was because he liked to pay attention to girls only my sister's age, when he was past sixty years old.

Maybe his idea of gallantries was ridiculous, but all the same," argued Morley, "it was because he was so prim and studious and fastidious that you couldn't associate it with him. It seemed a little—well, obscene."

Having delivered himself of these sentiments, as though he had been quoting a lesson, Standish bit hard on the stem of his pipe and regarded Dr. Fell in some defiance.

"Old rip with the ladies, was he?" inquired the doctor genially. "I don't suppose he did any real harm, did he?"

Standish's grim mouth slackened. "Thanks," he said in some relief. "I was afraid you'd take it—well, seriously, you know. Harm? Good Lord, no; but he annoyed a lot of people. . . . He especially used to put Hank Morgan's back up. A funny thing, because there are few people more broadminded than Hank. But I think it was Mr. Depping's pedantic mathematics-master way of talking that really annoyed him. This morning, when we got the news, Hank and Madeleine and my sister Patricia and I were having a game of doubles. The tennis courts aren't very far from here, and the first thing we knew Storer came running up the hill, and clawed at the wire, and babbled something about finding Depping dead in his study. Hank only said, 'No such luck,' and didn't even stop serving."

Dr. Fell was silent for a long time. The sun had drawn lower beyond the coppice, and the ugly deformities of the Guest House glittered in level shafts of light.

"We'll come back to that presently," he said, making a gesture of irritation. "Hum, yes. I think we had better go up and look at the body of this very odd combination. . . . But first, what was the remark you made when you arrived: something about 'They're my shoes'? You were examining—" He pointed with his stick to the edge of the brick path near the steps.

All this time, consciously or unconsciously, Morley Standish had been keeping one large foot dangling over a tuft of grass in the clayey soil beside the steps. He moved it now. He got up, large and stocky, and scowled.

"It's a footprint," he said. "I may as well tell you it must have been made with one of my shoes."

The bishop, who throughout the recital had been politely trying to see past that blocking foot, strode forward and bent over it. It was close to the edge of the brick path, its toe pointing towards the steps, as though somebody had strayed slightly off the path with the left foot. The impression was sharp and fairly shallow, with a tuft of grass trampled into it: a large square-toed shoe, having some faint but distinct markings in the heelprint like an eight-sided star. Whitish traces clung inside the print and along its edges.

"You see what happened," Standish explained uneasily. "There was the devil of a rain last night, a footprint would be effaced. But that thing is smack in the shelter of those steps. . . . I say, don't look at *me*. I didn't make it. But look here."

He swivelled round and lowered one foot gently into the lines of the impression.

"I must beg of you, Morley," said the bishop, "not to damage that print. If you will step aside . . . ? I have made quite a study of footprints, gentlemen. Hugh! Come here and let me have your assistance in examining this. We are fortunate. Clay, doctor, is by far the most accurate substance for recording an impression. Sand and snow, contrary to the popular impression, are almost valueless, as Dr. Hans Gross points out. The forward impulse of the foot in sand, for example, will lengthen the print anywhere from half an inch to two inches out of its natural dimension. As to breadth—stand aside, please, Morley." He looked round with a tight smile. "We shall certainly have an interesting exhibit to show Inspector Murch when he returns."

"Oh, Murch found it," said Standish, breaking off his effort to lower his shoe gingerly into the print. "He found it right enough. He and Hank Morgan got some plaster-of-Paris and made a cast of it. I knew they'd found a print, but I didn't even go to look at it until this afternoon."

"Oh, ah," said the bishop. He stopped, and rubbed his mouth. "Indeed! That was more of young Morgan's work, I dare say. Unfortunate. Most unfortunate."

Morley stared.

"You're jolly well right it's unfortunate!" he agreed, his voice booming out with sudden nervousness and annoyance. "Look here. It fits. I'm the only person hereabouts with a shoe as large as that. Not only that, but I can even identify the pair of shoes. . . . I'll swear *I* wasn't mucking about here last night, but you can see for yourself that's a fairly fresh print. I wonder if Murch is thinking—?"

Dr. Fell's voice struck in so quietly and easily that Standish paused. The doctor had lumbered over to blink at the impression in his vague, nearsighted way.

"How can you identify the shoes?" he inquired.

"By the marks on the heel. It's a pair I chucked away. . . . To understand that," explained Standish, pushing back his hat, "you'd have to know my mother. She's one of the best, mother is, but she gets notions. She is afflicted by the power of suggestion. The moment she hears of a new food over the wireless, we get it till we choke. If she hears of a new medicine for any ailment whatever, she becomes convinced that everybody in the house has got the ailment, and doses us all silly. Well," said Morley, with brooding resignation, "not very long ago she read a spirited article in a magazine about, Why submit to the tyranny of the cobbler? It proved what a difference you could make to your household budget if you bought rubber heels at cost and tacked 'em on your own shoes when the old heels wore out. It impressed her so much that she sent to town for great quantities of rubber heels; thousands of rubber heels; God knows how many rubber heels. I never knew there were so many rubber heels in the world. The house was swamped in 'em. They turned up everywhere. You couldn't even open the medicine chest in the bathroom without getting a shower of rubber heels. But worst of it was that you were supposed to nail 'em on yourself—that was a part of the diabolical design, to teach the British household a useful art. The result was—"

"Kindly come to the point, Morley," said the bishop; "I was about to go on explaining—"

"The result was," went on Morley, embarked on a grievance, "that you either soaked the nail clear through the shoe so that you couldn't walk on it, or put it in so loose that the heel would come off just as you started downstairs. I never heard my governor use such language before or since. Finally we rebelled. I told Kennings to take the only pair I'd mutilated and throw it away. . . . And that's *it*," he declared, pointing to the print. "I'd know it anywhere; the heel was too large for the shoe anyhow. All I'm sure of is that somebody is using them. But why?"

The bishop pinched at his lower lip. He said:

"This, doctor, begins to grow serious. It seems to indicate that somebody at The Grange itself is trying to throw suspicion on Morley . . ."

"I wonder," grunted Dr. Fell.

" . . . for it is obvious to the most elementary intelligence," the other went on benevolently, "that Morley himself never wore them. Stand over there, Morley, and put your foot down in the clay beside that print. Now walk in it—there. You see the difference?"

There was a pause. Morley examined the print he had made.

"What ho," said Morley, and whistled. "I see. You mean the print I make is too deep?"

"Exactly. You are very much heavier than the person who stepped there, and your own impression is half an inch deeper. You follow me, doctor?"

Dr. Fell seemed to be paying no attention. He had lumbered away, thoughtfully, his shovel hat pulled down on his forehead; and he turned again to examine the Guest House with a curiously blank, cross-eyed stare. "I'm very much afraid," he said, "that you miss the point of that footprint altogether. . . . When did you last see those shoes, Mr. Standish?"

"See—? Oh, months ago. I gave them to Kennings."

"And what did Kennings, whoever he is, do with them?"

"He's the first footman. He runs mother's junk closet. He . . . I say!" Morley snapped his fingers. "Got it! Ten to one he put 'em in the junk closet. That's mother's idea. It's for the heathen. Whatever there is in the house that we can't possibly want, it's chucked into the junk closet, and once or twice a year mother sorts everything out with the idea of sending it to the heathen. After six months' cool reflection, however, she generally decides she can find a use for most of the things that have been thrown away, so the heathen don't profit much after all."

"And this junk closet is accessible to everybody?"

"Oh, yes. It's a room, really." Morley glanced at the bishop, and one of his eyelids drooped. "It's next door to the room, by the way, where that poltergeist of ours made such a murderous attack on the Vicar of Puckle-church."

The bishop looked at Dr. Fell, and Dr. Fell looked at the bishop. Hugh Donovan had an uneasy feeling that nonsense was beginning to assume the colors of ugly purpose.

"Let's go inside," said Dr. Fell abruptly, and turned.

They went round to the front of the house. The marshy smell had grown strong with the declining sun, and gnats flickered in the shadow of the porch. All the dull-red blinds were drawn on the lower floor. Poking at the bell push with his stick, Dr. Fell glanced along the line of windows.

"There's more in this business," he said, "than shoes or poltergeists, or even murder. The queerest riddle of all is old Depping himself. H'mf. Look at this atrocity!" He rapped the stone wall of the house. "Here's a man noted for his fastidiousness of taste in dress, in letters, and in bearing. He is a *gourmet* who employs a special cook to prepare him dishes that must be exactly right. And yet he lives in a house like this! He's an austere fellow with the nicest sort of taste in wines, and yet he goes on periodical whooping sprees of secret drinking with a servant posted outside the door so that nobody may disturb him. In addition to this, he interrupts periods of hard study to go slobbering after girls young enough to be his granddaughters. This is bad. There's something mad and unholy about it, and this ascetic old satyr is the worst of all. Archons of Athens!—behold Hadley's idea of a nice, featureless, commonplace case. The eight of swords is only an item . . . Ah!"

The door, whose upper panel was made of red-and-black chequered glass, glowed out eerily as somebody switched on a light inside. It was opened by a thin man with a melancholy nose and an air of having looked on all the follies of earth without any particular surprise.

"Yes, sir?" said the nose; he talked through it.

"We're from the police," said Dr. Fell. "Take us upstairs.— Your name is Storer, isn't it?"

"Yes, sir. You will wish," observed the nose, exactly as though it spoke of a living person, "to see the corpse. Please come this way."

Now that they were approaching it, Hugh Donovan felt a nauseous reluctance to see Depping's body at close range. Nor did he like the hall through which Storer led them. It was without windows, and smelt of furniture polish: a mysterious circumstance, inasmuch as none of the heavy dark furniture ever seemed to have been polished. Two meagre-looking electric bulbs descended on a long chandelier from the high ceiling. On the floor and staircase lay matting which had once been yellow, and there were ghostly black portieres over several doors. A speaking tube projected from the wall beside one of them; Dr. Fell inspected it before he followed the procession upstairs.

The study was the front room on the west side. Storer seemed to resist an inclination to knock before he pushed open the door.

A large room with a high ceiling. In the wall facing the door by which they entered, Donovan could see the door to the balcony: its glass panel chequered, like the lower one, in red-and-black glass. It was flanked by two windows, their black velvet curtains drawn back, with the pot-bellied iron grilles outside. Three more windows were in the right-hand wall at the front, furnished in a similar fashion. And all the windows were open.

The trees round the Guest House were so thick that only a greenish twilight fell into the study, but it was sufficient to show dully the room's chief exhibit.

Hugh Donovan never forgot his first sight of violent death. In the left-hand wall—as he faced the door to the balcony—was a low fireplace of white marble. Three or four feet out from it, the late Dr. Septimus Depping lay forward across a flat-topped desk, with his face turned away from the newcomers and his back to the fireplace. He was leaning out of a low leather easy-chair. His legs were doubled back against it. His right arm hung down limp, shoulder on the edge of the desk, and his left rested out across the blotter. The late Mr. Depping wore an old-fashioned smoking jacket and a high collar; his trousers were evening trousers, and he wore black socks and patent-leather shoes. But, most prominent of all, the watchers could see the back of the head that was turned towards them. The hair was well-brushed, scanty, and grizzled-gray. On the crown there had once been a small bald spot, which was now scorched black where the bullet had been fired close against the head.

It was all quietly horrible, the more so because the birds were piping outside, and an indifferent robin was regarding something else from the top of the balcony railing beyond one window.

Hugh Donovan tried to look at something else also. He noticed that even his formidable father was much more human, and not quite so ghoulishly eager as before. Hugh tried to shake up his wits as he would have shaken up a medicine, sharply for sooner or later he would be required to express an opinion. But in the terrible grimness of that picture he did not understand how anybody could be cool and scientific. He peered round the study. The walls were lined with books, even between the window spaces, in neat sectional cases. Everything was scrupulously neat. On a side-table, with a straight chair drawn up before it, was a dinner tray covered by a white cloth; a silver bowl of roses, still unwithered, stood beyond it.

Donovan's eyes moved back, only skirting the desk. A leather chair had been drawn up facing the desk, as though X had been sitting there for a chat. There was a standing ash tray, without ashes or stubs, beside it. A metal filing cabinet stood against the desk; a small table bearing a covered typewriter; and another standing ash tray. Over the desk hung a single powerful electric bulb in a plain shade, which, with the exception of a bridge lamp in one corner, appeared to be the only means of illumination. On the large clean desk blotter was a wire basket containing several bundles of manuscript to which were clipped blue typewritten sheets; a tray of pens and colored pencils, an inkpot, a box of clips holding down several sheets of stamps, and a large silver-mounted photograph of a girl. Finally, almost in a line with the chairs of Depping and X, there stood on the edge of the table a holder containing a half-burned candle.

Yes . . . when the lights went out. Hugh saw another candle on the edge of the mantelpiece. On one side of this mantelpiece was a curtained door, and on the other a sideboard wedged cater-cornered in the angle of two walls of books. But his eyes always kept coming back to the bullet hole in the dead man's head; to the quiet orderliness of the murder, and to the glimmer of a painted card he could see just under the fingers of the dead man's left hand.

The first to move was Dr. Fell. He lumbered through the door, his stick bumping heavily on the carpet against stillness. Wheezing, he bent to peer at the body, and the black ribbon on his glasses brushed the candlestick. Then, still bent forward, he looked slowly round the room. Something seemed to bother him. He went to the windows, looked at the floor under them, and felt the curtains of each one. He was bothered still more.

"Why," he said, suddenly, "why are all the windows open?"

CHAPTER VI

The Wrong Visitor

STORER, WHO had been waiting patiently with his nose inclined, frowned at this beginning. He said:

"I beg your pardon, sir?"

"Were these windows open when you found the body this morning?"

"Yes, sir," replied Storer, after inspecting each one.

The doctor removed his shovel hat; and, on the sudden realization, everybody else did the same; though the doctor's action had been prompted less out of veneration for the dead than to mop his moist forehead with a gaudy bandana. And, as though that action had broken a sort of spell, everybody moved into the room.

"H'm, yes. The floor over here is half an inch deep in water, and all the curtains are soaked. . . . About this storm last night: What time did it commence?"

"About eleven o'clock, sir."

Dr. Fell seemed to be talking to himself. "Then why didn't Depping close his windows? Why leave all five of them open, with a thunderstorm blowing in? It's wrong; it's illogical; it's . . . What were you saying?"

Storer's eyes had grown sharp with a memory; his cheeks puffed slightly, and for a moment he looked less disillusioned.

"Go on, man," said Dr. Fell testily. "The storm begins at eleven. Depping is alone then. His visitor arrives shortly afterwards—the visitor goes upstairs, and is entertained—and all this time the storm is coming full blast through five open windows. That's wrong somewhere. . . . What were you thinking of?"

"Something Achille said, sir." The valet looked at Depping, and seemed puzzled. "I forgot it, and so did Achille, when the other police officer was speaking to us. That's Achille Georges—the cook, you know . . ."

"Well?"

Storer stood on his dignity, and would not be hurried. "After the storm had begun, and that American went upstairs to see Mr. Depping, you see, sir. I sent Achille out to see what had gone wrong with the electric wires. They put the lights out, you see—"

"We know all that."

"Yes, sir. While Achille was out in the rain, he saw Mr. Depping and the American up here going about and raising all the windows. He said they seemed to be waving the curtains too."

Dr. Fell blinked at him. "Raising all the windows? Waving the curtains?—Didn't that seem at least a trifle odd?"

Again the valet contemplated the follies of the world and was not surprised. "Mr. Depping, sir," he answered stolidly, "was a man of moods."

The doctor said, "Bah!" And the bishop of Mappleham, who

had recovered himself by this time, moved into first place with stately serenity.

"We can go into all that presently," he suggested. "Ah, might I inquire—Inspector Murch went over this room, I presume, for fingerprints? We shall not be disturbing anything if we investigate?"

"No, sir. There were no fingerprints," said Storer in a rather approving manner. He regarded the body as though he appreciated a workmanlike job, and then stared out of the windows.

"First," observed the bishop, "a look round . . ." He approached the desk, his son following, moved round it, and inspected the dead man's face. Death had been instantaneous. There was even a rather complacent expression on Depping's face, which was smirking out towards the windows with its cheek against the blotter. It was a long, dry, nondescript countenance, which might have borne any expression in life. The eyes were half open, the forehead bony, the mouth furrowed; and a rimless pince-nez still clung to his high-bridged nose.

From under his fingers the bishop drew the card. It was of white glazed cardboard, neatly cut out from a sheet such as you buy at any stationer's. Eight tiny broadswords drawn in India ink, their hilts painted black and their blades gray with water color, were arranged in a sort of asterisk along a blue painted line which was evidently meant to represent water. "If," said the bishop, as though offhand to his son, "Dr. Fell really has some notion as to what this means . . ."

Dr. Fell did not reply. He was lifting the white cloth over the dishes on the side table. After fingering the card impatiently, the bishop circled the desk, peering, and opened the right-hand drawer. From it he took out a thirty-eight calibre Smith & Wesson revolver with an ivory handle. He sniffed at the barrel, and then broke it open as though he had been handling firearms all his life. Then he replaced it, and closed the drawer with a bang. He seemed more at a loss than Hugh had ever seen him.

"Two shots," he said, "and no other bullet found here. . . ."

"No, sir," said the valet complacently. "The police officer and Mr. Morgan allowed me to stay here while they made their examination, sir. They even conceived an idea that it might have gone out one of the windows, and they sighted lines from all parts of the room to see if they could find its direction. But Mr. Morgan, sir—Mr. Morgan pointed out it would be most unusual if a bullet went out there without touching any of the bars. They are not more than half an inch apart, any of them. He said it would be freakish, sir," amplified Storer, testing the word with a little tilt of his nose, and finding it good; "freakish. If you'll excuse me."

"A very clever young man," said the other coldly. "But what we want are facts. Let us proceed to the facts." He stood heavy and sharp-jawed against his light, flapping his hands behind him, and his hypnotic eye fixed the valet. "How long have you been with Mr. Depping?"

"Five years, sir. Ever since he came to live here."

"How did he come to employ you?"

"Through a London agency, sir. This is not," replied Storer with a touch of austerity, "my part of the country."

"Do you know anything of his past life—before he employed you?"

"No, sir. I assured the police officer of that this morning."

He went over his story in a patient fashion. Mr. Depping had been a man of moods; touchy, irritated by trifles, apt to go into a rage with the cook if his meals were not shaded exactly to his fastidious palate, fond of quoting Brillat-Savarin. Very learned, no doubt, but not a gentleman. Storer appeared to base his sad deductions to this effect on the statements that (a) Mr. Depping tended to call the servants by their first names when he was drunk, and to mention his business affairs, (b) he used American expressions, and (c) he was freely and often—said Storer—vulgarly generous with his money. At one time (while devoted to his whisky drinking) he had said that the only reason why he employed Storer was because the valet looked so bloody respectable: and the only reason why he employed Achille Georges was because the world considered a taste for fine foods and wines to be the mark of a cultured man.

"That's what he said, sir," affirmed Storer, with an expression which on any less dismal face would have been sly. His nose sang on: "'The world is so full of fools, Charley,'—which is not my name, sir—'the world is so full of fools,' he said to me, 'that anybody who can get emotional over an omelette, or tell you the vintage of a wine, is considered a very superior sort of person.' Then he would glare over those half-glasses of his, and grip the whisky bottle as though he meant to throw it." The valet's eyes wheeled round his narrow nose as though he appreciated this too. "But I must say, sir, in all justice, that he said he would have kept Achille anyway, because of the soups he could make. They were good soups," agreed Storer, judicially. "Mr. Depping was very fond—"

"My good man," interposed the bishop testily, "I am not at all concerned with his tastes in food—"

"I am," said Dr. Fell suddenly. He had wheeled round as the valet's narrative went on. "Was he fond of crawfish soup, by any chance?"

"He was sir," replied Storer imperturbably. "It was his favorite. Achille had been preparing it frequently of late."

Dr. Fell removed the cloth again from the dinner dishes of last night, and nodded towards them. "Then it's damned funny," he said. "Here's crawfish soup, nearly untasted. On the other hand, he seems to have been especially rough on a kind of pineapple salad. He's eaten most of his dinner except the soup. . . . Never mind. Carry on."

The bishop of Mappleham, who had paid no attention to this, fixed on an idea which had been growing in his son's mind for some time.

"One thing is evident," he declared. "Every bit of evidence we have heard points towards it. I do not wish to defame the memory of the dead, but this man Depping was not what he seemed. His past life—his unaccountable past life—his actions, and contradictions, are all those of a man who is playing a part. . . ."

"Yes," said Dr. Fell, with a sort of obstinacy; "that's too evident to mention. But who's been eating his dinner?"

"Confound his dinner!" roared the bishop, letting off steam for the first time. "You know it, Storer. I believe you know it too, Morley . . ."

He swung round to young Standish, who had remained near the door with his hands jammed into his pockets. Morley lifted his eyes. Morley said equably:

"Sorry, sir. I don't know anything of the kind."

"It does not surprise me," pursued His Reverence, "that Depping should have been consorting with criminals. In all likelihood he has been a criminal himself in the past, and he has been living here to assume a guise of respectability. He knew Louis Spinelli. Louis Spinelli tracked him down for the purpose of blackmailing him. . . . Depping's 'business.' What *was* his business? Does anybody know anything about it?"

"Excuse me, sir," observed the valet. "He had—he informed me—a large financial interest in the publishing firm of Standish & Burke. But, as I told the police officer this morning, he was trying to get rid of that interest. You see, he told me all about it when he was—indisposed the last time."

"I meant his business previous to five years ago. He never mentioned *that* to you, I dare say? . . . I thought not."

His Reverence was regaining his self-confidence. He moved one hand up and down the lapel of his ponderous black coat. "Now, let us reconstruct what happened last night, if we can. Shortly after the storm began, around eleven o'clock, this stranger—I mean the American, whose name we know to be Spinelli—rang the doorbell and asked to see Mr. Depping. That is correct, Storer? Thank you. . . . Now, as a matter of form I must ask you to identify him. I have two photographs here"—he produced them from his inside pocket and handed them to the valet. "That is the man who called on Mr. Depping, is it not?"

Storer looked at the snapshots with care. He handed them back.

"*No, sir,*" he said apologetically.

With a feeling that somebody had gone mad, Hugh Donovan peered into the man's face. There was a silence, during which they could hear Dr. Fell unconcernedly poking with his stick in the fireplace behind the dead man's chair. Behind this chair Dr. Fell rose to the surface like a red-faced walrus, wrinkled his moustache with a beaming air, and sank down again. The bishop only stared, blankly.

"But this . . ." he said, and swallowed hard. He assumed a persuasive air. "Come, come, now! This is absurd. Utterly absurd, you know. This must be the man. Come look again."

"No, sir, it isn't the same man," Storer answered with an air of regret. "I only had a brief look at him, I know, and the candle didn't give a great deal of light. Perhaps, sir, I might not even be able to identify him positively if I saw him again . . . But—excuse me—this is *not* the same man. The whole face is different, except for the moustache. This man's face is very broad and low, and has heavy eyebrows. It doesn't look anything like the man I saw. And, besides, the man I saw had projecting ears, noticeably projecting, sir."

The bishop looked at Dr. Fell. The doctor was stirring a mass of heavy black ash in the fireplace, and one eye caught the ecclesiastical appeal.

"Yes," he said, "yes, I was afraid of that."

Somebody brushed past Donovan. Morley Standish had come up to the desk.

"This man's lying," he said heavily. "He's either lying, or else he's working with Spinelli. It must have been Spinelli. The bishop is right. There's nobody else—"

"Tut, tut," said Dr. Fell, rather irritably. "Calm yourselves a moment, while I ask just one question, and then I may be able to tell you something. I say, Storer, it's rather an important question, so try not to make any mistake."

He indicated the door to the balcony. "It's about that door. Was it usually locked or unlocked?"

"The door . . . why, always locked, sir. Invariably. It was never used."

Dr. Fell nodded. "And the lock," he said musingly, "isn't a spring-lock. It's the old-fashioned kind, d'ye see. Where's the key for it?"

The other reflected for some time. "I believe, sir, that it's hanging up on a hook in the pantry, along with some other keys for rooms that aren't used."

"Cut along then, and see if you can find it. I'll give you odds it isn't there, but have a look anyway."

He watched owlishly until the valet had left the room.

"Let's pass over for the moment," he went on, "the identity of the man who came to see Depping last night. Let's only assume that somebody came here for the purpose of killing Depping, not blackmailing him, and go on from there. Come here a moment, will you?"

They followed him uncertainly as he went over to the bridge lamp near the front windows.

"The electric fittings in this place," he continued, "are of a rather old-fashioned variety. You see that socket along the baseboard of the wall? This plug,"—he picked up a length of wire from the lamp—"this plug, which is loose now, is screwed into that socket. In the modern ones the plug has only two prongs, which fit into the socket, and the live part isn't exposed for somebody to touch accidentally and get the devil of a shock. But the live part is exposed there; you see?"

"Certainly," said the bishop. "What about it?"

"Well, I've found the buttonhook."

"*What?*"

Dr. Fell raised his hand for silence as Storer hurried back into the room. "The key isn't there, sir," he reported.

"H'mf, yes. Now, then, just let me get one or two points corroborated, and then you may go. Last night the storm began just before eleven o'clock. You didn't speak to Mr. Depping then, or he to you. You went downstairs to shut the windows, and you were down there when the lights went out. You rummaged after candles down here, which took—how long, should you think?"

"Well, sir, say five minutes."

"Good. Then you started upstairs, and were going up to see

whether your employer needed any candles when the knock came at the door, and you saw the mysterious man with the American accent. He wouldn't give any name, but pointed to the speaking tube and said to ask Mr. Depping whether he couldn't go upstairs. Which you did, and the visitor went up. Is all that correct, as we heard it?"

"Yes, sir."

"That's all. And be sure you go downstairs now, please." Pushing out his cloak, Dr. Fell lowered himself into an easy-chair near the lamp. He regarded his audience with an argumentative stare, and said: "I wanted to be sure of that, gentlemen. It struck me, when I heard it this morning, that the story had a distinctly fishy sound. Look here. Put yourselves in Depping's place for a moment.

"You're sitting here in this room one evening, reading or what not, and all of a sudden—without the slightest warning—every light in the house goes out. What would you do?"

"Do?" repeated the bishop. He frowned. "Why, I suppose I should go out and find out why—"

"Precisely!" rumbled Dr. Fell, and struck his stick against the floor. "It's the normal, inevitable thing. You'd be furious; people always are when that sort of thing happens. You'd go out and bawl over the bannisters as to what the thus-and-so was going on in that place. Depping, a man who was annoyed more than anything by trifles, assuredly would. But that's the point. He didn't. He didn't even call downstairs to inquire what was wrong.

"To the contrary, he evinced a singular lack of interest in those lights. He was willing to entertain a man—who wouldn't give his name—with only a candle or two for illumination. He even, you recall, instructed Storer not to bother about seeing that they were repaired. Now, that isn't reasonable. And, actually, what *was* wrong? Something had blown out the fuses. I thought it might be interesting to inquire into causes. Here is the cause."

From the floor beside the chair Dr. Fell took up a long steel buttonhook, now corroded and blackened. He turned it over in his palm, musingly.

"You see that live socket? Eh? Well, this buttonhook was deliberately thrust into it, in order to short-circuit the lights. You have only to look at the buttonhook to see that. I found it lying near the open socket. In other words, the lights were put out from this room. . . . What do you make of it?"

CHAPTER VII

"Who's Been Sitting in My Chair?"

THE BISHOP was a gentleman and a sportsman. He rumpled at the bird's nest of hair curling back over his big head, and then he smiled. "My dear doctor," he said, "it begins to be borne in on me that I should have done better to remain silent. Pray go on."

"Tut!" grunted Dr. Fell amiably. "Let's pursue this line of reconstruction a little further. *Il saute aux yeux la question:* Why under sanity should Depping want to put out his own lights? The obvious answer is that he wanted to entertain a visitor *who must not be recognized by his servants.*

"From this we proceed to inference that (1) Storer did know the person who was to call on him, but (2) he was in such fashion disguised that Storer would not know him if he were seen only by the very uncertain light of a candle. Hence the short-circuiting of the lights. This is decidedly supported by the conduct of the visitor. Mind, he is never supposed to have been inside the house before, and is a complete stranger. Yet he points to the speaking tube on the wall and tells Storer to speak to his em-

77

ployer. That isn't the ordinary behavior of a caller who wants an interview with the master of a house; far from it."

The bishop nodded. "Unquestionably," he agreed. "There can be no doubt of it. That is the explanation."

Dr. Fell scowled. His eyes wandered drowsily about the room, and then a capacious chuckle ran down the ridges of his waistcoat.

"No, it isn't," he said.

"I beg your pardon?"

"It isn't. I didn't say it was the explanation; I only said those were inferences to be drawn from the hypothesis that Depping put out his own lights. And I wish it were as simple as that. But let's proceed for a moment on that assumption, and see what we find.

"H'm. Harrumph. There is a very, very grave objection to this theory. If Depping wished to entertain a secret visitor, why did he indulge in all that elaborate and dangerous mummery? Why go to all the trouble of putting a loud check suit and a false moustache on his visitor, dousing the lights, and mysteriously bringing him in at the front door? Why not simply bring him up to the balcony, and through the balcony door unknown to anybody? Why not smuggle him in at the back door? Why not bring him through a window, if necessary? Why not adopt the simplest course of all: send the servants to bed and let him in himself—front door, balcony door, or back door?

"You see, that theory won't work. Nobody but a lunatic would have arranged a meeting like that. There must have been a very good reason why it was done in that way."

He paused for a long time.

"To see whether we can explain it, remember that the balcony door, which is always kept locked, was found open this morning. Not only was this door usually locked, but the key was not in it at all; it hung on a nail in a pantry downstairs. And it is gone now. Who took that key, and who opened the door? The murderer left that way, and it must have been unlocked either by Depping or by the murderer. Keep that fact fixed in your mind while we consider the problem.

"Whoever the visitor was, or why he was admitted under such circumstances of hocus-pocus, look at the facts and see what happened afterwards. Depping and X are closeted together, amiably enough to all purposes, and some very extraordinary things occur. They are seen by the cook putting up all the windows in the midst of a blowing thunderstorm. . . . What does that suggest to you?"

The bishop was pacing about at a measured and thoughtful gait.

"I can scarcely imagine," he replied, "that they did so because they wanted to air the room."

"But they did," said Dr. Fell. "That's exactly what they wanted to do. Haven't you looked in the fireplace? Haven't you wondered about a fire in the hottest part of August? Haven't you seen that heavy, clotted mass of ash? Haven't you wondered what must have been burned, so that all the windows had to be raised?"

"You mean—"

"Clothes," said Dr. Fell.

There was an eerie pause. "I mean," the doctor went on, his voice rumbling through the quiet room, "I mean that glaring check suit worn by the visitor. You can still see traces of it in the fireplace. Now, mark you, these two are acting in perfect accord and understanding. The more we examine the problems as it *seems* to be, the more we must realize that it's mad, and there must be something wrong with the facts as they have been presented to us. Here is Depping admitting a visitor as he does, when he could easily have let him in through the balcony door without fuss. Here are Depping and his visitor sitting down to burn the visitor's clothes: which, I can assure you, is a social pursuit somewhat rare in the British Isles. Finally, we have the visitor not only shooting Depping with Depping's own gun, but (a) taking the gun out of the drawer without any protest, (b) getting behind Depping with it, also without protest, (c) firing two bullets of which one has mysteriously vanished, (d) carefully replacing the gun in the drawer, and (e) leaving this room by means of a balcony door which is always kept locked, and whose key is downstairs in the pantry."

Wheezing, the doctor took out his pipe and tobacco pouch with an air of gentle protest. Morley Standish, who had been staring out of the window, turned suddenly.

"Hold on, sir! I don't follow that. Even if Depping didn't let the man in, he might have got the key out of the pantry and put it in the door so that he could let the visitor out afterwards."

"Quite so," agreed Dr. Fell. "Then why isn't the key there now?"

"Why isn't—?"

"H'mf, yes. It's not very complicated, is it?" the other asked anxiously. "If you're a murderer leaving a room in comparative haste, throwing the door open and ducking out, does it generally occur to you to pinch the key on your way out? Why should you? If you wanted to lock the door behind you, I could understand the position. Lock the door; chuck away the key. But why, if you intend leaving the door ajar, do you want a dangerous souvenir like that?"

He lit the dregs of his pipe.

"But let's not consider that just yet. Let's tear some more flimsy shreds out of the situation as it *seems*. If we come back to that problem of the mummery round the entrance of Depping's visitor, I think we shall see it isn't sensible either way. If for some reason the thing were an abstruse piece of deception, with all details arranged between them beforehand, look at the fantastic nature of one of the details! I refer, gentlemen, to Depping's apparent means of putting out the lights. I can think off-hand of several easy and perfectly safe means of short-circuiting 'em. . . . But what, apparently, does Depping do? He picks up an *all-steel* buttonhook and shoves it into a live socket—!

"There's the buttonhook. Will any of you volunteer to do it now?"

Morley ran a hand through his sleek dark hair.

"Look here!" he protested plaintively, "I mean to say, come to think of it, if you tried that you'd get a shock that would lay you out for fifteen minutes. . . ."

"If not considerably worse. Quite so."

Hugh Donovan found his voice for the first time. His father had ceased to be formidable now. He said: "I thought you'd just proved, doctor, that the buttonhook *was* used. And yet anybody would know better than to do a thing like that."

"Oh, it was used right enough; look at it. But go a step further. Can you think of any means by which it could have been used in perfect safety?"

"I confess I scarcely follow you," replied the bishop. "I cannot conjecture that it was in some fashion propped up so that it would fall into the socket at the required moment . . ."

"No. But what about rubber gloves?" inquired Dr. Fell.

There was a pause.

"H'mf. I'm only theorizing now, of course," the doctor rumbled, "yet, when you ally it with a few other points I shall indicate in a moment, it is an alluring theory. That's the only way the trick could have been worked. Yet again the total adds up to foolishness if we conceive that—as a part of this intricate design—Depping provided himself with a pair of rubber gloves to put out his own lights, when (as I have insisted) other and simpler methods were at hand. . . . Nevertheless, there is another connotation of rubber gloves. If a man desires to leave no fingerprints, and yet have a free and delicate use of his hands, rubber gloves are the best sort of protection."

The bishop made a massive gesture. "My dear Dr. Fell," he intoned, almost sepulchrally, "you are getting into the realm of fantastic nonsense. Why should the late Mr. Depping have cared whether or not he left fingerprints in his own study?"

Letting out a gust of smoke, Dr. Fell leaned forward with a sort of fierce intensity and pointed his pipestem. His wheezing breath grew louder. He said:

"Exactly! *Why should he?* There's another 'why should he' for this incredible collection. Why should he at least not make a pretense of wondering why the lights went out? Why didn't he play his part like an artist, and come out of his room to ask Storer what was wrong? Why didn't he show himself? Why did he help the visitor burn his clothes?—And last of all," said the doctor, lifting his stick and jabbing it towards the dinner tray, "why did he sample everything on that tray *except* his favorite soup?"

"I say, this bears a curious resemblance to the classic history of the three bears. 'Who's been sitting in *my* chair? Who's been drinking *my* porridge? Who—' Gentlemen, I think you are beginning to perceive by this time that the man in this room was not Depping at all."

The bishop muttered something to himself. A sudden dazzling suspicion seemed to make him wheel round and look at the smirking face of the dead man. . . .

"Then Depping—" he said. "Where was Depping all this time?"

"Why, I'll tell you," responded the doctor, and made a hideous pantomime face by way of emphasis. "He was decked out in an eye-splitting check suit, bogus jewellery, a wig, a false moustache, and actor's cement behind his ears to make them protrude. He was ringing his own doorbell and paying a call in his own house. . . . There it is, you see. In this masquerade the rôles were simply reversed, and that's what I meant by saying we should have to tear apart the facts as they seemed, or we should never understand the truth. It was X, the mysterious stranger, who posed as Depping in this room. And it was Depping—eh?"

"Can you—" said Morley Standish, "can you prove this?" He was breathing hard, and his heavy dark face, with its absurd-looking moustache, had a sudden look of relief.

"I rather think I can," said Dr. Fell modestly.

"But—ah," observed the bishop, "I—that is, I am bound to remark that this fresh approach would seem to make the matter quite as complicated and incomprehensible as it was before."

"Eh? No. No, I don't agree. Give me this reversal of rôles," urged Dr. Fell, with a persuasive air, "and I'll undertake to simplify it. Heh. Yes."

"I can understand," pursued the other, "how Depping's appearance could have deceived Storer with only one candle burning. The very clothes alone would have had the effect of distracting his eye much as a conjuror does; which is—ah—the first principle of disguise, and, I am told, the only really effective one." It was a struggle for the bishop to include that "I am told"; but he did it. He brooded. "I can even understand the change of voice, allied to the American accent. . . . But there is a more difficult imposture to account for. How do you account for the voice of the man in this room, imitating Depping's? Surely Storer would have known it was not the same?"

The doctor chuckled, and spilled ashes down his waistcoat.

"He would," the doctor agreed, "if he had heard it anywhere else but through a speaking tube." He pointed to the wall. "Of all the ghostly and disembodied effects in the way of communication, commend me to the speaking tube. You yourself would sound like a spirit-voice. Have you never used one?—It isn't like a telephone, you know. Go downstairs, and let each of us speak to you in turn; and I will defy you to identify your own son.

"And, you see, it was only over the speaking tube that the bogus Depping spoke to Storer. The 'visitor' went upstairs, entered this room, and the door closed. Afterwards, of course, the *real* Depping spoke, and there was no deception to puzzle our observant valet."

"For the present," said the bishop, "let's accept the hypothesis. . . . I must insist that we still have as inexplicable a situation as before. Why should Depping and X have put up this imposture between them?"

"I don't think they did."

The bishop remained calm. He said: "Most extraordinary, doctor. I was under the impression that you said—"

"I do not think they put it up *between them*, confound it," snorted Dr. Fell. "Remember, if you please, that we have only got a reversal of rôles. It doesn't alter any of the circumstances. If you say there was collusion between those two, you must explain the same riddles as before. The queer behavior of the man in this room isn't greatly altered because his name is X instead of Depping. Why, if X is working with Depping from the beginning of a carefully conceived plan, does he want the rubber gloves? If Depping brought a disguised X through the front door instead of smuggling him up the balcony, why didn't X do the same for a disguised Depping? . . . Be calm, my dear sir; I know you yourself pointed out those difficulties. So let's begin with the dinner. Depping didn't eat it, but X did. Whispering to the inner ear, echoing through the halls of consciousness," said Dr. Fell with relish, "comes the sinister question: Why didn't Depping eat his dinner?"

"Maybe he wasn't hungry," said Morley Standish, after considering the problem.

"Brilliant," said Dr. Fell testily. "The helpfulness of my colleagues is inspiring. Surely, gentlemen, your innate shrewdness, your native cunning, can provide a better answer than that—? It must have occurred to you that he didn't eat his dinner because he wasn't here, and X did eat it because he was here. The dinner was brought up at half-past eight. Depping was here then, restless and nervous, I think the report was. And he must have left the house shortly after that, *in his fancy disguise.* He must, therefore, have gone out the balcony door. Eh?"

"Quite," said the bishop. "And—that provides us, it is obvious, with an important piece of evidence. He had the key to the balcony door."

"Good. We progress. So what follows?"

"I do not agree with your statement that no plot was arranged beforehand between Depping and X," said the bishop. He was stalking about now, in a fervor of enlightenment. "Everything points to that. While Depping was away—"

"For nearly an hour and a half—"

"—for nearly an hour and a half, then, X was in this room.

Doctor, every detail fits into place. Depping, in disguise, left here for a nefarious purpose, an illegal purpose . . ."

Dr. Fell stroked his moustache. "It is considered so. Yes. He took his gun along, you see . . . Are you beginning to have a nebulous idea as to what happened to the missing bullet?"

"Oh, my God!" said Morley Standish suddenly.

"Ghosts of the past will now gather round," continued Dr. Fell, "to gibber that crusty old Depping was a very, very dangerous man on whom to try any games. I expect his use of American words, when drunk, came naturally to him. . . . It occurs to me that poor old Louis Spinelli will never try any blackmailing tricks again. If he isn't as dead as Garibaldi at this moment, I am very much mistaken."

They all looked at the dead smirk on Depping's face; at the neatness of his clothes, the orderly books, and the silver bowl of roses on the dinner table.

"My friend," declared the bishop, as though he were beginning a speech, "on the admirable completeness with which you have conjured a case out of evidence which does not exist and facts which have not been demonstrated, I must offer my sincerest congratulations. . . . Hem. On the other hand, you must be aware that everything you have said indicates a plot between Depping and X. Depping was going out to commit a murder. It is simplicity itself. He left a colleague here to prove him an alibi."

Dr. Fell ruffled the hair at his temples. For a long time he blinked across the room. A new, disturbing idea seemed to strike him.

"You know . . ." he said. "By the Lord, I believe it would be better, if for the present, we agreed on that. I don't believe it is precisely true; and yet my own idea—which is not so very different from yours in essentials—is open to such an overpowering objection that . . . Yes, let's assume what you say. Let's say Depping left somebody here, to growl something through the door in case he should be approached—"

"And this person," interposed the bishop grimly, "came here determined to kill Depping just as Depping meant to kill Spinelli."

"Yes. Now we are on safe ground. Gentlemen, no more beautiful opportunity for murder ever presented itself with a proof of innocence attached. Look at it! If Depping thought he was safe to kill Spinelli, then X must have roared with mirth to see how safely he could kill Depping. . . .

"Don't you see," he demanded, pounding his fist on his knee, "how it would work out? It explains our problem as to why Depping walked through the door in disguise. In the original plan, *Depping had never intended to do that.* To do that, after he had killed Spinelli, would have been idiotic and dangerous. His alibi was planted in his study. He should have returned there as he left—by the balcony door, unseen, to shed his disguise. A suspicious man in loud clothes, with a mysterious manner and an American accent, who deliberately walked in his front door . . . why, it would have started every tongue in the countryside wagging. If Spinelli were discovered dead—another suspicious American—then inquiries would lead straight to Depping to ask what *he* knew about it. They might not prove him guilty of murder, but your respectable, studious country gentleman would be in for an uncomfortable lot of explaining."

Morley Standish cleared his throat. "Then, hang it, why did he?" he asked.

"That's the infernal beauty of X's scheme. . . . Depping came in the front door because he couldn't get in any other way. Do you see it? X caught him in the neatest kind of trap. Depping had gone out the balcony door, leaving the key in it; instructing X to lock it behind him, and admit him when he returned. . . . Remember, that's *your* theory; I told you that in many features mine is different . . . but, anyway, Depping returns just as the thunderstorm breaks, and he can't get in—"

"Because X won't let him in," said the bishop.

"Well, it can scarcely have been so crude as that. That's where your hypothesis wobbles a bit; to keep Depping unsuspicious, X would have had to spin some yarn about losing the key. It would sound improbable. I think I have a better explanation, but it works out on the same principle . . . And there you are. There's the door locked, and bars on every window. There's Depping fairly caught out in a heavy storm, in a disguise he can't possibly explain!

"The stiff and scholarly Mr. Depping known hereabouts," he went on musingly, "wearing a music-hall suit. . . . Where can he go? How can he dispose of that garb? Picture yourself, Bishop Donovan, caught in an English village at night and in a storm, dressed up as Charles Chaplin just after having committed a murder . . . Depping was fairly in the soup. He'd *got* to get into his house unsuspected, and all the windows were barred. And he had to get in quickly; every minute his accomplice remained there increased the danger of detection both for himself and his accomplice. He could even talk to his accomplice, through the bars of the balcony window, but he couldn't get in . . .

"And here's X with a suggestion—you know what it was. Lights short-circuited, American visitor enters, identities are restored. It was a dangerous risk, but the lesser of two bad positions for Depping. For X it was the boon of an American visitor who would be supposed to have shot Depping when, later on, Depping was found murdered. And it very nearly succeeded."

The bishop went over the desk, and for a time he looked down at the dead man with an expression in which were mingled compassion and disgust.

" 'The Lord gave—' " he said, and stopped. When he turned again, there was a quizzical expression in his eyes.

"You are a persuasive speaker, doctor," he said. "An unusually persuasive speaker. All this has been explained so coherently that I have been forgetting the basis on which all the assumptions rest: that is, the death of Spinelli. I have read of brilliant pieces of deduction to unravel crimes. But I must compliment you on your brilliance in unravelling a murder we don't know has been committed."

Dr. Fell was not abashed. "Oh, I'm a bit of a charlatan," he acknowledged affably. "Still, I'll wager you two junior mathematics masters against a curate that it took place as I've indicated. That door over there leads to Depping's bedroom. If you care to make a search, you'll probably find evidence to support me. Personally, I'm lazy . . ."

"Look here," said Morley Standish. "There's something you've *got* to promise. You say old Depping was a crook in the past, and probably worse; that's what you believe, anyhow . . ."

His big stride brought him to the side of Dr. Fell's chair, and his face was painfully earnest; he had the uncertain look of a man who feels that showing an emotion would be an incorrect thing, but is determined to force it over by lowering his voice and speaking very fast.

"Well, I'll tell you the truth. I'm not surprised. I've been thinking—things, myself. You'll say that's disloyal—"

"Tut," grunted Dr. Fell. "Why?"

"—but there it is. Now do you realize what a mess we'll all be in when this gets out? Scandal, publicity, slime . . . My God, don't you see it? They may even try to stop my marriage; they will try, if I know my mother. They won't succeed, but that's not the point. Why does everybody have to be subjected to this? Why . . ." His puzzled expression as he glanced at each of them, puzzled and baffled and rather desperate, seemed to demand the reason for the injustice of having criminals in the world just when he was on the point of matrimony. "What good purpose will it serve to drag all this out? Can you tell me that?"

"I take it, my boy," said the bishop, "that you do not care whether your fiancée's father had been a criminal? Or a murderer?"

Two muscles worked up the sides of Morley's jaws. His eyes were puzzled.

"I don't care," he said simply, "if the old swine committed every murder in Chicago . . . But why does it have to be made *public?*"

"But you want the truth to come out, don't you?"

"Yes, I suppose I do," admitted Morley, rubbing his forehead. "That's the rules. Got to play fair. But why can't they just catch him and hang him quietly, without anybody knowing . . . ? I'm talking rot, of course, but if I could make you understand what I mean . . . Why do the damned newspapers have a right to splash out all the scandal they like just because a man's been murdered? Why can't you administer justice in private, the same as you make a law or perform an operation?"

"That, Mr. Standish," Dr. Fell said, "is a problem for discussion over half-a-dozen bottles of beer. But for the moment I don't think you need worry about scandal. I was coming to that: I mean our plan of campaign . . . Do you see what we've got to do?"

"No," said Morley hopelessly. "I wish I could."

"It's an ugly thing to face, then, but here it is. The murderer of Depping—X—the decidedly brainy person who worked out this design—is *here*. He's no fanciful gangster. He's a member of the community in an English village, and probably not a mile away from us now. That's why I've gone through this laborious explanation: so that we could center our activities. As it stands now—"

He leaned forward, and beat his finger slowly into his palm.

"—as it stands now, he thinks he is safe. He thinks we have laid the murder on Louis Spinelli. That's where we have the advantage, and the only way we shall be able to trap him unawares. Therefore, for the time being, we shall keep silent about everything we know, including our suspicions as to Depping's past. I shall have to report it all to Hadley, and the past can be investigated from London. But our information we will keep to ourselves.

"Besides, gentlemen, we have several valuable clues. The murderer made one or two mistakes, which I needn't outline at the moment, but his greatest mistake was leaving the eight of swords. It supplies a direction in which to look for the motive."

"Are you at last prepared, then," said the bishop, "to tell us what this eight of swords means?"

"Oh, yes. I don't know whether you've noticed on Depping's shelves a number of works dealing with—"

From outside the house there rose a murmur a voices and a trampling of feet. Morley and the bishop, who were near the windows, glanced out.

"Here comes a whole procession," said the former. "My father, and Inspector Murch, and my sister, and Dr. Fordyce, and two constables. I—"

Apparently the colonel could not restrain himself. Through the quiet of the coppice, eager and jubilant, his hoarse voice came floating from below.

"I say! Come down here! It's all up, you know; all up!"

The bishop tried to peer out through the rounded bars. He hesitated, and then called: "Kindly refrain from yowling like that, Standish. What's all up?"

"Why, we've got him, you know. Murch has got him. Make him talk now."

"Got who?"

"Why, Louis Spinelli, demmit! He's down in the village, and Murch has got him under technical arrest."

"Whoosh!" said Hugh Donovan, and turned to stare at Dr. Fell.

CHAPTER VIII

At the Chequers Inn

AT THIS point, the chronicler of Dr. Fell's adventures should, strictly speaking, apologize for introducing that luscious little ginch, Patricia Standish. "Ginch," Hugh Donovan has frequently assured the chronicler, is the word that best describes her; a mysterious term whose definition will presently be made clear. It is pronounced to rhyme with "cinch," for more reasons than one.

This apology should come from the fact that on one point all the leading authorities are agreed: to introduce a heroine (whether or not the tale be fact) is bad. Very bad. As Henry Morgan says, you know what I mean: the gray-eyed, fearless Grace Darling with the cool philosophy, who likes to poke her nose into trouble and use a gun as well as the detective, and who requires the whole book to make up her mind whether she is more than casually interested in the hero.

But in extenuation it must be urged, first, that this is a true story, and second—by the splendid grace of God—Patricia Standish had none of the traits just mentioned. She was not cool-headed or strong-minded. She could no more have accompanied the detectives with a gun than she could have brought down the villain with a flying tackle. Quite to the contrary, she was content to leave that sort of thing to the proper people; to beam up at you as though she were saying, "What a man!"— and you threw out your chest, and felt about nine feet tall, and said, "Ha, ha." Nor, in her case, were there all those persistent attempts to freeze or embarrass the hero until the very last. She tumbled into Hugh Donovan's arms from the start, and stayed there, and a very good thing too.

Some magnificent premonition of this stirred in his mind the moment he saw her. She was walking up the brick path, against the dark trees that were now glowing fiery with sunset, and she was in the midst of a small procession. Patricia Standish had her arm through that of the ruddy-faced colonel, who was expounding something to a large man in uniform. Behind them walked two constables and a melancholy medical man who seemed to be thinking glumly about a lost tea.

Against this background she stood out vividly. She was a blonde, but not a fluffy blonde or a statuesque blonde. And she was dexterously made, as though nature had added just that extra touch and fillip to the curves in the right places, for a frock to adhere to. Her air was at once hesitant and vigorous; and her skin seemed to glow with that brownish flesh tint which is so rarely to be seen in real flesh. Dark hazel eyes contemplated you with that interested, rapt, *"What-a-man!"* look already referred to; her high eyebrows gave her a perpetual air of pleased surprise; and she had a pink, rather broad mouth which always seemed to have just finished smiling.

Thus Hugh Donovan saw her coming hesitantly up the path, in a white tennis frock without sleeves, against the dark fire-edged trees. Along with the bishop, Morley, and Dr. Fell, he had come downstairs to the porch of the Guest House. And there she was, arching her neck to look rather fearfully at the balcony door, while the colonel spoke to Inspector Murch. Then she looked towards the porch, and at Donovan.

His immediate sensation was that of one who goes up a staircase in the dark, and puts his foot down on a nonexistent top step—you know. And this was followed by a sort of stupendous emotional *clang*: as though he had put a rifle to his shoulder, fired, and hit the loudest bell in the shooting-gallery first shot. *Clang*—like that, and hot and cold all at once, and a number of other mixed metaphors.

He knew, right then and there.

Furthermore, he knew that she knew also. You can feel that kind of thing emanating from ginches, in waves or vibrations or something, and the person who says you can't is a goof who does not deserve to have the vibrations launched in his direction. Hugh Donovan knew she knew, also, by the way their eyes did not meet. They took a sort of quick flash and slid away from each other. He and Patricia Standish made an elaborate pretense that they were not aware of each other's presence; that they would scarcely be aware of each other's presence after they had been properly introduced; and these are excellent signs indeed. Patricia was contemplating a stone peacock on the roof of the Guest House, her head high and her manner casual.

All these emotional fireworks were not obvious to Colonel Standish. The colonel made noises of satisfaction, and pushed forward Inspector Murch. Inspector Murch was large, and had a aggressive moustache; his method of standing at attention made him look as though he were tilted slightly backwards, and in danger of toppling over if you gave him a shove. His expression of conscientiousness remained fixed; but he seemed pleased with himself.

"Tell 'em, Murch," said the colonel. "Speak out, now. Oh, yes; that's Dr. Fell, and the Bishop of Mappleham, and Mr. Donovan . . . Inspector Murch, and this is Doctor Fordyce—goin' to take the bullet out now. Oh, yes, h'rrm—I forgot. And my daughter Patricia. Tell 'em, Murch."

Patricia gave a small inclination of her head. The inspector was more conscientious than ever; he fingered his sandy moustache, cleared his throat, and fixed a pale blue satisfied eye on Dr. Fell. He spoke confidentially, in a throaty voice.

"I would like to call this an honor, sir. And I would explain why I was unable to do me duty in being here to welcome you." He took a notebook. "After making investigations here, I took the liberty of going home for me tea. This was not a dereliction of duty, look; I took with me a selection from Mr. Depping's correspondence—letters, sir," he translated, tapping the notebook, "which were revealin'. Meanwhile, I had been making inquiries about the man who visited Mr. Depping last night.

"The landlord of the 'Bull' told me that a man answering to the description had been seen frequently in these parts for more than a week. He was often at the 'Bull,' and asking questions about everybody at The Grange; and news do get about, sir," observed Inspector Murch, shaking his head. "But this man had not been there last night.

" 'Owever, while I was drinking me tea, I received a call on the telephone from Detective Sergeant Ravens, at Hanham, saying he thought the man I wanted was stopping at the Chequers Inn—which I must explain is down Hanham way, by the river, about four miles from here. . . ."

"Interesting," put in the bishop, looking sideways at Dr. Fell. "The man is not dead, then?"

"Dead?" said Murch, blankly. "Dead? Gaawdblessmes'ul, no! Why should he be dead?"

"I was only endeavoring to ascertain the facts," said the other, with a negligent gesture and another satisfied look at Dr. Fell. "Go on, Inspector."

Dr. Fell was not at all disconcerted.

"It would seem that for the moment I am in disgrace," he wheezed affably. "H'mf. No matter. Sexton Blake will yet be triumphant. I don't think it matters in the least—did you go over to see him, Inspector?"

"Yes, sir. First I telephoned to The Grange, to ascertain whether Colonel Standish had returned. He had not. I then borrowed a car and drove to the Chequers Inn. At this time I did *not* know his name was Spinelli, or 'oo the chap was at all.

"He was known at the Chequers as Mr. Travers, and he'd not made any attempt to bolt. I found him sitting out on the porch, drinking his half-pint, as cool as you please. A very well-spoken person, sir; like a gentleman. In process of law," intoned Inspector Murch, "I cautioned him, informing him he was not under oath, but 'ad better answer such questions as I put in process of law. He made a certain statement, not under oath, which he initialled."

Clearing his throat, Murch opened his notebook.

"'My name is Stuart Travers. I am a theatrical impreesorrio, retired. I lived at the Deword, Broadway and Eighty-Sixth Street, New York City. I am travelling in England for pleasure. I do not know Mr. Depping. Yes, I know what happened last night; everybody here knows all about it. Yes, I know I am under suspicion. I was not near the Guest House at any time last night. If the man who called there was seen, they will tell you it was not me. I have nothing to be afraid of. I went to my room last night at half-past nine, and did not leave it until this morning. That is all I have to say until I have consulted my lawyer."

During the reading, Inspector Murch had been leaning farther and farther backwards. Now he looked up with a heavy and crafty smile.

"I had not any warrant," he pursued, "and could not hold the accused until properly identified. I asked him to accompany me 'ere to be identified, and he would not, sir, he said, until he had telephoned to London and talked to his lawyer. Very cool. Afterwards, the accused said he would come gladly, and meantime he would stop in charge of Sergeant Ravens. So he won't run away, sir, look—*but*, in secret, I obtained pieces of evidence which is most significant."

"Dashed good work, that," said Colonel Standish approvingly. "Hear that? Listen again. Hang him without a doubt. Eh, Murch?"

"Thank you, sir. We can hope so," replied Murch, with heavy modesty. "Well, sir, to go on. Mr. Travers was not in his room last night at the time indicated as per statement. It is true he be and went there at half-past nine. But he left it, because he was seen at close on ten o'clock, climbing *back* into the window of 'is room—which is on the ground floor. Funny thing; he was sopping wet, though the rain hadn't started, as wet as though he'd been and fallen in the river . . ."

"In the river," interrupted Dr. Fell, musingly. "Not bad, not bad. How do you explain that?"

"Well, sir, I don't. But that's not the important thing, you see. Mrs. Kenviss, the landlord's wife at the Chequers, saw him doing it when she was coming back from taking the cloths off all the little tables in a sort of restaurant arbor they have out-side. She wondered what was up, and watched. . . . In less than five minutes, *out* this Mr. Travers climbed again, with 'is clothes changed, and hurried off somewhere. That's the important thing. A good walker could easy cover four miles between the Chequers and this house here in less than an hour. He'd have reached here by eleven o'clock. . . ."

"So he would," agreed Dr. Fell. "In time for a blackmailer to have seen a great deal."

The inspector frowned. "Seen, sir?" he repeated, with a sort of hoarse jocosity. "'M! 'Tisn't what he'd 've *seen*, not much. That's the time he walked straight in that door there, after the lights went out, and upstairs—as we know. And shot poor Mr. Depping. He didn't get back to the Chequers until half-past one. Mrs. Kenviss," the inspector said virtuously, "said it was her bounden duty to sit up, and watch that window, and see what was what. Blessmes'l, she and Mr. Kenviss do get a scare when they learn this morning what's happened! And they didn't dare speak to Mr. Travers; so she hurries out after Sergeant Ravens, and that's how *I* know. But," announced Murch, tapping his notebook with heavy emphasis, "we don't give our knowl-edge away, Ravens and me. To Mr. Travers, I mean. I thought I'd best nip back here straightaway, get that Storer chap, take him and identify Mr. Travers, and we've got him."

He closed his notebook. "My superior officer, the chief con-stable," he continued, with an air of putting on the final touch, "has made the information against him as being one Louis Spi-nelli, and that completes it. I have now my warrants for arrest and search."

"Got him, eh?" inquired the colonel, glancing from one to the other of the figures on the porch. "Got him drunk on parade—dead to rights, damme! Sorry to have pulled you down here for nothing, Fell. Still . . . Hallo, I'm sorry; I forgot! . . . Let me introduce, Dr. Fordyce, my daughter Patricia . . ." He whirled round with an air of inspiration.

"How do you do?" said Hugh Donovan instantly.

"You've already introduced everybody," said the sad-faced medical man with some asperity. "And since the police seem to have finished, I'll be thankful to get on with my postmortem and be off."

"Oh, yes. Carry on, then," said Dr. Fell, with an absent-minded air. He waited until the doctor and the two constables had tramped past him into the house. Then he looked round the little group, and fixed Murch with a sombre eye. "So you came back here for an identification of Spinelli from the valet, Inspector?"

"Yes, sir." Murch wheezed out a breath of relief. "And, by Gearge, sir! I'm free to confess how glad I am it was this man Travers, or Spinelli; one of those there gunman chaps, that'd as soon shoot as look at you, like you see in the films; and not one of our own folk. Ah, ah, he'll soon learn you can't do that business over *here*, by Gearge!" Another breath of relief, which agitated the ends of his sandy moustache. "Ah, ay, a good thing. I'm bound to admit I was having ideas, sir."

"Ideas?"

"Ah," agreed the inspector. " 'Tis nonsense, sir, but there it is." A broader strain had crept into the good inspector's speech now that the burden of an official report had been removed. "Ah, but when an idea cooms to you, blest if you can drive 'ee oot. There he is, and there he stays. Eh zed to meself, Eh zed, by Gearge!" proclaimed Murch, illustrating what he said to himself by sweeping a big arm through the air and snapping his fingers as though he had just thrown a pair of dice, "*is* that true? Eh zed. 'Tis queer, when I heard some of the things that are being said hereabouts—hints, like—and had a look at his letters, then I had ideas. Both Mr. Morgan and I had ideas; yon's a clever lad, Mr. Morgan; he helped me this morning. Aa-hh-ha, yes. But Eh zed to meself. Eh, zed, 'Luther Murch, you'm dimp!' And a small matter now, too, with us having the murderer."

He threw out his big hands, dismissing it, but not without a frown. Dr. Fell regarded him steadily.

"I shall want to hear those ideas, Inspector. H'm, yes. Together with all the evidence you have collected today; we haven't done much but talk. Please come upstairs. I'm afraid I've bad news for you."

The colonel interposed. He said:

"Well, well, what are we waiting for, demmit?" in a querulous tone. "Time we were busy. I've got to drive six miles to a telegraph office, confounded nuisance, just to tell Hadley we've caught our man. . . . *Morley!* What the devil are you doing here, eh? Come along with me; *I* can't write telegrams; never could . . . You, Patricia! Dash it, this is no place for you, you know!" he protested, rather defensively.

She spoke for the first time. It was one of those warm, soft, ginch-like voices also. She looked down from her contemplation of the stone peacock.

"Of course not, Dad," she agreed, with such readiness that the colonel stared at her.

"Eh?" he said.

"Of course not." The hazel eyes grew sombre. They flickered past Hugh, and then looked squarely at him for the first time. They had such an overpowering effect that the shooting-gallery bell clanged six times in rapid succession, and with unnerving noise. Patricia went on in bright helpfulness:

"Shall I take Mr. Donovan up to The Grange and introduce him to Mother? And I'm sure he must be dying for a dr—for something to eat."

She smiled. The colonel caught up with the suggestion with his usual air of inspiration.

"That's it, by Jove!" he assented warmly. "Take him along. Introduce him. Oh, yes; and that reminds me . . . Patricia, this is Joe Donovan's son. Hugh, my boy, let me present my daughter Patricia. Patricia, this is Hugh Donovan."

"How do you do?" said Donovan obediently.

"Are you sure you've got it clear now?" she inquired. "Right-ho, then! Come along with me; do."

CHAPTER IX

The Deductions of Old John Zed

THAT WAS how, in a few short moments, he found himself walking away beside this lithe, bright-eyed, altogether luscious ginch in the tennis frock—walking rather hurriedly, because he was afraid he would hear his father's stern hail from the porch, bidding him back to duty and the lighthouse. If possible, that last remark of hers drew her closer to him than ever, a powerful, unspoken, dazzling sympathy. "He must be dying for a dri—" She knew. This must be the sort of thing Elizabeth Barrett Browning wrote about in the sonnets. It was not only sympathetic feminine intuition on her part, but he realized that the very sight of this girl had made him want to reach for a cocktail; some women have that effect. Such a glamour must have attended all the great sirens of the ages. In its absence there are unfulfilled romances. If, when Dante met Beatrice that famous time on the what's-its-name bridge, Beatrice had smiled at him and whispered, "Look here, *I* could do with a slug of Chianti," then the poor sap would have tried to find out her address and telephone number, instead of merely going home and grousing about it in an epic.

Here in the twilight coppice the strength and reasonableness of this theory grew on him; and, as he looked down at the hazel eyes which were regarding him inquiringly over her shoulder, he was struck with inspiration.

He burst out suddenly:

> "There once was a poet named Dante,
> Who was fond of imbibing Chianti—
>   He wrote about hell
>   And a Florentine gel,
> Which distressed his Victorian auntie."

Then he said, "Hah!" in a pleased, surprised tone, and rubbed his hands together as though he were waiting for the gods to throw him another.

"Hullo!" observed Patricia, opening her eyes wide. "I say, *that's* a nice opening speech from a bishop's son! Your father told me a lot about you. He said you were a good young man."

"It's a contemptible lie!" he said, stung to the depths. "Look here! I don't want you to go believing any such—"

"Oh, I don't believe it," she said composedly. "H'm. What made you think of it? That limerick, I mean?"

"Well, to tell you the truth, I think it was you. That is, it was a sort of inspiration—the kind that's supposed to soak you on your first sight of Tintern Abbey, or something of the sort. Then you rush home, and wake up your wife, and write it down."

She stared. "Ooh, you villain! You mean to tell me that looking at me makes you think of a limerick? I don't think that's nice."

"Eh? Why?"

"H'm. Well," she admitted, lifting an eyebrow meditatively,

"maybe we weren't thinking of the same limerick. . . . Why do you wake up your wife?"

"What wife?" said Hugh, who had lost the thread of the discourse.

She brooded, her full pink lips pressed together. Again she looked at him over her shoulder, with an air of a suspicion confirmed.

"So you've got a wife, have you?" she said bitterly. "I jolly well might have known it. Secret marriages are all the fashion. I bet you didn't tell your father, did you? One of those forward American hussies, I suppose, who—who let men—*h'm.*"

From experience on both sides of the Atlantic, Donovan was aware that one of the most stimulating qualities of the English girl is her bewildering use of *non-sequitur.* He wanted wildly to disclaim any foreign entanglement. Yet the statement roused his stern masculine pride.

"I am not married," he replied with dignity. "On the other hand, I have known any number of very pleasant ginches on the other side, who were certainly fond of *h'm.*"

"You needn't bother," she said warmly, "to regale me with any account of your disgusting love-affairs. I'm sure I'm not interested! I suppose you're one of those nasty people who think women are toys, and oughtn't to have careers and do some good in the world—"

"Right you are."

"Bah!" she said, and gave a vigorous toss of her head. "That's just it. I never thought anybody could be so stupid and old-fashioned in this day and age. . . . What are you thinking of?" she asked in some suspicion.

"*H'm,*" said Donovan enigmatically. "You are a little liar. And you keep straying away from the subject. What I originally said was that merely seeing you inspired me to burst into limericks, like Keats or somebody. The idea of you having a career is unthinkable. Preposterous. If you became a doctor, your patients would wake up out of the strongest anaesthetic the moment you felt their pulses. If you became a barrister, you would probably throw the inkstand at the judge when he ruled against you, and . . . What ho! That reminds me . . ."

Patricia, who was beaming, followed his expression.

"Go on," she prompted, rather crossly.

They had come out of the gloom in the coppice to the warm slope of parkland, drowsy, and almost uncannily still as the evening drew in. After the clanging of cities, this hush made him uncomfortable. He looked up at The Grange, with the poplars silhouetted behind it, and he remembered what Dr. Fell had said about a killer. He remembered that, after all, they were still as far away as ever from knowing the murderer's name. Old Depping made a pitiable ghost. These people went on their easy ways, interested in the gossip, but certainly not mourning him. And something that had persisted in Hugh's mind wormed to the surface again.

"Throw the inkstand . . ." he repeated. "Why, I was only thinking of your poltergeist, and what it did to the vicar . . ."

"Oh, that?" She raised her eyebrows quizzically, and grinned. "I say, we did have a row! You should have been here. Of course none of us believed your father was mad, really—except maybe my father—but we didn't believe him when he told us about that American what's-his-name—"

"Spinelli?"

"'M. But that's what made it worse when we heard this morning . . ." She dug the toe of her shoe round in the grass, uneasily. "And that reminds *me*," she went on, as though she would dismiss the subject. "We don't really want to go up to the house now, do we? If we went along to Henry Morgan's, and maybe had a cocktail . . . ?"

The power of sympathy showed the answer in both their faces. They were beginning to turn round and head the other way almost as soon as she had uttered the words, and Patricia gave a conspirator's gurgle of enjoyment. She knew, she said, a shortcut; a side gate in the boundary wall, not far from the coppice where the Guest House stood, which would lead them out to Hangover House.

"I don't know why," she continued, as though she hated thinking about the matter, but was determined to flounder through it; "I don't know why," she went on suddenly, "that Spinelli man should want to kill Mr. Depping. But he did do it; and Spinelli's an Italian, and probably a member of the Black Hand, and they do all sorts of queer things—don't they? You know. You know all about criminals, don't you?"

"Um," said Hugh judicially. He was beginning to feel remorseful. He wanted to explain everything to this little ginch, but for some reason he found he couldn't.

"All sorts of queer things," she repeated, evidently satisfied by this logic. "Anyway, I'd be a hypocrite—and so would most of us—if we pretended we'd miss Mr. Depping. I mean, I'm jolly sorry he's dead, and it's too bad, and I'm glad they've caught the man who killed him . . . but there were times when I wished he'd move away, and—and never come back." She hesitated. "If it hadn't been for Betty, the few times we've seen her, I think we'd all have flown against Dad and Mr. Burke and said, 'Look here, throw that blighter *out*.'"

They were skirting the boundary wall, and she slapped at it

with sudden vehemence. It was beginning to puzzle Hugh all the more.

"Yes," he said. "That's the queerest part of it, from what I've seen . . ."

"What is?"

"Well, Depping's status. There doesn't seem to be anybody who more than half defends him. He came here as a stranger, and you took him up and made him one of you. It sounds unusual, if he was so unpopular as he seems to be."

"Oh, I know! I've had it dinned into me a dozen times. Mr. Burke is behind it. He puts Dad up to speaking to us about it. Dad sidles up with a red face and a guilty look, and says, "Burpf, burpf, eh, what?' And you say, 'What?' Then he splutters some more, and finally says, 'Old Depping—very decent sort, eh?' And you say, 'No.' Then he says, 'Well, damme, he is!' and bolts out the most convenient door as though he'd done his duty. It's Mr. Burke's idea, but he never says anything at all."

"Burke? That's—"

"'M. Yes. Wait till you meet him. Little, broad-set man with a shiny bald head and a gruff voice. He always looks sour, and then chuckles; or else he looks just sleepy. Always wears a brown suit—never saw him in anything else—and has a pipe in his mouth. And," said Patricia, embarked on a sort of grievance, "he has a way of suddenly closing one eye and sighting at you down the pipe as though he were looking along a gun. It takes some time to get used to him." Again she gave the little gurgle of pleasure. "All I'm sure of about J. R. Burke is that he hates talking books, and he can drink more whisky with absolutely no change of expression than any man I ever saw."

Hugh was impressed. "That," he declared, "is a new one." He pondered. "I always had a sort of idea that everyone connect-

ed with a publishing house had long white whiskers and dou-
ble-lensed spectacles, and sat around in darkish rooms looking
for masterpieces. But then I also thought Henry Morgan—I've
met him, by the way—that is, the blurbs on the jackets of his
books said . . ."

She gurgled. "Yes, they're rather good, aren't they?" she inquired complacently. "He writes them himself. Oh, you're quite
wrong, you know. But I was telling you about Mr. Depping.
I don't think it was so much the money he'd invested, though
I gather that was quite a lot. It was a sort of uncanny ability
he had to tell what books would sell and what books wouldn't.
There are only about half-a-dozen people like that in the world;
I don't know where he got it. But he always knew. He was in-
valuable. The only thing I ever heard Mr. Burke say about him
was once when Madeleine and I were giving him what-for, and
J. R. was trying to sleep in a chair with the *Times* over his face.
He took the paper away and said, 'Shut up'; and then he said,
'The man's a genius,' and went back to sleep again. . . ."

They had come out into the main road now, cool and shad-
owy under the trees that lined it, and the high hedges of haw-
thorn. Almost opposite were the gables of Hangover House.
As they approached the gate there became audible an energetic
and muffled rattling, which appeared to proceed from a cocktail shaker.

"Light of my life," said an argumentative voice, between rat-
tles, "I will now proceed to expound to you the solution of this
mystery as it would be explained by John Zed. To begin with—"

"Hullo, Hank," said Patricia, "may we come in?"

A very pleasant little domestic scene was in progress on the
lawn before the house, screened by the high hedge. Madeleine
Morgan was curled up in a deck chair under the beach umbrel-

la, an expression of bright anticipation on her face. Alternately she raised to her lips a cocktail glass and a cigarette, and she was making noises of admiration between. In the faint light of the afterglow, the newcomers could see her husband pacing up and down before the table; stopping to administer a vigorous rattle to the shaker, wheeling round, slapping the back of his head, and stalking on again. He turned round at Patricia's greeting, to peer over his spectacles.

"Ha!" he said approvingly. "Come in, come in! Madeleine, more glasses. I think we can find you a couple of chairs. What's up—anything?"

"Didn't I hear you say," remarked Patricia, "that you were going to explain the murder? Well, you needn't. They've found that American, and everything seems to be finished."

"No, it isn't," piped Madeleine, with a pleased look at her husband. "Hank says it isn't."

Chairs were set out, and Morgan filled all the glasses. "I know they've found the American. I saw Murch on his way back from Hanham. But *he* isn't guilty. Stands to reason. (Here's loud cheers—down she goes!—)"

A general murmur, like the church's mumbled responses when the minister reads the catechism, answered the toast. The Martini's healing chill soothed Hugh Donovan almost at once. He relaxed slowly. Morgan went on with some warmth:

"Stands to reason, I tell you! Of course, I'm interested in truth only as a secondary consideration. Chiefly I'm interested in how this murder ought to work out according to story standards, and whether a plot can be worked up around it. You see—"

"I say, why don't you?" interrupted Patricia, inspired. She took the glass away from her lips and frowned. "That's a jolly good idea! It would be a change. To date," she said dreamily,

THE EIGHT OF SWORDS · III

"you have poisoned one Home Secretary, killed the Lord Chancellor with an axe, shot two Prime Ministers, strangled the First Sea-lord, and blown up the Chief Justice. Why don't you stop picking on the poor Government for a while and kill a publisher like Depping?"

"The Lord Chancellor, my dear girl," said Morgan with a touch of austerity, "was not killed with an axe. I wish you would get these things right. On the contrary, he was beaned with the Great Seal and found dead on the Woolsack. . . . You are probably thinking of the Chancellor of the Exchequer, in *The Inland Revenue Murders*. I was only letting off a little steam in that one."

"I remember that one!" said Hugh, with enthusiasm. "It was damned good." Morgan beamed, and refilled his glass. "I like those stories," Hugh pursued, "a lot better than the ones that are so popular by that other fellow—what's his name?—William Block Tournedos. I mean the ones that are supposed to be very probable and real, where all they do is run around showing photographs to people."

Morgan looked embarrassed.

"Well," he said, "you see, to tell you the truth, *I'm* William Block Tournedos too. And I thoroughly agree with you. That's my graft."

"Graft?"

"Yes. They're written for the critics' benefit. You see, the critics, as differentiated from the reading public, are required to like any story that is probable. I discovered a long time ago the way to write a probable and real story. You must have (1) no action, (2) no atmosphere whatever—that's very important—(3) as few interesting characters as possible, (4) absolutely no digressions, and (5) above all things, no deduction. Digressions are the curse of probability . . . which is a funny way of looking at life in general; and the detective may uncover all he can, so long as he never deduces anything. Observe those rules, my children; then you may outrage real probability as much as you like, and the critics will call it ingenious."

"Hooray!" said Madeleine, and took another drink.

Patricia said: "You've whipped your hobbyhorse to death, Hank. Go back to the problem. . . . Why couldn't this be a story; I mean, from your own preferences in stories?"

Morgan grinned, getting his breath. "It could," he admitted, "up to and including the time of the murder. After that. . . ." He scowled.

A sharp premonition made Hugh look up. He remembered that this was the person who had told them to look for the buttonhook.

"What do you mean, after that?"

"I don't think the American is guilty. And," said Morgan, "of all the motiveless and unenterprising sluggards to gather up as suspects, the rest of us are the worst! At least, in a crime story, you get a lot of motives and plenty of suspicious behavior. You have a quarrel overheard by the butler, and somebody threatening to kill somebody, and somebody else sneaking out to bury a blood-stained handkerchief in the flower bed. . . . But here we've nothing of the kind.

"Depping, for instance. I don't mean he had no enemies. When you hear of a man who is said to have *no* enemies, you can practically sit back and wait for somebody to murder him. Depping was a harder sort of problem. Nobody liked him, but, God knows, nobody hereabouts would have gone to the point of doing him in.—And in your wildest imagination, now, can you picture anybody as the murderer? The bishop? Colonel Standish? J. R. Burke? Maw? Let me fill up your glass again."

"Thanks," said Hugh. "Who's Maw?"

Patricia wriggled delightedly in the deck chair. The windows of the house behind her were still glowing, though the lawn was in shadow; there was a light on her blonde hair, and even that vibrant brownish-gold skin seemed to reflect it. She lounged back in the chair, her eyes bright and her lips moist, ticking the glass against her teeth. One bare leg in a tennis shoe swung over the side. Patricia said:

"Oh, yes. I'd better explain that before you meet her, so that you'll know how to handle her. . . . It's my mother. You'll like her. Nowadays she's a sort of tyrant who can't tyrannize, and it makes her furious. Coo! We all used to be afraid of her, until an American friend of Hank's found the solution . . ."

"Um," said Donovan. He resisted a powerful impulse to go over and sit down beside her on the foot-rest part of the deck chair. "Yes, I remember your brother said something about that."

"Poor Morley is still shocked. But it's the only way to deal with her, really. Otherwise you'd always be eating turnips, or doing exercises in front of an open window, or something. It only began by everybody calling her Maw. . . . So remember. When she comes sailing up to you and orders you to do something, or tries to dragoon you into it, you look her straight in the eye and say, firmly, '*Nuts, Maw.*' Just like that. And then even more firmly, '*Nuts.*' That closes the subject."

" '*Nuts,*' " repeated Donovan, with the air of one uttering a talisman. " '*Nuts, Maw.*' " He drew reflectively on his cigarette. "But are you sure it works? I'd like to try something like that on my old man, if I could muster up the nerve. . . ."

"It takes a bit of doing," Morgan admitted, rubbing his jaw.

"Colonel Standish can't manage it even yet. Of course, he got off on the wrong foot. The first time he tried it he only rushed up to her and said, 'Almonds, damme, almonds'; and waited for something to happen. And it didn't. So now—"

"I don't believe that story," said Patricia defensively. "He tells that to everybody," she appealed to Hugh, "and it never happened at all. It—"

"On my sacred word of honor," said Morgan, raising his hand with fervor, "it did. I was outside the door, and heard it. He came out afterwards and said he must have forgot the demnition countersign, and now he'd have to take cod-liver oil after all. But there you are; there's a good example. . . . Try to find a murderer among people like that! We know these people. I can't seem to find one who would fit into the part; not one of the whole crowd we could hang for murder—!"

"Certainly you can, dear!" his wife maintained stoutly. Her flushed face looked round at the others in some defiance. She swallowed a sip of her cocktail, said, "Urk!" and then beamed on them. "You just keep on trying, and you'll find somebody. I know you will."

"But you don't *need* to find anybody, old boy," said Patricia. "This is real life, you see; that's the difference. This American Spinelli shot him, and there's no detective story plot about it."

Morgan was stalking up and down, gesturing with his dead pipe. Even his striped blazer was growing indistinct in the dusk. He wheeled round.

"I am prepared to outline you a theory," he declared, "and to prove to you that what's-his-name didn't. I don't know whether I'm right. I'm only looking at it from poor old John Zed's viewpoint. But I shouldn't be surprised if it were true.

Anyway, it's what I meant by saying the first part of it would make a good story. . . ."

None of them had heard stolid footsteps coming along the road. But now an indistinct figure leaned over the gate, and seemed to be looking from one to the other of them. They could see the bowl of a pipe glowing.

"You still talking, eh?" growled a gruff voice, with a faint chuckle under it. "May I come in?"

"What ho," said Morgan. "Come in, J. R. Come *in*." He was apologetic but determined. "I'd like to have you hear this, if you think I generally talk nonsense. Mr. Burke, this is the Bishop of Mappleham's son . . ."

CHAPTER X

A Question of Keys

THE GREAT J. R. Burke came in with his short solid steps, head slightly down. Hugh could see him better when he moved out of the darkness near the gate, and into the faint glow that lingered over against the house. Patricia had correctly described him, except that now his large bald head was hidden under a sort of piratical hat with its brim turned up in front. A short, stocky man in a brown suit, who always seemed to be looking up at you in that squinting, sighting fashion over half-glasses. First he would preserve a Chinese-image expression, with the corners of his mouth drawn down. Then, as he seemed to see nothing dangerous on the horizon, he would grunt, assume a quizzical expression, and attain a faint twinkle of the eye.

This, as indicated, was the great J. R. Burke, potent discoverer of authors, manager of finances, and hater of books; urbane, genial, cynical, immensely well-read, frequently drunk, and always at ease. He stumped across now, sighting at everybody.

"I've been sittin' on a log," he grunted, with a sniff which seemed to indicate what he thought of nature in general. "I hate sittin' on logs. If I sit on a log for two minutes, all the rest of the day I think things are crawling all over me. . . . Hum. Let us have a little *causerie*."

Morgan brought out another chair, and he established himself. "Go on talking," he said to Morgan. "You will anyhow. Humph. Eh? Yes, whisky, please. Ah!—that's enough. Stop a minute. They tell me Scotland Yard's sent Gideon Fell down to look into this business. Is that true?"

"It is. Do you mean to say you haven't been about all afternoon?"

"Good man, Fell," said J. R. gruffly.

He spread himself out, squaring his arms; tasted his whisky, and then looked quizzically at everybody, blinking over the half-glasses. The pipe went back into his mouth.

"Humph," he added. "I've been taking a walk in quiet country lanes. I won't do it again. Every time I try to walk in quiet country lanes, they are suddenly as full of automobiles as Regent Street at five o'clock in the afternoon. Twenty times I was nearly run over by bicycles coming up behind. I hate being run down by bicycles; there is something insulting about being run down by bicycles, damn it. They sneak up on you. When you do see them, neither you nor the cyclist can decide which way to go; so you both stagger all over the road, and finally he sideswipes you with the handlebar. Humph."

"Poor Mr. Burke!" said Madeleine, keeping her face straight with an expression of concern. "Diddums get hit by a mean old bicycle?"

"Yes, my dear," said J. R., and squinted sideways with his rifle-barrel glare, "yes, I did. And on the main road. I was deliberately assaulted by a bicycle on the main road—*after* having successfully dodged twenty-four of them in all the back lanes of Gloucestershire. Fellow coming down this hill at a speed that ought to be prohibited. It's a blind corner. I didn't see him. *Bang.*"

"Never mind, sir," said Morgan consolingly. "You were just off your game, that's all. You'll fool him next time."

J. R. looked at him.

"Fellow got up off the road dizzy, and helped me get up. Then he said, 'Are you Mr. J. R. Burke?' I said yes. He said, 'I've got a telegram for you.' I said, 'Well, this is the hell of a way deliver it, isn't it?' Imagine his confounded nerve. 'What is your procedure,' I said, 'when unusual circumstances compel you to deliver a telegram at somebody's house? Is it necessary to use a tank, or do you only wrap the telegram round a hand grenade and chuck it through the window?'" Evidently satisfied by this retort, J. R. recovered some of his good humor. He growled something into his glass, and glanced sardonically at Morgan. "By the way, it was from Langdon, Depping's solicitor in London. You people at The Grange—I don't suppose anybody thought to do that, eh? Fine practical minds. Suppose you thought his affairs would take care of themselves."

"Any ideas," said Morgan, "about the murder?"

J. R. looked at him sharply. "No. It's a bad business, that's all I know. Going to hurt us—plenty. Why theorize? They've caught the murderer . . ."

"Have they?"

"If you're trying to apply theories . . ." The corners of the other's mouth turned down, and he surveyed his glass; looked around it, and over it, and under it. "I'll give you advice. Stick to John Zed, and let real life alone. Don't touch this business, anyway. It's mucky."

"Well, that's what I was wondering. The police are likely to be asking you what you know about Depping; his past, and the rest of it—"

"You mean Gideon Fell will. Humph . . . What of it? I can't tell him any more than I can tell anybody else. Depping's credit's perfectly sound and Bank-of-England. Otherwise he had— useful qualities. Standish vouched for him. If Fell wants any further information, he'll have to ask the solicitor. Langdon will be here tonight or tomorrow morning."

Morgan evidently saw that J. R. (if he knew anything) had no disposition to talk. But Morgan talked. He stood in the middle of the darkened lawn and proceeded with a recital which raised Donovan's hair—for, in essentials, it was inference for inference almost exactly the same explanation as Dr. Fell's.

Less closely reasoned, more discursive, and with a few points missing, he had nevertheless contrived to evolve the whole scene with the imaginative vividness of a story-teller. He started with the buttonhook, and went on with a multitude of details—after the fashion of the novelist—which were new to Donovan. When he announced his first surprise, Depping's disguise and imposture, Patricia gave a hoot of derision, and J. R. peered over his glasses in tolerant mockery. But presently he began pounding in his details, and the others were silent.

"And I can prove my assumptions," he went on, striding back and forth among them, and addressing himself to Burke, "on points I noticed when Murch and I examined the room this morning. I decided that there had been an imposture, and I examined the body first of all. . . ." He turned to Donovan. "You were with Dr. Fell when *he* went to the Guest House. Did he examine the body carefully?"

Donovan was cautious. "Well, no. That is—"

"On the upper lip," Morgan proceeded, "there were traces of spirit-gum for the moustache; you can't take it off with water. Traces of the actor's cement were behind his ears. In the fireplace were not only remnants of burned clothing, but a scorched tuft of black hair from the wig . . . Then I went into his bedroom and bathroom, which adjoined the study. If there had been any further need for confirmation, it was there. On either side of the mirror over the washbowl in the bathroom, two candles had been propped up—to give Depping light in taking off his make-up, immediately after his return. Stuck in the drain was one of those strips of transparent fishskin that are used for drawing in sagging flesh round the cheeks and eyes, to present an appearance of youth. There were wet socks and a suit of wet underclothing across a chair; the rest had been burned. I didn't find any box of cosmetics, but Murch was watching and I couldn't make a thorough search. All this puzzled Murch considerably." Again he peered at Hugh in the gloom. "What did Dr. Fell make of it?"

This time Hugh was caught off guard. "We didn't go in there," he replied. "When he deduced all you've said, it was only from the facts we'd heard—"

There was a silence. He heard his own words as though they had come back to him in an echo. Suddenly he tried to stumble into another explanation, but he could think of nothing. In the hush Morgan walked across, his head bent forward.

"Good God," he said, "do you mean to tell me that I'm *right?*"

There was a sort of staggered incredulity in his tone which puzzled Hugh still more.

"Right?" he repeated. "Well, if you've been saying all this—"

"I know," said Morgan, and passed a hand over his eyes.

Then he started to laugh. "I'd convinced myself of it, but . . . well, it seemed too good to be true. It was so exactly the way it should have happened according to romance that I didn't really believe it myself. That was why I was testing it out on all of you. Betrayed, by the Lord! Master mind betrayed into telling the true facts too soon." He picked up the cocktail shaker, found it was empty, and set it down irritably. "Why the devil couldn't I have waited and hit the bishop in the eye with it? I'll never forgive myself for this."

He sat down. J. R. was making protesting noises.

"Look here," he said, "do you mean to tell me Gideon Fell believes all this tommyrot?"

"I'd be willing to bet," said Morgan thoughtfully, "that you believe it yourself."

"Tommyrot!" snapped J. R. "You're making Depping out as an ex-criminal, who wanted to kill Spinelli—"

"I only said there was something highly unsavory in his past."

"Humph." After a time of lowering his head and grunting, the other's tone changed again to tolerant sarcasm. "It would look well enough for a book, my lad, but it won't do. There's one great big thundering hole in it. Know what it is? Shut up. Let me talk. I'll see to what lengths of nonsense you're willing to go before I explode the thing. . . . Suppose it's true. Which I don't admit, mind. What then?"

"Why, we come back to the fact that the murderer is somebody in our midst." Morgan got up again, stared at the darkening sky, and began to move about rather uneasily. He had the air of one who has started up more than was his intention. "That is . . . Look here, *is* this what Dr. Fell thinks? For God's sake, man, tell me the truth!"

Donovan, who had been cursing himself, made an attempt

at mysteriousness that was not very successful. He shrugged his shoulders. Patricia was brooding with her chin in her fists. Morgan went on:

"This was Depping's world. If he wanted a confederate to keep guard in his room while he went out after Spinelli . . ."

"Rubbish," said J. R. "And I'll tell you why . . . Assume what you say is true. His having a confederate for this business is fantastic. Worse than the idea he was a criminal in the past. Much. Pah! Listen to me." The red bowl of his pipe stabbed out in the gloom. "What did Depping most want to do?"

"About what? I don't follow you."

Patricia passed a hand over her hair and then gestured like one who wants silence in which to think. "I say, wait a bit. I think *I* follow." She turned accusingly to J. R. "At least you'll admit this. You've always thought he was playing some sort of part—now, haven't you?"

"Got nothing to do with it. Don't ask *me* questions," growled the other. "Go on."

"He wanted to be thought a scholarly and well-bred country gentleman; that's what he wanted," said Patricia with emphasis.

"Humph. Which he may have been, mind . . . Anyhow, that's what I meant. He wanted to establish his position for that; he'd been working towards it for five years. Humph." J. R. gathered his shoulders together. His face was barely visible in the gloom; but they could feel the Chinese-image expression hardening and staring out as though to convince them by weight of personality, like the bishop. "Then is what you say very likely?—Would he go up to one of the people hereabouts and say, 'Look here. Sorry to deceive you all this time, but the fact is I'm really an ex-criminal and baby-killer. There's a fellow I used to know, who's been trying to blackmail me, and I've got to bump him off. Give me a hand, will you? Take my place in the study while I go out and attend to him; there's a good fellow. I'll do the same for you sometime.'" He snorted. "Nonsense!"

Morgan had been lighting his pipe. The match abruptly stopped just above the bowl; it showed his face gone tense, and rather strained, and he was staring at the beach umbrella. Then the match went out.

He said slowly: "No. Depping needn't have said that at all."

"More theories—?"

"The only theory," Morgan answered in a queer voice, "that will account for all the facts. A theory that turns half-a-dozen of the most harmless people in England, including myself, into a group of potential murderers."

Another pause. Hugh stared at the sky, turning to colors of pale white and purple after sunset, and he was conscious of a chill that had taken hold of everybody. Madeleine said, "Don't talk like that—" all of a sudden, and struck the side of the deck chair.

"Let's hear it," said J. R. sharply.

"I'm rather muddled myself," Morgan admitted, with his hand over his eyes; "and there have been so many cross-deductions that we're apt to tangle up what we know with what we only suspect. But here it is . . .

"The last part of the hypothesis I told you—that is, the murder of Depping by his confederate—was based on the assumption that the confederate was *a willing accomplice, who knew what Depping meant to do;* and, second, that this accomplice *had meantime devised his own plan for killing Depping.* That he went to the Guest House prepared with rubber gloves. That he left

Depping locked out on the balcony, pretending that the key was lost; that he made Depping come up through the front door to provide an alibi . . . Is that correct?"

"Fair enough," said Hugh. "What then?"

Morgan replied quietly: "Only that the accomplice was nothing of the kind, and had at first not the slightest intention of killing Depping."

"But, look here—"

"J. R.'s objection is perfectly sound. It's convincing, and it's true. Depping would never have suggested to anybody hereabouts that they assist him in a murder; or even have hinted at an unsavory past, until . . . Wait a bit. *But there would have been any number of harmless people in this vicinity quite willing to assist Depping in what they thought was a lark.*"

Burke snorted. "A lark! You've an odd notion of the people in your circle, my boy, if you think they're addicted—"

"Have you forgotten the poltergeist?" said Morgan.

After a silence he went on steadily:

"Somebody was willing to cut up that row with the vicar, and probably enjoyed it. *I* should have enjoyed it, personally. . . . I still insist that several people could have been drawn in to assist Depping, unwittingly, if they had been persuaded it was a show of that sort. It wouldn't be hard to spin up a tale that would plant an unconscious confederate in that study. Depping meant to go out and kill Spinelli. But the accomplice didn't know that."

"In that case," said Donovan, who was trying to hold hard to reason, "what becomes of the plot to kill Depping? What about the rubber gloves—and the key that accomplice pretended to have lost—and—?"

"They are all suppositions," said Morgan coolly.

Hugh peered at him. "Good God, man, I know they are! They're *your* suppositions. What happens to them now?"

"Put it this way. Depping, in disguise, was locked out. He was locked out for an obvious reason which doesn't seem to have occurred to anybody: that the accomplice really couldn't find the key. Depping had sneaked out the front door of the house intending to return by the balcony. But he had forgotten the key—left it behind in his other clothes, and it couldn't be found. Meantime, Depping can't wait in the rain. He conceives the idea that he can get in through the front door, if the other person will blow out the fuses . . ."

"How?" demanded Hugh. "I thought we'd agreed about the buttonhook. Nobody with bare hands would have tried blowing the fuses like that."

"Certainly not. But it could have propped against that low socket, and pushed in to make a contact . . ."

"With what?"

"With the sole of a tennis shoe," said Morgan, and struck another match. "We mustn't be too sure of those rubber gloves, you know. And thus we destroy the only basis for believing that the accomplice intended to kill Depping . . . with the sole of any ordinary tennis shoe."

Donovan searched his mind for a suitable observation, and eyed his host with malevolence. "*Nuts!*" he said violently, after some consideration. "*Nuts!*"

Patricia let out a protesting gurgle.

"I say, Hank, it won't do!" she insisted. "I thought you said that, after Mr. Depping was shot, the murderer got out the balcony door, and the door was left open. . . . If that's so, and the murderer really couldn't find the key, how did he get out that way?"

Morgan was afire with his new idea. He went stalking up and down, banging into the table in the gloom, and bumping against chairs indiscriminately.

"As simple as that!" he almost shouted. "Ha. Ha. Of course. When his accomplice can't find the key, Depping is hopping mad. Depping is hop . . . 'm. Let the euphony pass. He comes upstairs in his disguise. He does exactly what you yourself would have done under the circumstances. 'Are you blind?' he says. 'Look here, you fathead!'—or words to that effect, however Depping would have phrased it. He goes in and finds the key himself, and produces it before the other person's eyes. In moments of great emotional stress, that's precisely the sort of silly thing a person would do. Can't you see Depping, wet to the skin, nervous, vicious; with his loud clothes and his wig coming askew; standing there shaking the key before the other person? Even with the murder of Spinelli on his mind . . ."

"I don't know whether you are aware of it," said Hugh with great politeness, "but Spinelli happens to be alive."

"Which," said Morgan, "Depping didn't know. *He* thought Spinelli's body was safe in the river . . . Murch told me what happened at the Chequers last night. Depping didn't know his attempt was a failure. And what then?"

Morgan's voice sank. "Now he has the accomplice utterly at his mercy. I can see Depping with that little smirk he used to have—remember it?—on his face, and the stoop of his shoulders, and his hands rubbing together. He goes into the bathroom and painstakingly removes his disguise. He brushes his hair and puts on other clothes. His accomplice is still mystified; but he has been promised an explanation, *after* the clothes and evidences have been destroyed. Presently Depping sits down, facing the other person, and smiles again.

" 'I have killed a man,' he says in that dry voice of his. 'You will never dare betray me, because I have made you accessory before and after the fact.' "

Morgan's voice had unconsciously fallen into an imitation. Hugh had never heard Depping's voice; but it was just such a one as he would have believed Depping to have possessed—level, thin, harsh, and edged with malice. The man had suddenly become alive here in the dusk: a puzzle and a monstrosity, rubbing his hands together. Donovan could see him sitting up stiff in his leather chair, with a candle burning on the desk before him, and the storm roaring outside. He could see the long furrowed face, the grizzled hair, the dry leer out of the eyes.

Across from him sat X . . .

"You know how he repressed himself when he was with us," Morgan went on abruptly. "You could feel it. You knew he hated us, that he was thinking differently, and his mind was boiling the whole time. He'd got his new life; but he could never get used to it. That was why he went on those drinking sprees.

"I don't know what there had been in his past life. But I think that murder had probably been one of the least of his offenses. I think he sat there and carefully explained to his accomplice what he had been, and what he was; that all his spite came out; and that he pointed out carefully how the accomplice was *caught*. He couldn't be betrayed, or Depping would swear both of them were concerned in the murder. What the confederate had thought a lark was really a crime that put him at Depping's mercy. Depping displayed the pistol, laid it on the table. And I think something was said—I don't know what; this is only a guess—that made one of our nice, harmless, inoffensive community go slightly insane. Maybe it was the way Depping smirked and moved his head. I don't know, but I could have killed him, myself, more than once. I think one of our harmless community found an excuse to get behind Depping—snatched up the gun from the table, and—"

"Don't!" cried Patricia out of the dark. "Don't say that! You almost sound as though you'd been there! . . ."

Morgan lowered his head. He seemed to catch sight of his wife, who was huddled back silently into the deck chair. Moving across, he sat down beside her and said in a matter-of-fact voice:

"What price horrors? Actually, what we all want is another cocktail. Wait till I get the lights on, and another bowl of ice, and I'll mix a new shaker . . ."

"You don't get out of it," said Hugh grimly, "so easily as that."

"No. No," the other replied in a reflective voice, "I didn't suppose I should. Well, the only question is: Which one of us would old Depping select for his lark?"

The implication of his remark was setting slowly into all their minds when, with only a preliminary grunt, J. R. Burke spoke out. He said in a meditative voice:

"I dare say I'm obstructing justice."

"Obstructing—?"

"Don't mind obstructing justice, I don't," growled J. R. "Officious, that's what the police are. Ought to be a law against it. Still—if Gideon Fell thinks all this, got to tell it. Young fella, you think there was an accomplice, do you? What time do you think this accomplice came to see Depping at the Guest House?"

Morgan peered at him oddly. "I don't know. Any time after Depping's dinner tray was taken up; half-past eight to nine o'clock, maybe."

"Humph. Well, you're wrong."

"How do you know?"

"Because," said J. R. equably, "I was talking to Depping at that time . . . Don't gape at me, confound it!" He unscrewed his pipe and blew down the stem. "Now you'll call it suspicious behavior, won't you? Bah. Man pays a perfectly ordinary visit, and there you are."

Morgan got up. He said: "Holy Saint Patrick! And the suspicious behavior had to come from *you*. . . . Did you tell this to Murch?"

"No. Why should I? But now they've brought on all this funny business . . ."

"Excuse me, sir," said Hugh, "but did you make any footprints?"

J. R. used some bad language. He said it was a matter of indifference to him whether he had made any footprints, and also that he didn't know, and what was this all about anyway?

"I mean," Hugh persisted, "did you go to see him in Morley Standish's shoes?"

J. R. dwelt fancifully on this theme. He pointed out the infrequency of his necessity for borrowing a pair of shoes in order to pay business calls on his associates. Then Morgan remembered the footprint of which he and Murch had taken a plaster cast; and Hugh explained its origin.

"But the valet," he went on, "didn't mention any other visit last night, and I only wondered whether you might have gone up by the balcony door . . ."

"I did go up by the balcony door," returned Burke. "Ah, I see, I see. You're itching to turn inquisitor on me; I can smell it in the air. There's no good damned reason why I should tell it, but I will." He craned his neck aggressively. "I went up because I saw his light, and that's the only room he ever uses. Why shouldn't I go up by the balcony door? Much easier."

There was a strained and polite silence. Morgan coughed. No better spur could have been applied.

"I'd just as soon break down your theories by telling you. Humph. All this business about keys—! Listen. I went to see Depping last night just after dinner; it was about a quarter to nine, and just getting dark. And I'll give Gideon Fell another tip, for what it's worth. Depping was leaving England.

"Don't ask me where or why. What I saw him about was business, and that doesn't concern you. But I'd be willing to swear he wasn't expecting anybody at all that night. . . . I went up on the balcony and looked through the glass in the upper part of the door; you can see through the white squares in the chequering. He was standing by the desk with his coat, shirt, and collar off, and rummaging in the desk drawer. I couldn't see what he had in his hand. Still, I'll admit it may have been a wig."

Morgan whistled.

"Pleases you, don't it," said the other, "when somebody really gets into a situation like that? Tell you frankly, it didn't please *me* when I heard about the murder this morning . . . Humph. I was telling you. When I tapped on the door, Depping almost jumped out of his shoes. He'd got a wild-eyed look about him. Wondered if he'd been drinkin' again. He said, 'Who's there?' Would he have looked like that if he'd been expecting somebody eh?"

"Well . . ."

"Well, nothing. He took a key out of his pocket—yes, out of his pocket—and came over and unlocked the door. He smelled of whisky. He said, 'I can't see you tonight.' I said,

'This is important, and I don't want you going off drinking again.' We talked for a while, but every minute or so he'd look at his watch; and he didn't ask me to sit down. Finally I said, 'All right, go to the devil,' and walked out. . . . He locked the door after me, and put the key in his pocket. That's all I know. It may be still there."

"It wasn't there," said Morgan, "when Murch searched his clothes. And it wasn't in any of the suits in his wardrobe. I wonder . . ."

They sat quiet for many minutes. It was Patricia who finally suggested that they ought to be returning to The Grange for dinner; and, when she put her hand on Hugh's arm as she rose, he thought that it trembled.

CHAPTER XI

The Poltergeist and the Red Notebook

THERE WAS no regular dinner that night at The Grange. When they hurried up to the house, well after seven o'clock, they received the news that Mr. Theseus Langdon, the dead man's solicitor, had arrived shortly before, accompanied by Miss Elizabeth Depping, who had taken the afternoon plane from Paris. The former was closeted in the library with Dr. Fell and Inspector Murch; the latter was indisposed, and kept to her room—probably, Patricia said with candor, less from her father's death than from her usual airsickness. But this indisposition was highly romanticized by Colonel Standish's good lady, who sailed about in a tempest of activity and set the house into an uproar. She presided at Betty Depping's bedside much as she might have presided at a ladies' club meeting; Patricia joined her, and there would seem to have been a row of some sort. Anyhow, only cold refreshments were set out on a sideboard in the dining-room, and disconsolate guests wandered about eating surreptitious sandwiches.

Of the celebrated Maw Standish, Hugh caught only a brief glimpse. She stalked downstairs to bid him welcome—a handsome woman, five-feet-ten in her lowest-heeled shoes, with a mass of ash-blonde hair carried like a war banner, and a rather hard but determinedly pleasant face. She told him firmly that he would like The Grange. She stabbed a finger at several of the portraits in the main hall, and reeled off the names of their artists. She tapped the elaborately carved frame of a mirror in the great alcove where the staircase stood, and impressively said, "Grinling Gibbons!" Donovan said, "Ah!" Next she enumerated the distinguished people who had visited the house, including Cromwell, Judge Jeffreys, and Queen Anne. Cromwell, it seemed, had left behind a pair of boots, and Jeffreys had smashed a piece out of the panelling; but Queen Anne seemed to have retired in good order. She fixed him with a stern, faintly smiling look, as though she wondered if he were worthy of this heritage; then she said that the patient required her attention, and marched up the staircase.

The Grange, he discovered, was a pleasant house: cool and sleepy, with its big rooms built on three sides of a rectangle. It had been modernized. The electric lights, set in wall brackets or depending from very high ceilings, had a rather naked look; but the only touch of antiquity—and a spurious one at that—was in the stone-flagged floor of the main hall, its great fireplace of white sandstone, and red-painted walls full of nonfamily portraits in gilt frames. Behind the main hall was a funereal dining-room, outside whose bay windows grew the largest ilex tree he had ever seen; and here J. R. Burke sat drinking beer in stolid thoughtfulness.

Wandering off into the west wing, Hugh found a drawing-room which some ancestor had decorated in opulent and almost pleasant bad taste. The walls were a panorama of Venetian scenes, with everybody leaning out of gondolas at perilous angles; gold-leaf mirrors; cabinets overlaid in china ornaments; and a chandelier like a glass castle. From across a hallway he could hear a mutter of voices behind the door to the library. A tribunal seemed to be going on there. As he watched, the door opened, and a butler came out; he could see momentarily a long room full of cigar smoke, and Dr. Fell making notes at a table.

The drawing-room windows were open on a stone-flagged terrace, where a cigarette was winking in the gloom. Hugh went outside. The terrace looked down over shelving gardens towards the rear, colorless under the white-and-purple dusk; and a few mullioned windows were alight in the pile of the west wing. Against the stone balustrade Morley Standish leaned and stared at the windows. He peered round as he heard a footstep.

"Who—? Oh, hullo," he said, and resumed his scrutiny.

Hugh lit a cigarette and said: "What's been going on? Your sister and I were down at Morgan's. Have they found—?"

"That's what I'd like to know," said Morley. "Seems to me they're devilish secretive. I don't seem to count for anything. Mother says I oughtn't to see Betty . . . Miss Depping, you know; she's here. *I* don't know what they're doing. They're had every servant on the carpet over there in the library. God knows what's going on." He flung away his cigarette, hunched himself up, and brooded over the balustrade. "Beautiful night, too," he added irrelevantly. "'Where were *you* on the night of the murder?'"

"I?"

"They've been asking us all that—just as a matter of form. Beginning with the servants to make it look better. Where would we be? Where is there to go after dark? We were all tucked up in our beds. I wish I could explain those confounded shoes."

"Did you ask about them?"

"I asked Kennings: that footman I was telling you about. He doesn't know. He remembers putting the shoes in the junk closet right enough, some time ago. Anybody could have taken 'em out. There's no mistake. They're not there now. . . . Hullo!"

Hugh followed the direction of his glance. Another light had appeared in the west wing. "Now I wonder," said Morley, rubbing his forehead with a heavy hand, "who's in the oak room at this time?"

"The oak room?"

"Where our poltergeist hangs out," Morley told him grimly. After a pause, during which he stared at the light, he said: "Am I getting idiotic notions? Or do you think we ought to go up and see?"

They looked at each other. Hugh was conscious of a tensity in the other's bearing; almost an explosiveness which the stolid Morley had been concealing. Hugh nodded. Almost in a rush they left the terrace. They were climbing the main staircase before Morley spoke again.

"See that fellow?" he asked, pointing to a bad portrait on the landing. It was that of a fleshy-faced man in a laced coat and full-bottomed periwig, with plump hands which seemed to be making an uncertain gesture, and an evasive eye. "He was one of the Aldermen of Bristol, supposed to have been concerned in the Western Rebellion of 1685. He didn't actually do anything—didn't have the nerve, I suppose—but he was rumored to have favored Monmouth. When Chief Justice Jeffreys came down for the assize to punish the rebels, he had all his goods forfeited. Jeffreys was staying here, with a Squire Redlands who owned The Grange then. That man, Alderman Wyde, came here to plead with Jeffreys against the sentence. Jeffreys foamed, and preached him a long sermon. So Wyde cut his throat in the oak room. Hence . . ."

They were moving along a passage that led off the main hall upstairs: a narrow passage, badly lighted, and Morley was peering about him as though he expected to find somebody following. The whole house might have been deserted. Morley stopped before a door at the end. He waited a moment, straightened his shoulders, and knocked.

There was no answer. An eerie feeling crawled through Donovan, because they could see the light shining out under the door. Morley knocked again. "All right!" he said, and pushed the door open.

It was a spacious room, but gloomy, because it was panelled to the ceiling. The only illumination was a lamp with a frosted-glass shade, which stood on a table by the bed: a canopied bed, unmade and uncurtained. In the wall facing them was a wooden mantelpiece, with leaded windows in embrasures on either side. There was another door in the right-hand wall. And the room was empty.

Morley's footsteps rattled on the boarded floor. He called, "Hallo!" and moved across to the other door, which was shut but unlocked. He pulled it open and glanced into the darkness beyond.

"That," he said, "is the junk closet. It—"

He whirled round. Hugh also had backed away. There had been a sharp creak near the fireplace, and a flicker of light. A section of the panelling between the fireplace and the window embrasure was being pushed open: a hinged section, nearly as high as a door. The Bishop of Mappleham, with a candle in his hand, appeared in the aperture.

Hugh had the presence of mind not to laugh.

"Look here, sir," he protested, "I wish you wouldn't do that. Mysterious villains have a monopoly on entrances like that. When *you* appear—"

His father's face looked tired and heavy over the candle flame. He turned to Morley.

"Why," he said, "was I not told of this—this passage?"

Morley only returned his gaze blankly for a moment. "That? I thought you knew about it, sir. It isn't a secret passage, you know. If you look closely, you can see the hinges. And the hole where you put your finger to open it. It leads—"

"I know where it leads," said the bishop. "Downstairs, to a concealed door opening on the gardens. I have explored it. Neither end is latched. Do you realize that any outsider could enter this house unseen at any time he chose?"

Morley's dark, almost expressionless eyes seemed to recognize what the other was thinking. He nodded, slightly. But he said:

"For that matter, an outsider could walk in the front entrance if he chose. We never lock doors."

The bishop set down his candle on the mantel-shelf, and fell to brushing dust from his coat. Again his face was heavy and clouded, as though from anger or loss of sleep. "However," he said, "it has been recently used. The dust is disturbed. And over there is the closet from which your shoes were taken . . ."

Heavily, with a forward stoop of his shoulders, he moved over towards the bed. Hugh saw that he was looking at a splattered red stain on the wall and on the floor. For a moment a vision of throat-cuttings, and periwigged gentlemen out of the seventeenth century, invaded the shrivelled old room; then, with a drop of anticlimax, Hugh remembered about the ink. This was where the poltergeist had been active. The whole thing was at once baffling, ludicrous, and terrible.

"Since our authorities," he went on with bitter heaviness, "Dr. Fell with his great knowledge of criminals, and that brilliant detective Inspector Murch, have not seen fit to take me into their confidence this afternoon—well, I have conducted my investigation along my own lines . . . Tell me: This room is not generally used, is it?"

"Never," said Morley. "It's damp, and there's no steam heat. Er—why do you ask, sir?"

"Then how did Mr. Primley happen to occupy it on the night of—on the night someone was assumed to be exercising a primitive sense of humor?"

Morley stared at him. "Well, you ought to know, sir! You were with us when it was arranged. It was because he asked . . ."

The bishop made an irritated gesture. "I am putting these questions to you," he said, "for my son's benefit. I wish him to understand exactly how the proper sort of examination is conducted."

"Oh!" said Morley. A slightly humorous look appeared in his eyes. "I see. Well, you and my father and Mr. Primley and I began talking about the story of the man who'd killed himself here, and 'the influence' or whatever you call it. So when Mr. Primley had to spend the night here, he asked to be put in this room . . ."

"Ah. Yes. Yes, quite so. That," nodded the bishop, drawing back his chin, "is what I want to establish. Listen, Hugh. But Mr. Primley had not originally intended to spend the night, had he?"

"No, sir. He missed the last bus back home, and he—"

"Consequently, I must point out to you, Hugh: consequently, no outsider could even have known of the vicar's intention to stay the night, even in the doubtful event an outsider knew he was here. It was a sudden decision, made late in the evening. Much less could any outsider have known Mr. Primley intended to occupy this room . . . Therefore this affair could not conceivably have been a joke put up on Mr. Primley by an outsider."

"What *ho!*" said Hugh, after a pause. "You mean somebody sneaked up that passage to get into the junk closet and steal those shoes; but he didn't expect to find this room occupied . . ."

"Precisely. I am afraid you run ahead of my logic," the bishop rebuked him in a somewhat annoyed voice: "a practice against which I must caution you. But that is what I do mean. He did not expect to find the room occupied; and, either coming in or going out—probably the latter—he woke Mr. Primley. He raised a very brief ghost scare to cover himself." The bishop's furry brows drew together, and he put his hand into his pocket. "What is more, I can tell you exactly the person who would be apt to do that, and I can prove that he was here."

From his pocket he drew a small notebook of red leather, smudged over with dirt. There were gilt initials stamped upon it.

"This interesting little clue was dropped in an angle of the stairs that go down inside that passage. Do me the favor of looking at it. It is unfortunate that it was lost; it bears the initials H.M. Do I need to expatiate at length on the traits of character belonging to young Mr. Henry Morgan, or to point out his suspicious eagerness to lead Inspector Murch by the nose in this case? It was he, I believe, who called Murch's attention to that footprint by the Guest House, and kindly offered to take a plaster impression of the evidence."

"ROT!" said Hugh violently. He swallowed hard. "I mean—excuse me, sir, but that's fantastic. It won't work. It's—"

Morley cleared his throat.

"You'll have to admit, sir," he urged persuasively, "that it takes some believing. I don't mean the evidence!—but about Hank. He would be quite capable of playing a joke of that sort on Mr. Primley or anybody else who slept here, but the rest of it can't be right."

The bishop spread out his hands. "Young man," he said; "I urge nothing upon you. I simply inform you. Did Henry Morgan know Mr. Primley was here at all that night?"

"N-no. But he could have seen him come in, possibly."

"Yet he could not under any circumstances have known Mr. Primley was staying the night?"

"I suppose not."

"Or, above all, the room he would occupy? Ah. Thank you." He placed the notebook carefully back in his pocket, patted his waistcoat, and assumed a benign air. "I think that I shall presently wait upon our good authorities in the library. Shall we go downstairs now? Morley, if you will blow out that candle . . . ? No, leave it there. We shall probably need it presently."

They were walking along the hall again before Morley spoke.

"I tell you, sir," he said, "your assumption is—well, ridiculous; not to put too fine a point on it. I told you Hank didn't like the old boy; all right; everybody will admit that, including Hank himself. But that's no reason for . . ." He hesitated, as though he could not use the word, and went on stubbornly: "And as for sneaking upstairs to get my shoes—! No, no. That won't work. That's pure theory."

"My boy, be careful. I wish it distinctly understood that I accuse nobody. I have not yet, even in my own thoughts, gone so far as any accusation or implication of—ah—homicide. But if this estimable gentleman, Fell, chooses to exert the letter of his authority in excluding me from his puerile councils, then he cannot be chagrined if I take steps to circumvent him."

Hugh had never before seen his father's hobby take such a violent and spiteful hold. More than this, he suddenly became aware that the bishop was growing old, and unsteady. Nobody in the past, whatever the satirical remarks about him, had ever doubted his fairness or his intelligence. Now Hugh seemed to see only a large grizzle-headed shell, with flabby jowls, and a bitter mouth. He had lived too long, too aggressively, and now there was a faint childishness creeping into him. In only a year . . . Hugh realized, only then, what must have been the effect on him of being betrayed—as though the very Providence he extolled were conspiring to make a fool of him—into the ludicrous antics over which everybody had got so much amusement. It wasn't humorous. The maddest joke of all was just that; he took it seriously. There must be a moral somewhere . . .

Nor did Hugh believe that Morgan was guilty, if only because he felt vaguely that people like Morgan do not commit murders; especially as they are always writing about them in books, and treat murderers as fascinating monstrosities apart from human life, like unicorns or griffins. He doubted whether his father believed it. But he had an alarming idea that the bishop was willing to accuse anybody, regardless of belief, if he could find any sort of case.

Meanwhile, his thoughts were complicated by the mess of the whole affair, and how soon he could see Patricia, and why the mess had to occur at just this time anyway. As he followed his father through the drawing-room, a door slammed violently. It was the library door. Stumping through the drawing-room came J.R. Burke, a sardonic expression on his face, and a reminiscent gleam of battle over his half-glasses. He peered at the newcomers, and grinned. Then he took the pipe out of his mouth to point over his shoulder.

"Evenin'," he said to the bishop. "They told me to fetch you. And also you, young fella. I've given *my* evidence, and they can put it in their pipes and smoke it. Hum, hum." He cocked his head on one side in pleased reflection. "Go on in. The more the merrier. There's hell poppin' in there."

The bishop drew himself up. "I fancied," he replied, "that sooner or later my presence might be requested. I also fancy I shall somewhat astonish them—What is going on in there, Mr. Burke?"

"It's about Depping's lawyer," explained J.R., chuckling. "It turns out that, in addition to being Depping's lawyer, he's also Spinelli's. And trimming both sides as neat as you please. . . . Join up. You and your son are both wanted."

CHAPTER XII

Spinelli Reads the Taroc

THE LIBRARY was a long, narrow room, on one side of which were windows opening on the terrace, and on the other built-in bookshelves and a built-in fireplace. Its color scheme was both dark and florid; there were heavy brown drapes at the windows, and across double doors at the far narrow end of the room. All the wall lamps were burning behind yellowish shades; and the glass chandelier was also in full blaze. Blue sheets of smoke hung under it. At a cluttered table beneath the smoke, Dr. Fell sat spread out with his chins in his collar, absently drawing pictures on a pad. Inspector Murch, a whole brief-case-full of papers spread out before him, was teetering backwards and bristling over his sandy moustache. His pale blue eye looked angry and baffled. Evidently he had just finished some remarks to the smiling gentlemen who sat on the divan beside the table.

"—and you will appreciate, I am sure," the latter was saying smoothly, "the difficulties, both ethical and legal, in which I find myself. You are a reasonable man, Mr. Murch. We are all (I hope) reasonable men. Ahem." He turned his head as the Donovans, *père et fils*, entered.

Dr. Fell blinked up from his drawing, and waved a hand. "Come in," he invited. "This is Mr. Langdon. Sit down. We're very much in need of help."

Mr. Theseus Langdon was one of those smiling and expansive gentlemen, smooth of gesture and rather too practised of poise, who are all of an engaging frankness. They seem always to impart confidences, with low-voiced diplomacy and a deprecating smile. They can speak of the weather as though they were telling international secrets. In person Mr. Langdon was inclined to portliness. He had a pink scrubbed face, thin brown hair brushed back from a low forehead, eyes like those of an alert dog, and a broad mouth. He sat back on the divan with both ease and dignity, his well-manicured hands in his lap. His cutaway and striped trousers were unwrinkled, and his wing collar looked cool despite the heat. He rose, bowing to the newcomers.

"Thirty-seven, Gray's Inn Square," said Mr. Langdon, as though he were making an epigram. "Gentlemen! At your service!" Then he sat down again and resumed in his easy voice: "As I was saying concerning this dreadful affair, Inspector, you will appreciate my difficulties. Whatever information I possess is at your disposal, I need not tell you. But, as Mr. Burke so admirably put it a moment ago, Mr. Depping was an oyster. Precisely so. A veritable oyster, I assure you."

Murch glowered at him. But his dogged, gruff voice persisted. "'Tes this, then. Which you won't deny. You'm the solicitor both for Mr. Depping that was, and for Louis Spinelli—"

"Excuse me, please. For Mr. Stuart Travers."

"Eh, eh! I be and told you his name is Spinelli—"

"So far as I have any knowledge, Mr. Murch," said Langdon, smiling composedly, "my client's name is Mr. Stuart Travers. You see?"

"But Spinelli has told us—"

At this point Dr. Fell rumbled warningly. Inspector Murch nodded, and fell back. For a time the doctor sat tapping his pencil against the writing pad, and blinking at it. Then he raised his eyes.

"Let's get this straight from the beginning, Mr. Langdon. We happen to know that Spinelli, or Travers, put in a trunk call to you this afternoon. What you advised him is neither here nor there, at the moment. Let's concern ourselves with Depping. You have told us"—he held out his pudgy fingers and checked off the points—"that you have been his legal adviser for five years. That you know nothing about him, except that he was a British subject who had spent some years in America. That he made no will, and leaves an estate which you estimate at about fifty thousand pounds—"

"Sadly depreciated, I fear," interposed Langdon, shaking his head with a sorrowful smile. "Sadly."

"Eh. Very well then. How did Depping come to you in the first place?"

"I believe I was recommended to him."

"Um," said Dr. Fell, pinching at his moustache. "By the same person who recommended you to Spinelli?"

"I really can't say."

"Now, it's a very curious thing, Mr. Langdon," rumbled Dr. Fell, after a time of tapping the pencil on the pad, "about this information you volunteer. After telling you nothing of himself for five years, according to what you say, Depping walked into your office about two weeks ago and told you several things of a highly private nature.—Is that what you told Inspector Murch?"

Langdon had been sitting back, all polite attention, smiling mechanically; but his alert eyes had been disinterested. They strayed. He touched the sharp crease in his trousers, and seemed pleased. But now the eyes came round sharply to Dr. Fell. His faint eyebrows rose. It was as though the satisfaction of some exceedingly shrewd piece of business gleamed out.

"Quite true," he said. "Shall I—would you like me to repeat my statement, for the benefit of these gentlemen?"

"Langdon," the doctor said suddenly, "why are you so damned anxious for everybody to hear it?"

He had raised his voice only slightly, but it seemed to boom and echo in the room. This somnolent fat man took on an expression which caused Langdon's own expression to veil immediately. But the doctor only said, between wheezes:

"Never mind. I'll repeat it. Depping said, in effect, 'I'm sick of this sort of life, and I'm going away; probably for a trip around the world. What's more, I'm taking somebody with me—a woman.'"

"Quite so," affirmed Langdon pleasantly. He glanced at the newcomers. "Say, however, a lady. A lady of your own charming community here, he told me."

Hugh looked at Inspector Murch, and then at his father. The inspector was muttering with suppressed anger, his eyes half-shut and his moustache bristling. The bishop sat upright, and all the muscles of his face seemed to stiffen with some thought that had come to him. His hand moved slowly towards his pocket . . . For possibly a full minute each of that group was locked up with his own buzzing thoughts. Then Inspector Murch's voice fell heavily into the silence.

He said to Dr. Fell: "I don't believe it. S'help me, sir, I don't believe it."

Langdon turned on him. "Come, come, my friend! This won't do, you know—really it won't. I should have thought that the word of an honorable man would be sufficient. Have you any reason for doubting it? No? I thank you." He went on smiling.

"And he told you all this—?" Dr. Fell prompted.

"À propos the matter which Inspector Murch was mentioning a while ago. Those rather spirited letters between Mr. Depping and Mr. J. R. Burke," he nodded at the papers on the table, "which the inspector found in Mr. Depping's files. Mr. Depping had invested quite a large sum in Mr. Burke's firm. When he decided to leave England, he wished to withdraw it: a sudden and highly irregular proceeding; but then Mr. Depping was never a business man. You heard what Mr. Burke said a moment ago—it would have been highly inconvenient, not to say impossible, to allow this at the present time; especially on such short notice. Besides, as I pointed out, it was an excellent investment."

"What did he decide?"

"Oh, it was settled most amicably. Mr. Depping was content to let it stand. He was—may I say so—a strange combination of wisdom and irresponsibility."

Dr. Fell leaned back in his chair and asked offhandedly:

"Got any explanation of his death, Mr. Langdon?"

"Ah. Unfortunately, no. I can only say that it is a dreadful business, and shocks me beyond words. Besides"—again the solicitor's eyes narrowed, and his voice grew soft with suggestion—"you can hardly expect me to express an opinion, either private or professional, until I have had the opportunity of conferring with my other client, Mr. Travers."

"All right," said Dr. Fell. He hoisted himself to his feet, wheezing. "All right. That's fair enough . . . Inspector, bring in Louis Spinelli."

There was a silence. Clearly Langdon had not expected this. One of his well-manicured hands moved to his upper lip and caressed it; he sat stiffly, but his eyes followed Murch as the inspector went to the windows. Murch put his head through the curtains and spoke some words outside.

"'Mf. By the way," the doctor remarked, "you'll be interested to know that Spinelli is willing to talk. I don't think he's satisfied with your legal counsel, Mr. Langdon. In return for certain favors—"

Murch stood aside. Followed by a constable, Spinelli moved into the room and looked round him coolly. He was a thin and wiry man, but with a broad, low face. His chin was weak, and his eyes had a look of assumed easiness. Hugh Donovan could understand at once why the rather vague descriptions of him always insisted on "loud clothes," though, strictly speaking, it was erroneous. In no particular was he noticeably loud, yet the effect of the whole—a trick of gesture, a ring on the wrong finger, a necktie adjusted too studiedly at one side—was blatant. His fawn-colored hat was a little too narrow in the brim, and too rakish; his sideburns were exaggerated, and his moustache shaved to a hairline. Now he looked coolly round the library, as though he were appraising it. But he was nervous. Most unpleasant of all, Hugh was conscious of a faint medicinal smell which clung to him.

"How are you?" he said to the company in general, nodding. He removed his hat, smoothed back his sharply parted hair, and looked straight at Langdon. "Fowler told me you were a crook, Langdon. But of all the crude work I've ever had pulled on me, your advising me to hand over my passport to 'em was the worst."

Spinelli's air was compounded of vindictiveness and a nervous desire to please. His voice had a rasping softness. He turned to Dr. Fell. "That fellow—my counsel; my counsel, mind you!—didn't waste any time. I knew I was in a spot. And then I knew he was out to sell me. 'Certainly, let them see your passport.' So they'd cable to Washington, and then where am I?"

"In Dartmoor," replied Dr. Fell blandly. He seemed to be enjoying this. His sleepy eye wandered towards Langdon. "Why should he be trying to sell you, do you think?"

"Cut it," said Spinelli, with a curt gesture. "That's your business to find out. All I want is to understand your proposition—the proposition this fellow," he nodded at Inspector Murch, "put up to me. I'm not running foul of any English dicks if I can help it, and that's flat."

Langdon had risen, and was smiling paternally. He began:

"Tut, tut! Come, you mustn't misunderstand me, Mr. Travers! Be reasonable. I advised you for your own good . . ."

"As for you—" said Spinelli. "You're thinking, 'How much does he know?' You'll find out . . . So this is the proposition. I'm to tell you everything I know. In return for that, you promise not to prosecute for using a faked passport, and allow me one week to get out of the country. Is that it?"

Langdon moved forward. His voice went up shrilly. He said: "Don't be a fool—!"

"Knocks the wind out of you, does it?" asked Spinelli. "I thought it would. Keep on thinking, 'How much does he know?'"

The American sat down opposite Langdon. With the lights just above his head, his face was hollowed out in shadows; under the eyes and cheekbones, and in sharp lines down his jaws; but his hair had a high gloss like his small defiant eyes. Then he seemed to remember that he had not been acting exactly in the character of a cultured and cosmopolitan traveler. His manner changed, with a jerk. Even his voice seemed to change.

"May I smoke?" he inquired.

This attempt at suavity, considering the haze of smoke round him, was not a success. He seemed to know it, and it angered him. He lit a cigarette, twitching out the match with a snap of his wrist. His next remark was obviously more sincere; as his eyes were roving round the room, he appeared surprised and rather puzzled. "So this," he said abruptly, "is an English country house. It's disappointing, I don't mind telling you. That thing"—his cigarette stabbed at another of the bad Venetian scenes—"is an eyesore. So is that. Your imitation Fragonard over the fireplace would disgrace Pine Falls, Arkansas. Gentlemen, I hope I'm in the right place?"

Inspector Murch was insistent. "Never mind that. You see you do stick to the subject; look." He scowled. "I don't mind saying, myself, that I do favor no bargains with you. 'Tes Dr. Fell who's done it, and it's done, and he's responsible to Scotland Yard; now we'm here to get the benefit from it . . . *if* you do satisfy us that you'm not the one who shot Mr. Depping. First, we want to know—"

"Nonsense, inspector!" said Dr. Fell affably. His wheezy gesture bade Spinelli continue on whatever line he liked; he folded his hands over the ridges of his stomach and assumed an almost paternal air. "You're quite right, Mr. Spinelli, about the pictures. But there's a more interesting one, in water color, on the table beside you—that card. Look at it. What do you make of it?"

Spinelli glanced down; he saw the card with the eight swords painted on it, and forgot his lethargy.

"Hell's bells! The taroc, eh? Where did you get this?"

"You recognize it? . . . Good! That was better than I had hoped for. I was going to ask you whether Depping, when you knew him, ever dabbled in pseudo-occultism of this kind. I presumed he did; he had several shelves of books dealing with the more rarified forms—people like Wirth, and Ely Star, and Barlet, and Papus. But nobody seemed to know anything about his interest in such matters, if—h'mf—if he had any."

"He was a sucker for it," Spinelli answered simply. "Or for anything in the line of glorified fortune telling. He didn't like to admit it, that's all. Actually, he was as superstitious as they make 'em. And the taroc was his favorite."

Inspector Murch lumbered over and seized his notebook.

"Taroc?" he repeated. "What's this taroc?"

"To answer that question, my friend, fully and thoroughly," said Dr. Fell, squinting at the card, "you would need to be initiated into the mysteries of theosophy; and even then the explanation would baffle any ordinary brain, including my own. You'll get some idea of the modest functions it is supposed to have if I tell you some of the claims they make for it. The taroc reveals the world of ideas and principles, and enables us to grasp the laws of the evolution of phenomena; it is a mirror of the universe, wherein we find symbolically the threefold theogonic, androgonic, and cosmogonic theory of the ancient magi; a double current of the progressive materialization or involution of the God-mind, and the progressive redivinisation of matter which is the basis of theosophy. It is also—"

"Excuse me, sir," said Inspector Murch, breathing hard, "but I can't write all *that* down, you know. If you'd make yourself a bit clearer . . ."

"Unfortunately," said the doctor, "I can't. Damned if I know what it means myself. I only inflicted that explanation, as I have read it, because I am fascinated by the roll and stateliness of the words. H'm. Say that according to some people the taroc is, *in summo gradu,* a key to the universal mechanism . . . In substance it is a pack of seventy-eight cards, with weird and rather ghastly markings. They use it like a pack of ordinary playing cards, for what Mr. Spinelli has called glorified fortune telling."

Murch looked relieved and interested. "Oh, ah. Like reading the cards? Ah, ay; done it meself. Me sister's cousin often reads the cards for us. And tea leaves as well. And, lu' me, sir," he said in a low earnest voice, "if she don't 'ave it right, every time . . . !" He caught himself up, guiltily.

"Don't apologize," said Dr. Fell, with a similarly guilty expression. "I myself am what Mr. Spinelli would describe as a sucker for such things. I am never able to pass a palmist's without going in to get my hand read, or my future revealed in a crystal. Hurrumph. I can't help it," he declared, rather querulously. "The less I believe in it, I'm still the first to howl for my fortune to be told. That's how I happen to know about the taroc."

Spinelli's lip lifted in a sardonic quirk. He sniggered. "Say, are you a dick?" he asked. "You're a funny one. Well, we live and learn. Fortune telling—" He sniggered again.

"The taroc pack, inspector," Dr. Fell continued equably, "is supposed to be of Egyptian invention. But this card has the design of the French taroc, which dates back to Charles VI and the origin of the playing card. Out of the seventy-eight cards, twenty-two are called major arcana and fifty-six minor arcana. I needn't tell you such a pack, or even the knowledge of it, is very rare. The minor arcana are divided into four series, like the clubs, diamonds, hearts, and spades; but in this case called . . . ?"

"Rods, cups, pence, and swords," said Spinelli, examining his finger nails. "But what I want to know is this: Where did you get that card? Was it Depping's?"

Dr. Fell picked it up. He went on: "Each card having a definite meaning. I needn't go into the method of fortune telling, but you'll be interested in the significance . . . Question for question, Mr. Spinelli. Did Depping ever possess a taroc pack?"

"He did. Designed it himself, from somebody's manual. And paid about a grand to have it turned out by a playing-card company. But *that* card didn't come from it . . . unless he made a deck for himself. I'm asking you, where did you get it?"

"We have reason to believe that the murderer left it behind, as a sort of symbol. Who knows about high magic in the wilds of Gloucestershire?" mused Dr. Fell.

Spinelli looked straight in front of him. For an instant Hugh Donovan could have sworn the man saw something. But he only sniggered again.

"And that card means something?" Murch demanded.

"You tell him," Dr. Fell said, and held it up.

The American relished his position. He assumed a theatrical air; glanced first to one side and then the other. "Sure I can tell you, gentlemen. It means he got what was coming to him. The eight of swords—*Condemning justice.* It put the finger on old Nick Depping, and God knows he deserved it."

CHAPTER XIII

Bullet-Proof

AGAIN THEY were all locked up with their own thoughts, because each new development seemed to lead the case in a different direction; and each box opened up like a magician's casket, to show only another box inside the last. It was growing hot and stuffy in the library. Somewhere in the house a clock began to strike. It had finished banging out the hour of nine before Dr. Fell spoke again.

"So that's established. Very well. Now tell us what you know about Depping himself, and what happened last night."

"As your legal adviser, Mr. Travers—" began Langdon, suddenly thrusting himself into the conversation as he might have made up his mind to jump out of bed on a cold day; a more incongruous fancy because the man was sweating—"as your legal adviser, I must insist that you confer in private with me before taking any unwise steps . . ."

Spinelli looked at him. "Burn, damn you," he said cryptically, leaning forward in fierce vindictiveness. "Burn. Sweat. Go on; I like it . . .

"I can give the whole thing to you," he went on, relaxing

154

again, "in a couple of words. Nick Depping—he didn't call himself Septimus then—was the slickest article that ever came out of England. By God, he had brains! I'll give him that. He came over to the States about eight or nine years ago with the idea of making his fortune, like a lot of Britishers; only he'd thought it all over, and he'd decided that the best way was to teach them new rackets in the home of rackets. I don't know how he got hold of Jet Mayfree. Mayfree didn't amount to a row of beans then; he was one of those two-for-a-nickel ward heelers that hang around speakeasies and maybe can get a few muscle-men to do somebody else's dirty work—but that's all. Well, I'm telling you, Depping made Mayfree a big shot as sure as God made little apples. Depping blew into New York and lived in speaks until he found the man he wanted for his front, and in a year . . ." Spinelli gestured.

"I don't mean booze, you understand. That's small change. I mean protection, politics, swindles, blackmail—holy Jesus, he could put a new angle on each one of 'em that nobody else would have thought of in a million years! And he wasn't crude: no guns, unless it couldn't be helped, and even then no stuff that looked like a gang killing. 'Why advertise?' he said. 'Let somebody else take the rap.' At one time he was running a real badger-game syndicate: twenty-two women working the hotels for him. An assistant district attorney got nosey. Nick Depping worked it out, planted evidence, and had the man poisoned so that there was clear proof his wife had done it; and the d.a.'s wife went to the chair for it."

Spinelli leaned back and smoked with a sort of malignant admiration.

"Do you get it? He organized all the little rackets, that the big shots had never bothered with. He never tried to muscle in on them, and they let him alone. Extortion, for one thing. That was how he ran into me. *I* wouldn't join his union. And what happened? Why, he got me sent up the river for five years."

The man coughed on some smoke. He brushed a hand over his eyes, which had become watery. Sideburns, hair-line moustache, broad face with nostrils working, all the offensiveness of the man seemed to gather into one lump; to grow poisonous, and writhe on the brown sofa.

"All right!" he said hoarsely, and then controlled himself. He remembered his suavity. "I've forgotten that, now. All I was thinking—it was queer to see that dry old bird . . . He looked and talked like a college professor, except when he was drunk. I had one interview with him, the first time I ever saw him; and I was curious. He had an apartment in the East Sixties, lined up with books, and when I saw him he was sitting at a table with a bottle of rye and a pack of taroc cards . . ." Spinelli coughed.

"Steady on," said Dr. Fell quietly. His dull eyes opened wide for a moment. "There's a lavatory just off here. Would you care to, humph, retire for a minute or two. Eh?"

The other rose. At Dr. Fell's gesture, a mystified Inspector Murch followed to stand at the door. During the heavy silence of the room, when he had gone, Dr. Fell glanced round the group. He picked up a pencil, placed it against his arm, and made a motion of one pressing a plunger.

"Let him alone," he said gruffly. "He'll be with us shortly."

All during this recital, the bishop had been sitting with his head in his hands. He straightened up, and said, "This is sickening. I—I never realized . . ."

"No," said Dr. Fell. "It isn't pleasant when you really see it at

close range, is it? Far different from looking at criminals all pre-
served and ticketed behind glass cases; and reading the Latin titles on the reptile exhibits with your handkerchief to your nose?
I've found that out. I found it out long ago, for my sins. But I
ought to have warned you that you will never see clearly to the
heart of any crime until you can honestly repeat, 'There but for
the grace of God—'"

Mr. Theseus Langdon again took his jump, but this time
with more ease.

"Come!" he said persuasively. "I am afraid I must insist, in
justice to my client, that we must not place too much credence
in what he says at this time. If you will allow me to join him and
speak to him in private, as my prerogative is . . . ?"

"Sit still," rumbled Dr. Fell. He made only a slight gesture
with his pencil, but Langdon subsided.

Spinelli was soothed and urbane when he returned,
though a muscle seemed to jump in his shoulder. He stared
round with a toothy smile; apologized, and lowered himself
with a sort of stage grace into another chair. After a time he
went on:

"I was—ha, ha—speaking of poor Nick Depping the first
time I saw him. He said, 'They tell me you're a man of some education. You don't look it. But sit down.' That was how I came to
know him, and, take my word for it, I knew him pretty well. So
I entered his organization . . ."

"Stop a bit!" said Dr. Fell. "I thought you told us a while ago
that you refused—?"

The other smirked. "Oh, I had outside interests. Listen!
I still think I'm as smart as he was; yes, and as well educat-
ed too, by God, though you mugs wouldn't believe it . . ." His

wrist jerked viciously as he lit another cigarette. "Never mind. He found it out, and I went to the Big House. But in the meantime I was his sparring partner for what he thought of books, and I read his fortune in that taroc pack until I knew it better than he did. Mind, I expected him to go far. He used to call me the court astrologer, and once he nearly shot me when he was drunk. If it hadn't been for the drinking, and for one outstanding weakness—"

"What was that?"

"Women. He blew in plenty of money on them. If it hadn't been for that . . . yet," said Spinelli, who seemed to be jabbed by an ugly memory, "he honest-to-God had a real fascination for them. They fell for him. I told him once, when I'd had a few drinks myself, 'I'm a better man than you, Nick; by God, I am. But they don't seem to fall for *me*. It's your money.' But, somehow . . ." Spinelli fingered his sideburns. "I used to hate that conceited old rat because the women did go after him, and they wouldn't admit it. They'd pretend to laugh at him in public. But he—he hypnotized them, or something. Why can't *I* have his luck?" he demanded, almost at a whine. "Why won't they go for me? He even had one highclass dame with a Park Avenue manner, even if she did come from Ninth Avenue—and stuck to her—and she stuck to him; until he threw her over . . ."

Spinelli checked himself, as though he had just remembered something. He glanced at Langdon.

"You were saying—?" prompted Dr. Fell.

"I was telling you." He drew a deep breath. "I got sent to the Big House. But he was blowing in his money. And if he'd kept his head, and not thrown it around everywhere, he'd have been worth about six million, instead of only fifty thousand pounds in your money."

Dr. Fell opened one eye. He wheezed thoughtfully, and then said in a gentle voice:

"That's very interesting, my friend. How do you happen to know he left an estate of fifty thousand pounds?"

Nobody moved. Spinelli's eyes remained fixed and glazed. At length he said:

"Trying to trip me up, are you? Suppose I won't answer?"

They could hear his harsh breathing. Dr. Fell lifted his cane and pointed with it across the table.

"I wish you would endeavor to get it through your head, my friend, that there is at present quite enough evidence to hang you for the murder of Depping . . . Didn't I mention that?"

"No, by God, you didn't! You said—"

"That I wouldn't press the passport charge; that's all."

"You can't bluff me. This dick," he nodded at Murch, "told me this morning I was supposed to have visited Nick Depping last night. Well, I didn't. Show me that servant who says I came to visit him, and I'll prove he's a liar. You can't bluff me. And, if you try, I'll be damned if I tell you what did happen."

Dr. Fell sighed. "You'll try to avoid telling it anyway, I'm afraid. So I shall have to tell you, and I am afraid you'll hang anyway. You see, there are points of evidence against you which Inspector Murch neglected to mention. We don't think you were the man who rang Depping's doorbell and went upstairs at all. The evidence against you concerns that visit you paid to his house late on the same night—during the rainstorm—when you followed him back after he'd tried to kill you."

Spinelli jumped to his feet. He said shrilly: "By Christ, if any squealer—"

"You'd better listen to me, I think. Personally, I don't care a tuppenny farthing what happens to you. But if you value your own neck . . . Ah, that's better."

There was something rather terrifying in the wide-open stare of the doctor's eyes. He got his breath again, and went on:

"While you were in prison at Sing Sing, Depping left the States. He was tired of his new toy called racketeering, tired of making his fortune—just as later he tired of the publishing business. He cut loose from Mayfree and returned to England." Dr. Fell glanced at the bishop. "You remember remarking this morning, Bishop Donovan, how Mayfree suddenly lost all his power and influence about five years ago? Umph, yes. I think Spinelli has provided us with a reason. You, Spinelli . . . After you got out of prison, you went in with Mayfree; you discovered his influence was gone; and you very prudently deserted also. Then you came to England . . ."

"Listen, you," said Spinelli, jabbing his forefinger into his palm. "If you think I came over here to find Depping—if anybody thinks that—it's a lie. I swear it's a lie. I was only—on a vacation. Why shouldn't I? It was an accident. I—"

"That's the odd part of it," Dr. Fell observed reflectively; "I think it was. I think it was completely by accident that you ran across your old friend Depping, while you were looking for fresh fields in England. Although, of course, you had prudently provided yourself with a solicitor in case of trouble. Somebody recommended you the same solicitor who had been recommended to Depping; rather a natural thing in the fraternity . . . Of course, Mr. Langdon may have told you about Depping . . ."

Spinelli's lip twisted. "No fear. Say, no fear of *him* telling about a good thing! I didn't know he had anything to do with Depping, until—" He checked himself. A sharp glance passed between him and Dr. Fell; it was as though they read each other's thoughts. But the doctor did not press the obvious lead. Besides, Langdon was sputtering.

"This," he said, with a sort of gulp, "all this is outrageous! Insufferable. Dr. Fell, I must ask to be excused from this conference. I cannot any longer sit and listen to insults which—"

"Park yourself," said Spinelli coolly, as the other got up, "or you'll wish you had. . . . Got any other remarks, Dr. What's your name?"

"H'mf, yes. You found Depping posing as a respectable country gentleman. It struck you as a heaven-sent opportunity to exercise those peculiar talents of yours—eh?"

"I deny that."

"You would, naturally. Let us say that you wanted to present your compliments to Depping and arrange a meeting to chat about old times. But the terms of the meeting, as suggested by Depping, roused suspicions in your none-too-trusting nature. He didn't ask you to his house, for this chat. A meeting in a lonely neighborhood, beside the river half a mile from the inn where you were stopping; *and* so far away from where Depping lived that, if your body were found floating in the river some miles still further down, he would scarcely be connected—"

Dr. Fell paused. He flipped up his hand as though he were tossing something away.

"You know a hell of a lot, don't you?" the other asked quietly. "Suppose I admitted it? You couldn't prove any blackmail charge. We arranged a friendly little conversation; that was all."

"Agreed. . . . Well, how did you manage it?"

The other seemed to come to a decision. He shrugged his

thin shoulders. "O.K. I'll risk it.—Bulletproof vest. I trusted old Nick Depping about as far as I can throw that desk. Even so, he nearly got me. I was standing on the river bank—that little creek they call a river—at the foot of a meadow where there's a clump of trees. We'd arranged to meet there. It was moonlight, but clouding up already. I didn't *know* he was going to start anything. I thought maybe he'd come to terms, like any sensible man who was caught with the goods . . ." He thrust out his neck and wriggled his head from side to side; his collar seemed to be too tight. They could see his teeth now.

"And then I heard a noise behind a tree. I whirled around, and there was somebody steadying a rod against the side of a tree, and taking a flat bead on me so close he couldn't miss. It didn't look like Nick—this guy with the rod, I mean. He looked young, and had a moustache, from what I could see in the moonlight. But I heard Nick's voice, all right. He said, 'You'll never do it again.' And then he let me have it, and I saw one of Nick's gold teeth.

"I didn't think of falling in the river. The slug knocked me in; square in the chest—through the heart if I hadn't been wearing that vest. But once I was in the water I got my senses back. It's deep, and there's hell's own current. I went downstream underwater as far as I could, and came up round a bend. He thought he'd got me."

"What then?"

"I went back to that little hotel where I'm staying. I changed my clothes, and I went to bed. Now get this!—get it straight. You're not going to pin any rap on me. This talk about my following Nick Depping home is bluff, and you know it." He was fiercely trying to hold Dr. Fell's eyes, as though to drive belief in like a nail. "Bluff. Every word of it. I didn't stir out of that room.

You think I wanted more heat? *I* wasn't going to face Nick Depping. I never handled a rod in my life, and I never will. Why should I?"

His voice was cracking with intensity. "Look up my record and see if I ever handled a rod. I'm as good a man as Nick Depping ever was, but I wasn't going back there; I wasn't mad at him for trying to iron me. Fortunes of war, see? Kill him? Not me. And if I *did* want him to—ah, advance me a little loan, do you think I'd be crazy enough to try anything like that?" He hammered the arm of his chair. "Do you?"

Throughout all this, Inspector Murch had been trying to take rapid notes; he seemed to be struggling with the idiom, and several times on the point of protest. But now there was a tight smile on his sandy moustache. Hugh Donovan could see what was going on in his mind; he had still against Spinelli that evidence of his having changed clothes and crawled out the window of the Chequers Inn a second time . . . Then Hugh saw that Dr. Fell was also looking at the inspector. Murch, who had just opened his mouth to speak, stopped. His boiled eye was puzzled.

And Dr. Fell chuckled.

"Bluff?" he said musingly. "I know it."

"You—you know . . . ?"

"H'm, yes. But I had to persuade you to talk, you see," the doctor said. "As a matter of fact, we are fairly well satisfied that you had nothing to do with the murder. I neglected to tell you," he beamed, "that you were seen by the landlord's wife at the Chequers, climbing back into the window of your room, soaking wet, at about ten o'clock."

"And not leave it again—?" Spinelli asked the question after a very brief pause; he seemed almost to have stopped breathing.

"And not leave it again. There, my friend, is your corroboration."

After this thundering lie, Dr. Fell looked as benevolent as Old King Cole. Spinelli's shoulders jerked.

"You mean—I can go? You're not going to hold me? Even as a material witness?"

"You may go. Get out of the country in forty-eight hours, and you shall not be held."

A sort of wild, malignant hope was in Spinelli's face. He had drawn himself back, with one hand against his chest. You could see that he was thinking fast, sifting chances, wondering, feeling for a trap; but he could not help saying: "Say, you told me a week! A week to leave the country, that's what you said. A week—"

"Man," interposed Dr. Fell softly, "will you never let well-enough alone? There are a number of dangerous questions I could have insisted on your answering; and you evaded them. Very well. Since I don't believe you shot Depping, I am willing to let that pass. But, by God, my friend!—if you question me, or argue with me, or try to quibble about time limits, you will get no mercy at all." He struck the handle of his stick on the table. "Speak up! What's it to be? Freedom, or gaol?"

"Oh, I'll go! Listen, governor, please! I didn't mean anything. I wasn't trying to give you any back-talk . . ." The man spoke with a sort of eager and slobbering whine. "All I meant was—well, it's sudden. And I'd like," here he spoke slowly, as though he were watching the doctor with furtive care to see the effect of his words, "I'd naturally like to speak with my mouthpiece—my lawyer—and sort of—arrange things, you know; but he's tied up here, and I thought maybe I might have more time. That's all I meant."

For an instant, as the doctor bent over to pick up a matchbox he had knocked on the floor, Hugh saw the faintest twitch of a smile under his moustache. With a grunt Dr. Fell hoisted himself again.

"Humph. Well, I see no objection to that. Unless, of course, it comes from Mr. Langdon? I think he said a while ago that your conduct was insufferable, and that he was inclined to wash his hands of—"

Langdon was instantly all smiles and deprecation. For some reason he seemed as relieved as Spinelli at the turn matters had taken. He almost clucked. Rolling his dog's eyes about, talking with a glutinous ease, he assured them that his first duty (after all) was to his client; that he had spoken with unintentional warmth, and under pardonable stress; finally, that he would be most happy to assist his client with any advice in his power.

"I mean," insisted Spinelli, still watching Dr. Fell, "could you let us talk now—in private? Listen, if I've got to get out of England in a hurry, then I won't have *time* to see him . . . !"

The doctor seemed reluctant, but allowed himself to be persuaded. Murch, who was plainly mystified, agreed. The drawing-room was put at the disposal of Spinelli and Langdon, and they were ushered out by the constable. Langdon stood in the doorway to deliver a little speech, flashing his smile and assuring them that he would be only a few minutes; then he faded out after Spinelli with a rather ghostly effect of disappearance. The door closed.

Inspector Murch watched it close. He swung round on Dr. Fell.

"Well, sir! You'm got some idea in this! What is it? Ah, but now yon pair do have a chance to put their heads together!"

"Yes," agreed the doctor. "Never have I accomplished a design with less trouble. They clamored for it. Gentlemen, the game is getting rapid now, and somebody is going to lose a number of tricks in a very short time. I wonder—"

"Eh, sir?"

"I wonder," said the doctor musingly, and poked at the table with his cane, "whether Spinelli is still wearing his bullet-proof vest? I rather suspect he will find it valuable before long. Steady, now! In the meantime, I want to talk about ladies."

CHAPTER XIV

The Devil and Maw Standish

UNEASILY MURCH rubbed a hand across his sandy cropped hair. He glanced at the bishop, as though he wondered whether such matters should be discussed in the episcopal presence.

"About ladies, sir? You mean—what Mr. Langdon said about a lady from hereabouts? Ah, ah! S'help me, I hate to say it—!"

The bishop, who all this time had been staring at the windows, turned heavily. His face looked dull and uncertain.

"Is all this necessary?" he asked. "I confess, doctor, that I am—much troubled. And confused. Villainy—ah—in general I have always regarded as an abstract thing, like a chemical reaction. Seeing it here . . ."

"Nevertheless, we have got to talk about it. Those remarks between Spinelli and Langdon, especially the things they didn't say, were the most revealing clues we have had up to this time. I am interested now not so much in what things were said, as *why* they were said. H'm." A thoughtful sniff rumbled in the doctor's nose. "For instance, Langdon's insistent statement that a lady from what he calls 'your charming community' was prepared to run away with Depping. True or untrue—

why did he say it? Definitely he had some purpose, in desiring that everybody should know he knew it. I don't think we can doubt that Langdon knew a great deal more about Depping than he was willing to tell us. But he chose that little item to parade before us."

"To throw suspicion on a woman, one would think," suggested the bishop. "To let us know he knew more about the murder than he was willing to tell."

"And yet I doubt it. Surely it leads in another direction as well . . . It's an unpleasant business, but I think we shall have to listen to a little gossip and opinion. Humph, brr-r, yes. Preferably strong-minded gossip and opinion. Inspector, will you step outside and tell the butler to ask Mrs. Standish to step downstairs? We haven't yet heard her views. And I lack something. I know who the murderer is, but—"

The bishop lifted his head. "You *know*, doctor?"

"I'm afraid I do. I knew it this afternoon. You see," Dr. Fell's hands slid out and played with the silver inkstand, "you see, the murderer made one terrific slip, which has not received the proper attention . . . Never mind. We can discuss that later. Stop a bit, Inspector! Before you go, in case Spinelli and Langdon should get through their conversation prematurely, you must have your instructions."

"Yes, sir?" said Murch gruffly.

"When Spinelli comes back to this room, you will be informed that neither you nor your constable will be needed further tonight. Both of you will leave here, ostentatiously . . ."

"Ah! And follow Spinelli?"

"Tut, tut, Nothing of the kind. Those uniforms of yours would be spotted half a mile, especially if Spinelli has reason to believe he is under surveillance. The constable will go home.

You, after pretending to do so, will take a long way round and go to the Guest House. This is merely a guess of mine, but we shall have to play a long chance."

Murch stroked his moustache. "But there's nobody at the Guest House, sir! You be and sent the man Storer away to the 'Bull'—"

"Exactly. You won't go inside, but keep in concealment close to the house, and watch what may happen. Meanwhile . . ."

He turned to Hugh Donovan, and smiled quizzically. "You look like a stout young fellow who could take care of himself if it came to trouble. So I'll tell you why I wanted you here to listen to what we've heard tonight. You've—hum—studied academic criminology, they tell me." He coughed meaningly, and as Hugh met the glance over the doctor's spectacles he knew that this fat bandit knew his own particular guilty secret. "Would you like to try a little practical work?"

"Would I!" said Hugh fervently.

"Think you could follow Spinelli wherever he went, and keep out of sight?"

"Absolutely."

"I don't like to do this, but you're the only person here who might conceivably do it. And before you agree, I want to impress on you exactly what you're doing." Dr. Fell looked sharply at him, at the bishop, and at the scowling Inspector Murch. "If I'm right, you see, that man Spinelli is going to walk straight into a death trap."

He waited to let that statement sink in, and for his listeners to use their imaginations on it. The bright, hot library had become full of suggestion.

"In other words, my boy, this placid little rustic corner— where nobody has any motive—contains a killer who would just as soon put a bullet into you as into Spinelli. A killer possibly without deep intelligence, but a quick thinker with an incredible amount of nerve. I can't say for certain whether Spinelli will try the same tactics as he tried with Depping, but I believe he will. And if he attempts it at all, it will have to be immediately, because I've forced his hand; he has got to leave England, and he must act at once . . . Do you understand?"

"Enough to try it, doctor."

"Very well." He turned and nodded towards the closed portieres over the doorway at the far end of the library. "I don't want Spinelli to see you when he comes back. Go into the billiard-room there, and keep watch behind those curtains. We'll maneuver him out the same way he came in: through the windows to the terrace. The terrace runs all the way round this side of the house, including the billiard-room, and there's a door opening on it from there. When you see Spinelli leave, slip out the door from the billiard-room to the terrace, and follow. Whatever you do, *for God's sake don't lose him.* That's all. Very well, Inspector; go and see if you can find Mrs. Standish."

Hugh was already feeling the excitement of the thing, as though it had been a game. He had a wholesome love of play-acting, and he could not even yet bring himself to believe that following people was anything else. If he had not seen that dead man . . . but the image flashed across his mind as he put his hand on the portieres at the end of the room. It was effective.

There was a bright moon that night. Its light fell into the dark billiard-room through a row of diamond-paned windows high up on the wall to the right, and there were other windows at the far end. In the right-hand wall there was also a glass-panelled door standing open on the terrace. Like the library, this room was high and narrow. He could dimly see the billiard table in the middle, and the marking-board and racks of cues against the wall.

It was cool here, after the stuffy air of the other room. The portieres had a sound-deadening effect; he could hear his father's voice only faintly as the bishop expounded something to Dr. Fell. Parting the curtains about half an inch, he groped into the shadows after a chair. Cool here, and a faint breeze. The glass door moved slightly; a swish of trees went murmuring round the house; and the thin line of light from between the portieres trembled across the billiard table. This, it occurred to him, would be an excellent house in which to play any sort of game that entailed wandering about in the dark; say that noble pastime called sardines. Which suggestion turned his thoughts inevitably to Patricia Standish and the pleasures of darkness. But he had to attend to business. Discovering a chair, he had just drawn it up to the opening between the curtains when a new voice rose, commanding and majestic, from the library.

"I do not ask to know what this means," it proclaimed; "but I *demand* to know what it means. Certain remarks and hints have been made to me, which, in justice to the memory of dear, dear Septimus—to say nothing of poor, poor Betty—I *will* have explained. Furthermore . . ."

Hugh peered through the opening. Standing before Dr. Fell was the handsome and aggressive figure of Maw Standish. Her chin was up, her ash-blonde head and square face determined; she was a Matterhorn in white lace, staring down over the icy slopes of herself. She stood with her arm round the shoulders of a pretty little brown-haired girl who, Maw's gesture indicated, was Betty Depping. Betty Depping looked tired, and nervous, and, most of all, embarrassed. Instinctively Hugh liked her. In appearance she would not have qualified for the name of Ginch:

despite her neatness, her pale fine face, and dark blue eyes set rather wide apart, she looked sturdy and capable. Her lips were full, but her chin strong. The brown hair was drawn back severely behind her ears, and—had he been closer—Hugh would have expected to find a freckle or two round her nose. As she glanced at Maw Standish, there was in her eyes a sort of weary cynicism. You felt that she would never shed many tears; but that they would be bitter ones.

Her presence complicated matters. Hugh could only see the back of Dr. Fell's head, but he could imagine the doctor rumbling and scowling at bringing in Depping's daughter at this juncture. However, Maw Standish was giving nobody a chance to protest.

" . . . furthermore," she continued, shaking Betty by way of emphasis in spite of the girl's efforts to free herself, "I demand to know the reason why this house has been filled with objectionable people. In the drawing-room at this minute—at this very minute," said Maw Standish, as though that made the fact more sinister, "there is a horrible creature with a fawn-colored hat and a red pin stripe in his suit. Why must this house be filled with objectionable people? Think of the dear, dear bishop's feelings. Think of my own feelings. I am sure the dear, dear bishop must be outraged . . ."

The dear, dear bishop made a coughing noise, and backed his chair away.

"Ma'am," said Dr. Fell urbanely, "one of the most unfortunate features of police work is that it brings us into contact with people whom we should otherwise run a mile to avoid. Pray accept my assurance, ma'am, that nobody appreciates this more than I do."

Maw sniffed, and after considering this she looked at him sharply.

"Is it possible, Dr. Fell; can it *be* possible—and in the presence of the dear, dear bishop at that—that I scent an ulterior meaning in what you say?"

"Ma'am, ma'am," said the doctor, with a touch of reproof. "Heh. Heh-heh-heh. Pray control yourself. I am sure His Reverence must resent your statement that his presence stimulates your olfactory senses. I must ask you to respect his cloth."

Maw stared at him as though she could not believe her ears. She stiffened, turned livid, and emitted a sound like the whistle of a peanut vendor's machine on a cold day.

"Well, of all—!" she gasped, "of all the—of all—Go-rooo! Sir, will you trifle with me?"

"Madam!" rumbled Dr. Fell. He chuckled. Hugh could imagine his wide-open eyes as he looked at her. "Reluctantly, I am afraid I must decline. I trust you are familiar with that classic anecodote which concludes, 'Ma'am, I am a married man myself, and I would rather have a glass of beer?' Just so. *Nunquam nimis quod nunquam satis.* Speaking of beer—"

Maw was in a dangerous condition. She turned to the bishop, as though to appeal for assistance. That worthy gentleman narrowly missed doing something which would forever have condemned him in the maternal presence; he turned mirth into a cough at just the right time. Then he looked very ecclesiastial.

"Of all," said Maw, breathlessly, "of all the insufferable—"

"Yes. So Mr. Langdon said. Now, I'll tell you what it is, Mrs. Standish," said Dr. Fell sharply. "You are here for the purpose of giving evidence; not orders. You were expressly instructed to come here alone, furthermore. Certain things we have discovered today will not make very pleasant hearing for Miss Depping."

Betty Depping looked up. There had been a sort of weary humor in her eyes; but now she spoke dully, in a pleasant voice which always seemed to ask a question of her future mother-in-law.

"Isn't that," she said, "why I have a right to be here?"

Subtly, it brought a new element into the conversation. You could feel in what she was thinking a vitality, an intensity, even a tragedy about which nobody had bothered to think. Maw's attack was broken, but she went on in a lower voice:

"I wish this nonsense dispelled, that is all. If you cannot be sufficiently courteous—! I refer to hints. From Patricia, and especially (in a mealy-mouthed fashion, which I detest) from Morley. As though to prepare me for something." Maw shut her jaws hard, and looked from Dr. Fell to the bishop. "If I *must* speak of it, it concerns rumors of poor dear Mr. Depping's past life."

Again Betty Depping looked at her, curiously.

"Could it make any difference?" she asked in a low voice.

For a time Hugh could hear the slow tapping of Dr. Fell's pencil on the table. "My dear," he said suddenly, "since you are here . . . did you ever have any knowledge of your father's past life?"

"N-no. No knowledge. I—suspected something. I don't know what."

"Did you tell this suspicion to anybody?"

"Yes. I told Morley. I thought it was only fair." She hesitated, and a sort of puzzled, protesting fierceness came into her face. "All I wanted to know is, why should it matter? If father had lived—if he were living now—nobody would have known it or asked questions about it. Now that he's dead, if there's anything against him it's bound to come out . . ."

She looked away, at a corner of one window, and added in a very low voice: "I never had a great deal of happiness, you see. I thought that I was going to have it, now. Why should—somebody—have spoiled it?"

Again the night breeze went wandering through the trees round the house, with a rustling of turmoil far away; and you knew that it was agitating the beeches and maples round the Guest House as well. All the time Dr. Fell's pencil was slowly clicking against the desk; *tap—tap—tap*—as though it were a brain endlessly asking the same question.

"How long have you suspected anything in your father's past, Miss Depping?"

She shook her head. "There never was anything definite. But I think I started to wonder as much as five years ago. You see, he sent for me to join him in London suddenly. I thought he had always been there; I wrote him once a week, in care of Mr. Langdon, and he would reply about once a month, with a London postmark. So I came over from France; naturally I was pleased to get away from school. He told me he was retiring from whatever it was he did in the City, and going into the publishing business with a Mr. Standish and a Mr. Burke.

"Then—we were sitting in the lobby of the hotel one afternoon, and all of a sudden he caught sight of somebody walking towards us, and he was—I don't know—flustered. He said, 'That's Burke; he didn't say he was coming here. Listen: don't be surprised at anything I say to him in the way of business. So far as you know, I've spent a year in India, where—remember this—where my closest friend was a Major Pendleton.' Then he hushed me." She brushed a hand back across her shining brown hair. It was as though she had an insupportable headache, and tried to smile in spite of it. "You . . . well, you wonder about things like that. But I never knew. That's why I say I have a right to know."

Again she hesitated, stared at Dr. Fell, and could not ask the question. It was Maw Standish who fired it out.

"That's precisely it. That's why I demand to know. I still tell you this is impossible! Poor Mr. Depping . . . I have even heard rumors from the *servants' hall*—from the *servants' hall*, I assure you. To the outrageous effect that he was a criminal. A criminal." Maw gulped out the word.

"We had better settle this," declared Dr. Fell, "before we can go on." His voice became gruff. "I am sorry that I must give you the facts brutally, but it will be best this way. The rumor was correct. Depping was not only a criminal; he was a criminal of the meanest and most damnable variety; a racketeer, an extortionist, and a killer. Do not ask for any of the details. They are not pretty."

"Impossi—" said Mrs. Standish, and stopped. She stared at the bishop, who nodded slowly.

"I am sorry, madam," he said.

"God—help—us . . ." She touched her white face, her handsome face where you could see the faint wrinkles now. "This—this alters—this—that is . . ." Her gaze turned towards Betty Depping, who was looking blankly at Dr. Fell.

"Betty darling!" said Maw, with a brisk abrupt smile. "I see that I should not have brought you down here at all. You were upset enough to begin with. These trying events, these monstrous accusations . . . Child! Do as I tell you. Go upstairs this instant, and lie down. Now, now; I won't hear a word! Lie down like a good child, and tell Patricia to put the ice bag on your head. I will stay here and thrash this matter out. There is a mistake somewhere—surely there is a mistake. You will need all your strength presently. Depend on it, I will do my best for you. Run along, now!"

She disengaged her arm from the other's shoulder. Betty Depping was looking at her steadily. Again Betty was sturdy and capable; with the cool cynical eyes and the strong chin. She smiled.

"Yes, it does alter matters, doesn't it?" she asked softly. "I—I don't think I care to hear anything more."

She inclined her head to the group and walked to the door, but she turned there. She had become tense and fierce, with color in her cheeks: a fighter, and dangerous, and her eyes had a hot blue brilliance. Yet her lips hardly seemed to move.

"The only one who matters in this affair," she said, still in a low voice, "is Morley. Understand that. What he thinks, and what he cares"—her breast rose and fell once, with a sort of shudder—"is what I think and care. Remember that, please."

"Child!" said Maw, lifting her chin.

"Good night," said Betty Depping, and closed the door.

The warmth and strength of her personality was still in that room. Even the colonel's lady felt it. She tried to adjust herself to the new state of affairs; to stare down Dr. Fell and the bishop; to preserve a high-chinned dignity and yet keep an appropriate aloofness.

"Will you kindly," she said in a tense voice, "stop tapping that pencil on the table? It has been driving me insane . . . Thank you so much. Now that Miss Depping has gone, will you be so good as to substantiate these lurid statements of yours? They *can* be substantiated, I hope?"

"Unquestionably."

"Dear, dear, dear, dear . . . and—and will there be a scandal?"

"Why should there be a scandal, ma'am?"

"Oh, don't be so dull-witted! This is the most abominable and—and—incredible thing I have ever heard. I can't believe it. Poor, dear Mr. Depping . . . why, the filthy wretch! The—"

Tap-tap-tap-tap, as measured as the ticking of a clock, Dr. Fell's pencil clicked on the table. Hugh Donovan wished he could see his face. The doctor was gathered together into a great mass, his head down.

"Mrs. Standish," he said, "who was the lady whom Depping had persuaded to elope with him?"

CHAPTER XV

A Man Walks in the Dark

THE BISHOP got up abruptly from his chair, went to one window, and pushed it open for more air. Mrs. Standish did not seem to grasp the question. After a sideways glance, she repeated:

"Lady? Elope?—What on earth do you mean? My dear sir, you must be mad!" She edged backwards to a chair, and sat down.

"The ancient and melodious refrain to which," said Dr. Fell musingly, "to which I have got accustomed after all these years. 'Fell, you must be mad.' It is Chief Inspector Hadley's favorite ditty. Well, I don't mind. Believe me, ma'am, the subject is distasteful. I mention it only because I believe it has rather a terrible bearing on the murder."

"I'm sure I don't know what you mean."

"H'm. Perhaps I had better start from the beginning. Do you mind if I smoke?"

She sniffed the air. "It does not seem to have been necessary for you to get permission, doctor. Do not let my presence interfere with you, please . . . What were you saying?"

Dr. Fell sat back with a grunt of satisfaction, and clipped the end of a cigar. "Thank you. Beer and tobacco, ma'am, are the twin warming pans of my declining years. Both have curious histories. To the first I have devoted an entire chapter of my work, *The Drinking Customs of England from the Earliest Days.* Do you know, for example, the first time that what is humorously called a prohibition law was ever in effect in history? Heh-heh. It affords me amusement to think that our friends the Americans believed they had something new. The first prohibition law was enacted in Egypt by the Pharaoh Usermaatre, or Rameses the Great, about the year 4000 B.C. It was an edict designed to prevent his subjects from getting sozzled on a species of barley beer and manufacturing whoopee in the streets of Thebes. Prohibitionists asserted that the next generation would never know the taste of the villainous stuff. Ha, hum, alas. The law failed, and was revoked. Tobacco, now . . ."

He struck a match, argumentatively. "Tobacco, now—h'rrm; puff—puff—aaah! Tobacco, as I was saying, has a history which has been much distorted. Christopher Columbus saw American natives smoking cigars as early as 1492. It is a curious and fantastic picture, almost as though they had been described as wearing top hats and gold watch chains. Jean Nicot . . ."

"*Will* you get on with what you were saying?" she interrupted, clenching her hands.

"Eh? Oh, if you like . . ." He seemed to reflect. "I am given to understand, Mrs. Standish, that Mr. Depping was much addicted to gallantries."

" 'Gallantries' is precisely the word. He was gallant, in an age where men seem to think it most unnecessary."

"I see. And the ladies liked it?"

"Humph. *I* thought him a very charming man. The old hypocrite."

"Undoubtedly a man of singular gifts. But there was no one to whom he paid particular attention, was there?"

"There was not," she answered decisively. The lines tightened round her handsome mouth. "For instance, he took pleasure in reciting selections from the great poets to my daughter Patricia. I approved the practice. Young people are entirely too prone to neglect matters cultural in this lax generation; dear Canon Dibson said so over the wireless only last week, and I must say that I agree with him . . . But Patricia did not like Mr. Depping, and Madeleine Morgan positively detested him. H'm. H'm." She pondered, one eye narrowing. "Now I wonder . . . it couldn't, of course it *couldn't* have been dear Lucy Mellsworthy, from Bath. One of my very dearest friends, Dr. Fell, though of course much older. Nevertheless, I have always said there was a little something—something—something suspicious about that whole family, since her cousin Nell ran away with that dreadful man who was owl-catcher for the zoo. Heredity tells; that's what I always say to my husband. Don't you agree?"

"I hardly think we need consider this Miss Mellsworthy—"

"Mrs. Mellsworthy," she corrected stiffly. "Indeed not. Besides, I do not think they were acquainted. All I said was, heredity tells. And I will tell you frankly, doctor: I do not like gossip. This nonsensical rumor of Mr. Depping running away with somebody: I will not stand for it in my house, and I wish you distinctly to understand that.—Where did you hear it?"

Dr. Fell chuckled. "You don't believe it's true, then?"

"I am bound to admit *I* never saw anything." She shut her lips firmly, peered over her shoulder, and edged forward. "Though, if the man was a criminal, I would not put anything past him.

When I think that a son of mine almost married the daughter of a man who might have cut our throats any night, why, why—!" She shuddered. "I needn't tell you that I shall instruct my husband to take immediate steps about *that*. Such silliness in young people should be shaken out of them, anyhow. Besides . . ."

Trying to make no noise, Hugh slid his chair back. It was here now. Behind Maw Standish the door giving on the passage to the drawing-room had opened. Spinelli, twirling his hat on one finger, a satisfied smirk on his face, preceded Langdon into the room. The solicitor, Hugh noticed, did not look so happy. Spinelli's gaze rested briefly, without recognition, on Mrs. Standish; flickered past, and rested good-humoredly on Dr. Fell.

"Thanks, governor. I'm all set now," he vouchsafed. "So I'll be pushing off. Got a hired car down by the 'Bull'; I'll get back to Hanham, check out, and hop a night train to London. I'll be on a boat tomorrow, if there is one. If not, I'll see if they'll let me into France before I head back to the States. Well . . ."

"Dr. Fell," the colonel's lady said with mounting exasperation, "will you kindly inform me what this objectionable person is doing in my house?"

Spinelli looked over his shoulder. "Kind of feeling your oats, aren't you, mother?" he asked coolly. Then he turned back. "*Tiens, qui est la vielle vache? Je crois que son mari a couché sur la pin de sa chemise.* Which reminds me, doc. Be a sport and don't try to keep me out of France, will you, eh? I'd like to brush up my French. I noticed you sent that fellow Murch and his harness-bull away; saw 'em go. Thanks. That's a square guy. Well, I'll be seeing you. If you'll show me the front door of this joint—"

"Indeed?" said Maw Standish. "You have great presumptions, I think, my man. Doctor, will you ring for somebody? If we can arrange to show this person out by way of the cellar—"

Spinelli hid his face with his hand, and took it away in a gesture of his wrist. On his face there was plastered such a quirk of impudence that Hugh had a strong inclination to assist his progress with a kick.

"O.K., mother. *O.K.!* I'll use the window, then. I don't think much of your country houses anyway. Lousy pictures, imitation antiques, Bowery manners—"

"Get out of here," said Dr. Fell, and surged to his feet.

It was the last Hugh saw. He hurried across the billiardroom to the glass door, kept himself in the shadows, and peered along the terrace. Fortunately, he was wearing a dark suit. The luminous dial of his wristwatch showed that it was half past nine. And he was a trifle surprised to find his heart beating heavily.

No wind now, but a cool moist air that smelt of grass and flowers. The moon was still low, but very bright; long shadows were close at hand, lawns dully gleaming, and a haze in the hollows of trees that sloped down towards the east. Half a mile away he could make out the lights of a bus passing along some unidentifiable road. A dog was barking faintly.

Along the terrace a window creaked open, letting out yellow light. Spinelli stepped out, pushing aside curtains, and closed the window behind him. He hesitated, and seemed to be staring up at the moon. Hugh could dimly see his face; he was smiling. The smile died. He looked sharply left and right; saw nothing, and seemed reassured. Leisurely he struck a match and lit a cigarette. Then he descended some shallow steps to the lawn, looked round again, and finally sauntered along below the terrace towards the direction in which Hugh was hiding. As he passed the door to the billiard-room, he was trying to read his watch by the moonlight, and humming, "The Gay Caballero." His footsteps crunched on the gravel path.

Hugh was after him as he turned the corner of the house. Keeping to the grass border against the house, the pursuer was entirely in shadow, and could move soundlessly; though once he nearly tripped over a playful lawn mower. The crunching steps moved ahead, steadily and jauntily. As the driveway curved down through the avenue of elms towards the lodge gate, Hugh had to negotiate a broad patch of moonlight to cross the drive and duck into the shelter of the trees on the right hand side. He jumped the stretch of gravel and dodged behind a laurel bush. What he believed to be the absurdity of this performance began to grow on him. He liked it well enough, this crawling about wet lawns on the knees of your trousers, and peering round bushes as though you were playing I Spy. But you would look damned silly if anybody happened to see you . . .

His blood was heating already. He slid into the shadow of the elm avenue and walked upright in comparative safety, though Spinelli was only twenty yards ahead. Spinelli's feet were making such a rattling noise on the gravel that any minor noises Hugh might make, a breaking twig or a crackly leaf, would go unnoticed. His quarry was muttering to himself; scuffling the gravel, and frequently giving it a kick. Once he cursed to himself, and stopped to assume some sort of defiant attitude, swinging back his cigarette as though he faced an adversary. Then he muttered again as he continued down the drive. At length he said aloud, "Ah, to hell with it!" and fell to whistling, loudly. But often again he would throw out his narrow shoulders for a heroic posture.

Hugh was forced into more sprinting and dodging when they reached the open lodge gates. Without hesitation Spinelli struck off down the hill in the direction of the village. There were no cars or pedestrians; the asphalt road ran bare under the moon and the high hedgerows; and Spinelli, a strutting little figure in an absurd hat, had not once looked around. As they came to Morgan's house, Hugh was in a sweat lest somebody should be hanging over the gate, and hail him as he crouched past in the shadow of the hedge. But he passed it in safety, passed the ghostly church, and came down to the cluster of dull lights that marked the village.

Here there was real danger of being seen, even though there were no street lamps. The only tolerable illumination (all of which came from oil lamps anyway) was in the public house. This building was set back from the road in a muddy yard, smelling of straw and dung: a low, heavy stone structure that had once been whitewashed, with a thatched roof and two wings running out to form a court in front. Its lattices were all open, and shadows passed the smoky oil flames inside.

Hugh slipped off the road about thirty yards away. From the pub issued a noise of jollification; people were stamping time to a piano and an asthmatic accordion, and roaring with applause as somebody sang a comic song. Hugh remembered that it was Saturday night. This was a fool game anyhow, stumbling about in the mud; his nerves crawled for a smoke, and he thought passionately of cool beer. In complete darkness he moved round towards the side of the 'Bull,' and bumped into an automobile parked there with its lights out. The pain of the collision brought his wits alive again. Probably Spinelli's car. God knows what the man meant to do; go back to the Guest House, Dr. Fell thought; but it might not be a bad idea to take out the spark plugs, just in case he tried to use it.

Meantime, Spinelli was standing in front of the "Bull," his

186 · JOHN DICKSON CARR

shoulders hunched, smoking reflectively. He seemed to come to a decision. The red end of his cigarette sailed away, and he sauntered up towards the steps that led into the court. Hugh had edged round to the front of the two-seater, lifted the clamps that held down the bonnet, and was raising it softly, to avoid creaks, when he heard footsteps squashing towards him. An unpleasant (and unreasonable) qualm took his stomach as he looked up. Spinelli had altered his direction, and was making straight for the car.

The bonnet seemed to scrape with hideous loudness as he lowered it. He ducked back towards a maple tree and waited, conscious that his heart was beating heavily again. It was impossible that he could have been seen. Then he heard Spinelli fumbling with the car in the dark not a dozen feet away; a door opened, there was a click, and the lights went on, off, and on again, until only the dashboard lamps were glowing. Clear in that little spot of light, Spinelli raised his head to peer about. Hugh could see his face clearly . . .

For the first time that night, dread took hold of him. The man's lower lip was shaking, and there was sweat on his forehead. A bead of it dropped down past his cheek and sideburn as he twisted his head. Spinelli tried to mutter a little laugh, and failed. His hand slid into the side pocket of the front seat; fumbled, and pulled out a belt and shoulder holster that showed the butt of a heavy automatic pistol.

Hugh whispered, almost aloud: "By God, it's *not* a game . . ." And his heart bumped for fear he had been heard. Crouching down over the dashboard, Spinelli drew out the automatic and examined it. He slid the cartridge clip into his palm, turned it over, replaced it. Finally, with a timorous finger, he released the safety catch and stuffed the weapon back into its holster. Peering round again, he removed his coat and began to buckle the holster under his left armpit. He was wearing a blue-and-white striped shirt, which clung to him damply. Even at that distance Hugh could hear him breathing.

A dim wind rustled in the trees. From the "Bull" issued a roar of merriment, and an applauding rattle of glasses on wooden tables. The accordion let out a few preliminary bleats, as though it were clearing its throat, and then began to punch out the accompaniment to somebody's song. The uproar died down; a mincing tenor voice floated out on the silence:

> "I'm Burlington Bertie,
> I rise at ten-thirty
> And saunter about like a toff . . ."

Somebody laughed. The accordion hit each syllable with rising and falling emphasis. A voice called, "*Eigh!* Two more bitters, *eigh!*" Spinelli, breathing hard, buttoned up his coat again. Whatever sort of rendezvous he would meet, he intended to keep it, then. Wiping off his forehead with a silk handkerchief, he adjusted his hat, switched off the lights of the car, and moved away.

He was going into the "Bull." Circling the car after him, Hugh was not certain what to do. There was undoubtedly a back entrance to the place, and, if he had any reason to throw off an even imaginary pursuit, the pursuer might be lost. On the other hand, Hugh did not wish to risk coming face to face with him.

But there seemed to be a large crowd inside, and he wanted a drink. He waited only long enough to complete his original design of removing the spark plugs. Then, as the door closed behind Spinelli, he strolled up the court after him.

CHAPTER XVI

The Puzzle of the Shoes

THUS GUILTILY excusing himself from the fact that, even in the midst of adventure, he could not resist the temptation to stop and have a glass of beer, Hugh walked up the court and through a low door. The place smelt heavily of beer, earth, and old wood; and the walls, he judged, must be four-feet thick. Nobody could tell when or why this house had been built, except that two cloister-like structures along the court, full of disused hay carts and straw, suggested a stable. Inside there was an even larger crowd than he had expected, comfortably tipsy, wandering and bumping in the narrow passages. Through the windows he could see a public-room in each wing, and there was a bar at the rear. Spinelli had turned into the room on the right.

Lowering his head in the passage, Hugh penetrated back to the bar. A couple of oil lamps smoked against perspiring walls. Most of the crowd had gathered in the room across the way, where somebody was strumming the piano, and two loud voices were arguing about a song. The room Hugh entered was low and raftered, with high-backed settles and long tables; polished brass jugs along the tops of the settles; walls patched up in grimy linoleum of different patterns; a wooden mantelpiece bearing an ancient clock without hands; and, squeezed into one dark corner, a fly-blown picture of Prince Albert in Highland costume. Prince Albert looked disapproving. Just beneath him, two or three grimy sages in cloth caps huddled about a table, flourishing pewter mugs as they argued, their long necks rising and wriggling above brass collar studs. One said: "Don't 'ee be a bloody fool, now!" and turned sulkily and banged his mug down on the table. "Tell 'ee 'tes *nowt* 'ow the *Princess Mary* was blowed up, and if the' can't take the ward of a gunner in 'Is Majesty's Sarvice, look, then Gawd bless me, look! I'll—" Bang! went the tankard again, and he glared at his opponent. A stout harassed barmaid hopped past with a tray of glasses; she seemed to be moving her head to avoid the layers of tobacco smoke, and giving an absent-minded smile to everybody. She said, "Tcha, tcha!" to the contestants, who then appealed to the proprietor. This latter was a pacifying dignitary in shirt sleeves, with a wary eye out: he stood behind the bar in a wilderness of beer cases, his arms folded; but he would jerk to life the moment a hand was raised for more beer. He sprang forward as Donovan approached the bar.

Hugh changed his mind, said, "Whisky and soda," and fixed his eyes on a polished brass plate on a shelf beside him. Despite the smoke and blur, he could see the door to the passage and the other room reflected there. Spinelli was directly in line with it. The other room seemed to be a sort of parlor; and Spinelli slouched in a large tasselled chair, defiantly. Even Hugh could hear the whispers in the noise there—"that gen'lman," "dreffle murder," "Sh-shh!" drowned out by the bang of the piano. Subtly, the news was going all around. Even the three sages finished their beer all together, as at a drill order, and peered round . . .

190 · JOHN DICKSON CARR

Squirting soda into his glass and watching the brass plate from the corner of his eye, Hugh turned quickly towards plate and wall. Spinelli had got up. He strode out of the room, into the passage, and through to the bar; he looked angry. People drifted out to follow him, obtrusively interested in their drinks. An insistent voice kept calling, "Sing 'Old John Wesley!'"

Spinelli strode up to the bar.

"Is it possible," he said in a voice of freezing dignity which somehow reminded Hugh of Maw Standish, "is it possible, my man, or isn't it, to get any service in this place?"

A part of the clamor had died down to a buzz; there were many people straining their ears. Spinelli's elaborate unconsciousness of everything, his airs and dignity, made a rather ludicrous spectacle. The proprietor sprang forward.

"*I'm* sorryzir! I'm sorry! Thought they do be and attended to 'ee, zir! *Yes*zir?"

"I'll have brandy," said the other, aloofly fingering his tie. "If you have any. Your best. Bring the bottle, and give me a glass of beer with it. Would you like a drink?"

"Ah! Thank 'ee zir. Eh don't mind."

If Spinelli got a good view of him, Hugh was thinking . . . He turned still farther away. But the American was not noticing. Pouring out a large dose of brandy, he swallowed it neat and followed it with a draught of beer. Then he poured another. The landlord, with a great carelessness of manner, was opening a bottle of home-brewed.

"Nice weather we'm 'aving, Mr. Travers," he observed critically.

"Uh."

"Ah! Bit waarm, though," the landlord qualified with a judicial air. The bottle cap went *Sss–t!* and the landlord frowned still more judicially as he poured out his beer. "Still, zir, the' get him much waarmer in the States, I expect?"

"Plenty. Fill up that glass again."

"Ah! Fine country, the States! Did Eh tell 'ee, zir, Eh've a wife's cousin's step-brother that lives in Kansas City?—Ah, ay!" He nodded approvingly. "Lived there farty year' now, 'e 'as. Gearge Loopey 'is name is. Maybe you've 'eard of him, zir; Gearge E. Loopey? 'E do run a big lumber yaard, I've 'eard. No! Ah, well; 'tes a big place . . . Your good 'ealth, zir!"

Never before had Hugh appreciated so thoroughly the restraint of the English people. Everybody in that house was exploding with curiosity as to what had been happening at The Grange; it must have been the chief topic of conversation all evening; and here was the chief actor—supposed to have been already under arrest—in their midst. Yet conversation, even though strained, went on as usual. Not a glance was obviously turned towards Spinelli. The landlord pattered on.

"The 'll be staying with us some time, now, I hope, Mr. Travers?"

"No," said Spinelli. "I'm leaving tonight."

"Ah?"

"Tonight. And damned glad to get away. Listen . . ."

He finished his third brandy with a swaggering gesture, and leaned against the bar. Whether it was the brandy, or some deliberate purpose, or merely a love of being in the limelight—for, as he spoke, a rustling quiet settled down, and his voice rang loud against it—Hugh never knew. But Spinelli was aware that he was talking to the house. And three double-brandies, on top of his nervous strain, did things to his tongue. He cleared his throat. His spiteful little eyes rolled round at the assembly with some satisfaction, but he turned back to the landlord.

"Come on, admit it! Don't stand there lapping up that beer and trying to be polite. I know what you're thinking about. The murder. Yeah. And wondering, in your charitable way, why they haven't got me in the can for it right now. Eh?"

The landlord tried to play his part by also seeming unconscious of all the others. He assumed a look of diffidence.

"Well, zir, now that you do mention it—! Of carse, us've 'eard all about it, and what a 'orrible business he was," he polished the bar vigorously, "and, ah, ah, we do feel sorry for the poor gen'lman . . ."

"Push that bottle over here. Horrible business, nuts! They tried to hook me in on it. And couldn't. Tell *that* to your friends. Because I didn't happen to have anything to do with it, and I proved it."

The landlord beamed. "Why, Eh'm sure Eh do congratulate you, Mr. Travers! Us thought nothing against 'ee, mind, zir! Only 'twas said 'ereabouts—you know what gossip is!—" he lowered his voice, "only that you'd paid poor Mr. Depping a visit, and a lot of dimp people—"

"You're telling me? Listen." He drained his glass, set it down with a thump, and poked the proprietor in the chest. "I was never inside his house. The man they thought was me was old Nick Depping himself, got up into a fancy disguise so nobody would recognize him. Tell *that* to your friends, and your dumb flatfeet too."

"Zir?"

"It was Depping, I tell you! Trying to tell me I'm a liar?"

The landlord was so obviously puzzled that even Spinelli did not press it. He grew confidential, almost paternal.

"Listen. I'll tell you how it was. Old Nick Depping wanted to get out of his house; see? Never mind why. I'm not telling that. But he wanted to get out of his house; see? All right. He goes up to London and buys a make-up box at a theatrical outfitter's, and he goes to a ready-made clothes store and buys a suit there. All right; you can do all that without anybody being suspicious of you. But Nick was an artist, see?—a real artist; I'll give him credit for that. And, if he left any footprints anywhere, he didn't want the footprints traced to him. He even wanted to have the shoes a different size from his own. All right! But you can't go into a shoe store and ask for a pair of shoes three or four sizes too large. That's nutty; and they're going to remember it in the store, and, if there's any trouble afterwards, maybe the dicks can trace you; see?"

Spinelli leaned across the bar and thrust a flushed countenance within an inch of the landlord's. He went on rather hoarsely:

"So what does Nick do? He goes up to that big place they call The Grange; the one with the lousy furniture in it, and pictures I wouldn't put in my coal cellar. Well, he goes up one afternoon with a satchel that's supposed to have books in it; get me? He goes back to a room where they store a lot of junk, and swipes an old pair of somebody's shoes to wear; and then if he does happen to make any footprints anywhere, why, it's going to be just too bad for the bird who owns the shoes. See? That's what Nick does, and all because he wants too get out of his house and . . ."

Hugh did not hear the last part of the sentence. He was so startled that he almost faced round and spoke to Spinelli. He remained motionless, his empty glass to his lips, staring at a placard behind the bar whereon a high-stepping figure of Johnny Walker grinned back with a rather sardonic leer. Down came one of the props of the case, shattering every hypothesis built on it; a clue blown up, shot to pieces; ashes and smoke: *viz.*, the mysterious shoes that belonged to Morley Standish. All sorts of explanations had been, and might be, propounded. The simplest explanation of all—that Depping himself had used them for his masquerade—had been overlooked or at least not mentioned. What became now of his father's fantastic picture of Henry Morgan playing poltergeist in order to steal the shoes?

He risked a short sideways glance at Spinelli. The latter was too preoccupied; too malicious, too full of new alcoholic courage, to greedy of the limelight, even to turn his head or lower his voice. Spinelli laughed. His foot groped vainly for a rail under the bar.

"And that's how it was," he said, tapping the counter, "that he got mistaken for me, see? Because he wanted to get out of his house, and nobody to know it. That's old Nick Depping for you! And when he got back to his house he couldn't get in. Because why? Because he'd lost the key out of his pocket while he was on his little expedition, that's why. Ha. ha ha ha. Don't tell *me*. I know."

All this was so much gibberish to the landlord. He stole a look at the brandy-bottle, thoughtfully, and coughed.

"Ah, ay. Well, zir, after all," he suggested in a persuasive manner, "after all, Mr. Depping was a strange sort of gentleman, look. Ah, ay. (Shall Eh sarve the' some Gearges' home-brewed, zir? Mind, he's good!) And if poor Mr. Depping do wish to dress 'imself up 'ow 'e likes, why, we've no right to complain, have us?"

Spinelli whirled. "You don't believe me, eh? Listen. I'm telling you this, I'm telling the world, just what kind of a heel Nick Depping was. I'm going to tell you about him, and I want everybody to know it, by God! Because—"

"Mr. Travers, zir! Ladies present!"

"And, anyway, somebody was smarter than he was. Somebody'd got in there with a duplicate key while he was out, and then pretended they had no key. But that's not what I want to tell the world. What I'm going to tell all you people who thought Nick Depping was a nice, high-hat, Park-Avenue swell; well, I'm going to tell you . . ."

Exactly how far he would have gone Hugh could not guess. He realized that Spinelli's idea was to take the only revenge on Depping now possible. But the proprietor interrupted it. He glanced at his watch, gave a start of realization, and with a voice of surprising power bellowed through the house: "Last or-ders! Last or'rders, ladies and gentlemen, *if* you please! Ten minutes apast closing! Come, come *if* you please—!" His voice held that note of extraordinary agony which seems to galvanize publicans like a cramp, and comes as suddenly as a cramp at ten o'clock. In an instant he had become all bustle. He exhorted his listeners, in almost lachrymose entreaty, not to make him lose his license. In the ensuing rush on the bar for final drinks, Hugh was able to crowd himself out into the passage unseen, and wait there to see which direction Spinelli would take.

From the darkness he could see his quarry's face. Indubitably there had been a let-down in the man's elation. There was an oil lamp just over his head; and he looked hunted. The old fears were coming back. This man wanted desperately to cling to lights and company; now they were all fading, and he would have to walk down a dark road to his interview. There could be no doubt that he was meeting the murderer; meeting him tonight, and at the Guest House. Hugh Donovan had at that moment a cold premonition, a conviction so growing and certain that he could have spoken it aloud.

This man is going to his death.

He had, furthermore, an almost maniacal impulse to elbow his way to Spinelli, grab him by the shoulder, and shout, "Look here, you damned fool, don't do it! Stay away from there. Stay away from there, or you'll get what Depping got as sure as he got it." He could have sworn to his conviction. In this babbling crowd, death was as palpable as the tobacco smoke round Spinelli's frightened face.

Spinelli was buying the bottle of brandy, stuffing it hurriedly into the pocket of his coat. And he was buying two packs of cigarettes, which probably meant that there was still some time to pass before his interview. Nobody paid any attention to him; each was elaborately unconscious of his presence. As the first to leave began drifting out the door, he took a sudden resolution and followed them.

Groups were breaking up in the moonlit road before the house. An argument waxed, passed, and faded away under ringing footfalls down the road. Somebody, in an unmusical baritone, was singing, "Me Old Corduroys"; and the countryside was so quiet that the loud voice almost seemed to have an echo from the sky. A woman, giggling-tipsy, went skipping towards the bus stop on somebody's arm. Already the lights were going out in the house.

Presently it was dark and silent again; an incredible silence, in which Hugh hardly dared to breathe. He was against the side of the tavern, wondering vaguely whether they let loose a dog at night. Somebody raised a window over his head, and afterwards he could even hear a creak as somebody tumbled into bed.

Spinelli was sitting in the front seat of his parked car, no lights on. He had not attempted to start it. He shifted constantly; at intervals he would strike a match for a cigarette, and peer at his watch; and he seemed to be steadily drinking. Afterwards Hugh could never tell how long a time it was, but he had a cramp in every muscle. The moon had begun to decline: a watery moon, with heat clouds banking up around it. . . .

There was a faint thunder, as stealthy as somebody's footstep. Hugh could hear cattle stirring in the stable yard. Stiff and half drowsy, he jerked alert as he heard the door of the car opening softly. His quarry slid down, and the bottle bumped against the door. Then he was off up the road; he seemed cold sober.

Until he was out of hearing of the tavern, Spinelli moved with great care, and Hugh had to exercise a greater. But halfway up the hill Spinelli stepped out into the center of the road. At the low stone wall bordering the churchyard he unexpectedly stopped, and leaned on the wall. He giggled to himself. He looked up at the square church tower, where the moon made shadows with the ivy, the queer little porch, and the toppling headstones in the yard. Then he made a magniloquent gesture.

"'Each in his narrow cell forever laid,'" Spinelli said aloud, "'the rude forefathers of the hamlet sleep.' *Nuts!*"

Something described a circle in the air, and there was a smash of a bottle breaking against stone.

Spinelli moved on.

That defiance, which had genuinely shocked Hugh, seemed to give Spinelli a fresh courage. For the pursuer's part, his impulse was now to overtake Spinelli, tap him on the shoulder, measure him for one on the jaw, and lay him out senseless along the side of the road. A neat, clean proceeding which anybody must approve of, and which would avoid endless trouble; certainly ease the strain of this night. He had no particular fear of the man's gun. He doubted that Spinelli, even in an extremity, would have the nerve to use it. In a rather vague way, as he considered his idea, he puzzled over the intricacies of the man's character as he had seen them revealed that night; Spinelli was a case for either a well-administered beating or a mental specialist, according to your view of the matter. He—

Hugh drew up short. Almost opposite Morgan's dark house, Spinelli had stopped. He moved to the left-hand side of the road, towards the boundary wall of The Grange park, groped, struck a match, and touched the wall. Towards the Guest House, no doubt of it. Hugh was pressing back against the hedge on the opposite side. He crept forward softly. . . .

Somebody grasped his arm from behind.

It was the most horrible shock he had ever had. Hugh stiffened, momentarily unable to think; motionless, without turning round. All he could think of was a murderer. He gathered himself to pivot suddenly and hit out. Then a voice spoke close to his ear, in such a whisper that he thought he must have imagined it; it was lower than the rustle in the hedges.

"It's all right," the voice said; "I've been watching. May I come along? You might need help."

The almost inaudible whispering ceased. Turning softly, Hugh saw that his back was directly against the gate in the hedge round Morgan's house. A fugitive spark of moonlight struck Morgan's glasses. He was leaning over the gate, invisible except for that. Hugh bent his shoulders to indicate an assent, and risked a whisper for silence. He wanted company. To his strained nerves he thought the gate creaked perceptibly as Morgan vaulted it, and landed on tennis shoes in the wet grass outside.

No; it was another gate creaking, a little way up the wall. Spinelli had found the entrance to the Guest House in the boundary wall. They could hear his foot scraping in coarse grass;

he was striking a match now, and propping the gate open. A good job. With Morgan following, Hugh went down on his hands and knees to dark across the moon-splashed road; he dodged into the shelter of the wall, breathing hard. The touch of rough stone was reassuring. Then they worked their way up and through the gate . . .

A momentary uneasiness gripped him. He could not see or hear Spinelli now. Damp trees overhung the path, and seethed faintly; the clouded moon could not penetrate, and only distorted the darkness. There were queer strands of cobweb floating across the path; they caught in your mouth as you moved. Hugh felt Morgan poke him in the back, and he crept on up in this wild game of hide-and-seek, up an endless path under the trees. . . . The end of it came abruptly, at a turn. There was the clearing, with the fantastically ugly house in the middle. Its barred windows were gleaming dully. And they saw Spinelli again.

He had come out into the clearing, slowly, and this time he had the pistol in his hand. He was bracing himself against a sundial, moving the gun about in a slow circle as though he were searching the whole open space. Nothing stirred . . .

Then he moved out of their line of vision, over towards the brick path that lead away in the direction of The Grange. They could hear the low *swish-swish* of his feet in wet grass; hesitant, exploring.

Silence. Then it was as though the air were full of vibrations; as though they could feel the jerk and gasp he gave. His voice rose, not loudly, but muffled and yet of piercing intensity:

"Come out of there! Come on, step out! No tricks—no tricks, now, by God—yes, I've got you covered—come on—"

The murderer . . . ?

CHAPTER XVII

No Longer Bullet-Proof

HUGH'S UPPERMOST thought was that he had got to see this, even if he blundered and wrecked all the plans. It occurred to him—where was Inspector Murch? Murch was supposed to be here, in hiding. If by any ironical chance Spinelli had stumbled on Murch in mistake for the man he hoped to meet, there was an end to everything. . . .

He swallowed hard; tried to control his inexplicable trembling; and slid forward boldly into the mouth of the clearing. Mud squished under his foot, but he paid no attention to it.

Its scrolls and deformities darkened, but its barred windows gleaming almost hypnotically, the Guest House seemed to be watching too. Hugh had a sharp feeling that this was not fancy at all; that it literally was watching, or that somebody was watching in a dead man's place. The cool air struck his face again. He peered to the right, and drew back.

About thirty feet away, back turned towards him, Spinelli was standing and facing a thick oak tree beside the brick path. His pistol was held close in against his side, to avert its being knocked away.

"Come out," he was muttering, with a rising inflection that sounded like hysteria. "I can see your hand—give you just a second more—don't stand there; I'm not going to hurt you; but you're going to pay me, and keep on paying me, get me?"

Some faint words were whispered, too indistinct to be heard at that distance. Hugh dropped on his hands and knees and wriggled closer. Spinelli was backing away, towards a dappling of moonlight.

"Know you?" said Spinelli. For the first time Hugh saw him sway a little; the man was almost blind drunk, and holding himself together on sheer nervous excitement. He lost all caution, and his voice screeched out aloud. "Know you? What the hell are you trying to do? You try any tricks on me, and see what you get. . . ." He gulped; he seemed hardly able to breathe. "I got your gun first last night, or you'd 've got me the way you got Nick. . . ."

Closer yet in the long grass . . . Hugh raised his head. He was touching the brick path, but he had had to circle backwards, sot hat Spinelli was now turned partly sideways to him, and whoever stood behind that oak tree was completely hidden. A dappling of moonlight touched Spinelli's face; he could see the loose mouth, and he even noticed that there was a little colored feather stuck in the man's hatband. Now a voice spoke, very low, from behind the oak. It whispered:

"Thank you, my friend. I thought so. But I'm not the person you think I am. Put up your gun, put up your gun—! Sh-sh!"

Spinelli's hand shook. He lurched a trifle, and tried to rub clear sight into his eyes. Twigs cracked as somebody stepped out.

"You dirty *rat*—" said Spinelli suddenly. He choked; it was as though he were going to weep as he saw the other person.

The word "rat" had an incredulous, shrill, despairing echo. He took a step forward . . .

It was pure chance that Hugh looked round then. He wanted to see whether Morgan was behind him. As he craned his neck round, his eyes fell on the house some distance behind Spinelli, and he stared. Something was different about it. Even his vision seemed blurred with doubt, until he realized that the difference was in the line of shimmering windows. There was a half-blank where one of the windows should have been, growing slowly, because one of the windows—that nearest the front door—was being slowly pushed up.

Spinelli did not see it. But the other man, the man behind the oak tree, let out a sound that resembled a gurgling, "*Chua!*" followed by a horrible rattling of breath. He jumped forward, seizing Spinelli by the shoulders as though he would hide himself.

From that window there was a tiny yellow spurt, less than a needle flash, but an explosion that shook the moonlight; so shattering in that hush that it was like a blow over the head. Hugh tried to lurch to his feet. He heard Morgan say, "Chri . . . !" behind him; but he was conscious only of Spinelli. The man's hat, with its little colored feather, had fallen off. His leg gave; he suddenly began to reel round like one who had been thrown off the end of the line in a game of crack-the-whip; then his other leg buckled; and Hugh saw that the man was being sick at the very moment he pitched forward with a bullet through the brain.

The other man screamed. It blended horribly with a squawking and stirring of birds roused out of the ivy by the crash. His body seemed paralyzed, though with one hand he wildly gestured towards the window as though he would push Death away. He fell on his knees and rolled, kicking; he tried to dive for the underbrush . . .

Crack! There had been another cool pause, as though the person in the window were taking deliberate aim. The man behind the oak was staggering to his feet just as the bullet took him; he flapped against the bole of the tree, screamed again . . .

Crack! The cool, inhuman precision of the sniper in the window was adjusted with hideous nicety; he fired at intervals of just five seconds, drawing his sights to a fraction of an inch . . .

Crack!—

Somebody was thrashing through the underbrush, still screaming. Hugh couldn't stand it. He got to his feet just as Morgan seized his ankle and brought him down toppling. Morgan yelled: "Don'tbeabloodyfool; he'llpickusoffas-we-get-up—! Ah!"

He grunted as Hugh jerked loose. Nobody would have believed that mere birds could have made such a racket; the clearing was alive with their noise, and they wheeled in clouds on the moonlight. Round the side of the house ran a clumsy figure, making indistinguishable noises. It was a wild-eyed Inspector Murch. He ran up the side steps of the porch, waving a flashlight whose beam darted crazily over the house, and he had something else in the other; and even then he was shouting out some nonsensical words about the name of the Law.

Nobody has a clear recollection of exactly what happened. Morgan gasped something like, "Oh, all right!" and then he and Hugh were running up the lawn, zigzag fashion, towards the house. Murch's light glared momentarily in the sniper's window, and something jerked back like a toad. The sniper fired high, off balance, shattering the glass in his own window. They saw it spurt and glitter out against a white mist of smoke and the pot-bellied bars that guarded the window. Then there were more flashes in the smoke, because Murch forgot police rules, and he was firing in reply. When the three of them came together on the porch, he was dangerously ready to drill anybody he saw; but Morgan cursed him in time, and prevented a shot as the inspector whirled round. The sniper was gone. All Murch did was stand and shake the bars of the window, until somebody said, "Door!" and they all charged for it.

It was unlocked. But even as Murch kicked it open, a faint bang from another door at the rear of the house announced which way the sniper had gone. . . .

Five minutes later they were still aimlessly beating the brush, and finding nobody. The only result was that Murch had stumbled on something and broken his flashlight. Not, they silently agreed as they looked at each other, a very dignified spectacle of a man hunt. Even the querulous birds were angrily dozing off again. The sharp mist of smoke had begun to dissolve before a shattered window; a breeze had come back—rather complacently, you felt—to the long grasses; and the clearing was quiet. But, from the porch where they had reassembled, they could see Spinelli's body lying spread-eagled on the brick path near the oak. That was all.

Morgan leaned against the porch. He tried to light a cigarette, shakily.

"Well?" he said.

"'E can't get away, I tell the'!" insisted Inspector Murch, who was nearly unintelligible from wrath and uncertainty. He shook his fist. "We know! He's going to The Grange, every time! We know it—we—aaah!" He panted for a moment. "You two see if the' can do anything for them that was shot, down there. I'll go to the big 'ouse. That's where our man is, and we know it."

"Do you think you hit him?" Hugh asked, as calmly as

he could. "When you fired through the window, I mean? If you did—"

"Ah! I was off me head for a moment, d'ye see." Murch looked blankly at the weapon in his hand. "I don't know. 'Twas so sudden; I don't know. Stand guard, now. There's an other one that was shot at—where's he? *Who* was 'e?"

"Damned if I know," said Morgan. He added bitterly: "We're a fine parcel of men of action. This is one to remember for the book. All right, inspector; cut along. We'll look for your missing body. Though, personally, I'd rather take castor oil."

He hunched his shoulders and shivered as he went down the lawn. Hugh could still hear the stupefying crash of the shooting; and the emotional let-down was fully as stupefying. He accepted one of his companion's cigarettes, but his hand was not steady.

"Is this *real*?" Morgan demanded in an odd voice. "Hell-raising—gunplay—all over in a second; feel like a wet rag . . . No, no. Something's wrong. I don't believe it."

"It's real enough," said Hugh. He forced himself to go close to Spinelli's body. All around there was a smell of sickness and the warm odor of blood. As Morgan struck a match, the glimmer shone on bloodstains in the brush round the oak tree, where the second man had tried to crawl for safety. Hugh added: "I don't suppose there's any doubt . . . ?"

Spinelli lay on his face. Morgan, who was looking white, bent over and held the match near his head. It burned his fingers, and he jumped up again.

"Dead. No doubt. They—they got him through the back of the head, just over the hair line. Euh . . . I imagine," he said blankly, "that's rather like what a battle must be, that business. I can't tell just yet what did happen." He shivered. "I don't mind admitting that if anybody leaned out and said 'Boo!' to me at this minute, I'd jump out of my skin. But, look here . . . H'm. One thing about it, that little marksman in the window was out to get Spinelli and the other chap; deliberately knock over those two, and nobody else. He didn't take a shot at either one of us, though he must have seen us easily."

"He shot at Murch."

"'M, yes. But a wild shot, over his head, to keep him back. Not the way he picked off Spinelli. Like a sitting bird. Ugh! And the other fellow. Or maybe he lost his nerve. *I* don't know. God, I don't know anything . . ."

He began to pace back and forth. "Come on. We've got to look for the other man, if it kills us. Who was he? Do you know?"

"I didn't see him either; at least, to recognize him. Here, I've got a cigarette lighter. That will be better than matches. If," said Hugh, feeling a little sick, "we follow that trail of bloodstains . . ."

But neither of them was anxious to start. Morgan made a gesture which said, "Let's finish our cigarettes." He said aloud:

"I was just thinking who it might be." The thought, to Hugh, was as terrifying as anything that had gone before. They would need to penetrate only a little way among the trees, because the sniper had been too deadly a shot for his second victim to have got very far. But his mind was full of formless conjectures that were all horrible. Morgan seemed to meet his thought. He went on swiftly:

"Uh. A dead shot, and cool. My God, what's going on in this nice placid corner of the universe? Who's the maniac can sit at a window and break people's heads like clay pigeons? I told you how impossible it was. And yet it *happened*. 'Keep your stories probable.' I'd like to know what the hell a probable story is," he said rather wildly, "if this is one . . . Keep on talking; it'll whistle our spirits up. That reminds me, I'm carrying a flask. Like a drink?"

"Would I!" Hugh said fervently.

"Two amateur criminologists," jerked out Morgan, handing over the flask, "afraid of the bogey man. The reason is, you and I are afraid there's somebody we know only too well lying in there with a couple of bullets through him."

Hugh drank whisky greedily, shuddered at the bite in his throat; but he felt better. "Let's go," he said.

The pocket lighter made a surprisingly broad flame. Holding it low, Hugh stepped across the brick path towards the oak tree. The path here was bordered with foxglove, white and reddish-purple above the fern; but it had been torn and kicked about, and much of the red was blood. It was not difficult to follow the trail. Somebody had ripped himself loose from the thorns of a blackberry bush, and penetrated in where the trees were thickest. It was chill and marshy now, and there were gnats. More blood in a clump of bracken, which bore an impress as though somebody had dragged himself forward on his face, weakening . . .

Something rustled. The flame moved right and left, writhed in a draught, and almost went out. Their feet crackled on dead plants. Branches scratched past Hugh's shoulder; their snap and swish knocked his arm, and he had to spin the wheel of the lighter again.

"I could have sworn," said Morgan. "I heard somebody groan."

Hugh almost stepped on it. It was a highly polished black shoe, scuffing in dead leaves at the bole of a maple tree. As they looked it jerked once, showed part of a striped trouser leg, and became only a shoe again. There were whitish rents in the bark of the tree where the owner of the shoe had scratched it as he fell. He was lying on his side in a clump of foxglove, shot through the neck and shoulder. They heard him die as Hugh's light flickered on him.

Morgan said: "Steady. We can't go back now. Besides—"

Kneeling, Hugh wrenched the portly figure over on its back. Its face was dirty, the mouth and eyes open; and blood had not made it more attractive. There was a long silence as they stared at it.

"Who the devil is *that?*" Morgan whispered. "I never saw . . ."

"Hold the lighter," said the other, gagging in sudden nausea, "and let's get out of here. I know him. He's a lawyer. His name is Langdon."

CHAPTER XVIII

Dr. Fell Meets the Murderer

THEY GOT back into the clearing somehow. Even then, Hugh remembered accidentally kicking Spinelli's hat as they crossed the brick path. By common consent they made for the Guest House. It was full of ugly suggestions and memories, but it was better than that area where the sniper had left his messy trophies.

Morgan peered at the house, and stopped. "I know what's wrong," he said. "Funny. It never occurred to me before. Do you know what we've done? The lights, man!" He pointed. "We've chased somebody we couldn't find all over the house and the grounds, and we never once thought to turn on the lights inside. . . . Add psychological quirks, if you can add anything. What am I talking about anyway? Anyway, what we need is light. . . ."

He ran up on the porch, and groped round inside the open front door. The electric lights of the hall glowed out; gloomy enough, but better than the darkness. They stood in the light as they might have stood before a fire on a cold day.

"All we can do," said Hugh, sitting down on the step, "is

to take it easy and wait until Murch gets back with some—some minions." (That, he thought, was an idiotic word to use; like somebody in a bad play. "Minions!" What put that into his head?)

Morgan nodded. He stood bracing himself against the doorway, the collar of his blazer drawn up, and his face turned away.

"Uh. Yes, that's all. Question is, who is this Langdon down there, and why should he get killed?"

"I don't know why he should get killed. As to who he was, you'd have to hear all about what happened tonight. It's a longish story, and I don't feel up to it. Not just yet, anyhow. But—" an idea occurred to him, "but at least there's something about it you ought to know."

Automatically Morgan took out his flask and handed it over.

"Fire away," he said.

"Well, the fact is that my old man—the bishop, you know—got an idea into his head that you were the murderer; or, at least, a pretty suspicious character."

The other did not seem surprised. He let out a long breath, as though facts were being faced at last. "Ah! *Enfin.* I've been waiting for that. It was sure to occur to somebody, and I'm not surprised it was your father; I could see he had his eye on me. But why?"

"Chiefly it was about that footprint; the one around the side of the house here, made with Morley Standish's shoe. He had a theory that you had gone up to The Grange to steal those shoes; gone in through the secret passage in the oak room to get to the junk closet, without knowing anybody was sleeping there; and, when you find it had an occupant, you played poltergeist to cover your retreat."

Morgan turned, staring.

"Holy—!" he said, and struck the back of his head. "Now there's a suggestion that hadn't occurred to me. About the shoes, I mean. But the rest of it—yes, I was expecting it to happen."

"The idea's all wrong, of course. Spinelli proved that tonight. It was Depping himself who wore the shoes for his masquerade; I heard Spinelli say so. Afterwards he probably hid them somewhere in the house. But my old man worked up rather a plausible theory, proving that you couldn't have known the vicar was in the house, and the rest of it. Doesn't matter now. We know you weren't the poltergeist . . ."

Morgan frowned. "Certainly I was the poltergeist," he said. "That's just it. Do you mean to say you didn't find the clue I deliberately left? That's what I was worried about. I wanted to be true to tradition, and, besides, I was full of cocktails; so I dropped a little red notebook with my initials on it. After all, damn it," he pointed out argumentatively, "the sleuths ought to have something to work on."

"You mean . . ."

"Uh. It gave me some bad moments, when I thought about it afterwards." He kicked moodily at the jamb of the door. "Penalty of childishness. It makes me want to kick myself when I think of—of this. Not so entertaining, is it, when it's real? But I was the poltergeist, all right. And it's perfectly true: I *didn't* know the vicar was sleeping in that room. I didn't know he was in the house at all."

After a pause, he turned again with a guilty expression.

"As a matter of fact, that demonstration was intended for your old man . . . It was like this. I've got a habit of taking about a six-mile walk every night, late—incidentally, I was caught out in that storm last night, and hadn't any alibi; never mind. Well, I knew the bishop was staying at The Grange; he'd made a point of sitting on me hard and frequently, because of the detective stories. On the poltergeist night I was coming back from my walk, and cutting across the park, when I saw a light go on in the oak room. I thought, 'What ho!' and I put two and two together, because the room isn't usually occupied. And the bishop knew the story of the haunting. But, just to make sure, I sneaked round to the side door of the servants' hall, and collared old Dibbs—that's the butler. I said, 'Where is His reverence sleeping?' And Dibbs said, 'In the oak room.'"

Wryly Morgan moved his glasses up and down his nose. "Well, what did I naturally think? I didn't know it was poor old Primley. I swore Dibbs to silence with a new, crisp jimmy-o'goblin—and I'll bet he hasn't betrayed me yet. Ha. The more I thought about it, the better I liked the idea. I went home, and had a few drinks with Madeleine, and the idea got better and better. You know the rest."

He came over and sat down on the step.

"And I saw Spinelli that night," he said abruptly. "Going down over the hill to the Guest House here, just as the bishop said. But I couldn't tell the colonel so, could I? And nobody believed the bishop—and this business came on." He stabbed his finger down the lawn.

The moon was low now, a deathly radiance through the trees towards the west. A mist had begun to creep over the lawn, in the hour of suicides, and the black despair of those who lie awake; a cold, luminous mist, that came out to take Spinelli's body. Hugh felt an increasing sense of disquiet. A party from The Grange should have arrived by this time. "It's a wonder," he said, "that the whole county wasn't wakened by that shooting. Why there isn't anybody here—why we've got to sit like a couple of corpse-watchers—"

"Madeleine!" said Morgan, sitting up straight. "My God, she must have heard it as plainly as we did. She'll be picturing me . . ." He jumped up. "Look here, this won't do. Post of duty or no post of duty, I've got to hop back to my place—for a few minutes, anyhow—and tell her I'm alive. I'll be back in five minutes. Is it all right?"

Hugh nodded. But he wished very fervently that half-a-dozen people, talkative people, would come into that clearing with lights and set about removing the sniper's trophies. As Morgan strode off down the misty lawn, he moved into the exact center of the light that streamed from the open door. What he ought to do was go into the house and switch on every lamp. Besides, it was devilish cold; he could see his breath. But whether it would do any good, even if the whole house blazed like a cinema theatre . . .

Hesitantly he went into the hall. It was even more depressing than it had looked that afternoon: the soiled yellow matting, the black portieres, the black furniture smelling of stale furniture polish, the speaking tube in the wall. He understood a little better now. It was not only empty at this moment, but it had always been empty. Old Depping had never actually lived here. It had only been the place where he hung up one of his masks; an unsatisfied genius, as brilliant as unpleasant, whose fingers had touched everybody in this case, and whose fury was the one thing that made it vivid. You might think to see him coming down those stairs now in his high, prim collar: a sort of grizzle-haired satyr, peering over the bannisters.

Uneasily Hugh wondered whether the body upstairs had been removed. He supposed it had; they were speaking of it this afternoon; but you did not like to think the old man might still be lying with his dead smirk across the desk . . . Automatically Hugh did what he and Murch and Morgan had done when they first entered the house a while ago: he went to the door on the right and glanced through to the room where the sniper had hidden.

There were no electric lights here. Hugh did not try to put on the gas; he kindled his pocket lighter and saw, as before, nothing. A dreary and unfurnished place, which might once have been a drawing-room, smelling of damp wallpaper. But they had kept it clean and dusted. The floor, varnished round the edges and bare-boarded in the middle where a carpet should have been, held no footprints. Nor were there any traces that the sniper had been hit by Murch's fire, though the mantelpiece was gouged with bullets and one of them had smashed the mirror that was a part of it. Only stale cordite fumes, and slivers of broken glass round the window.

His foot creaked on a loose board. In the act of blowing out the lighter, he whirled round. Somebody was moving about in the house.

Impossible to tell the direction of sounds. The noise he heard seemed to have come from upstairs. It would be . . . queer how these inapt words struck him. What he had thought was, it would be embarrassing if old Depping were to walk down the steps now. The bright hallway was full of creakings. Another explanation occurred to him. There was no actual evidence to prove that the murderer had ever left the house at all. They had seen nobody. A slammed door; nothing else. And, if the sniper were still here, there would still be a bullet or two in reserve . . .

"Good morning," said a voice from the back of the hallway. "How do you like your job?"

He recognized the voice, as well as the lumbering step that followed it, in time to be reassured. It was Dr. Fell's voice; but even then there was a difference. It had lost its aggressive rumble. It was heavy, and dull, and full of a bitterness that very few people had ever heard there. Stumping on his cane, catching his breath harshly as though he had been walking hard, Dr. Fell appeared round the corner of the staircase. He was hatless, and had a heavy plaid shawl round his shoulders. His reddish face had lost color; his great white-streaked mop of hair was disarranged. The small eyes, the curved moustache, the mountainous chins, all showed a kind of sardonic weariness.

"I know," he rumbled, and wheezed again. "You want to know what I'm doing here. Well, I'll tell you. Cursing myself."

A pause. His eyes strayed up the dark staircase, and then came back to Donovan.

"Maybe, yes, certainly, if they'd told me about that passage in the oak room . . . Never mind. It was my own fault. I should have investigated for myself. I allowed this to happen!" he snapped, and struck the ferrule of his cane on the matting. "I encouraged it, deliberately encouraged it, so that I could prove my case; but I never meant it to happen. I intended to set the bait, and then head off . . ." His voice grew lower. "This is my last case. I'll never play the omniscient damned fool again."

"Don't you think," said Hugh, "that Spinelli got not very far off what he deserved?"

"I was thinking," said Dr. Fell in a queer voice, "of justice, or what constitutes justice, and other things as open to argument as the number of angels that can dance on the head of a pin. And I couldn't see my way clear as to what to do. This new business"— he pointed toward the door with his cane—"has almost decided it. But I wish it hadn't. I tried to prevent it. Do you know what I've been doing? I've been sitting in a chair in the upstairs hallway at The Grange, after everybody else had gone to bed. I've been sitting there watching the entrance to a passageway giving on a line of bedrooms, where I knew Somebody's bedroom was. I was convinced Somebody would come out of there when the house was asleep, go downstairs, and out for a rendezvous with Spinelli. And if I saw this person, I would know beyond a doubt that I was right. I would intercept this Somebody, and then . . . God knows."

He leaned his great bulk against the newel post of the stairs, blinking over his eyeglasses.

"But in my fine fancy conceit I didn't know about the secret passage in the oak room, that leads outside. Somebody did come out—but not past me. It was very, very easy. Out of one room in a step, into another, down the stairs; and *I* suspected nothing until I heard the shots down here . . ."

"Well, sir?"

"Somebody's room was empty. Across the corridor, the door of the oak room was partly open. A candle had been indiscreetly left there, lighted, on the edge of the mantel—"

"My father put that candle there," said Hugh, "when he explored—"

"It had been lighted," said Dr. Fell, "against Somebody's return. When I saw the piece of panelling open—"

There was something odd in the doctor's manner; something labored; he went on talking as though he were giving a long explanation for the benefit of some person unseen, and using Hugh only as an audience.

"Why," said the latter, "are you telling me this?"

"Because the murderer did not return," replied Dr. Fell. He had raised his voice, and it echoed in the narrow hall. "Because I stood at the entrance to the secret passage on the outside, and waited there until Murch came up over the hill to tell me the news. The murderer could not get back. The murderer was locked out of that house, with all the downstairs windows locked, and every door bolted; shut out tonight as certainly as Depping was shut out here just twenty-four hours ago."

"Then—"

"The whole house is aroused now. It will only be a matter of minutes before the one room is discovered to be empty. Murch knows it already, and so do—several others. A searching party, with flash lights and lanterns, has begun to comb the grounds. The murderer is either hiding somewhere in the grounds, or"— his voice lifted eerily—"is here."

He took his hand off the newel post and stood upright.

"Shall we go upstairs?" he asked gruffly.

After a pause Hugh said quietly, "Right you are, sir. But I suppose Murch told you the fellow's a dead shot, and he's still armed?"

"Yes. That is why, if Somebody is here, and could hear me, I would say: 'For God's sake don't commit the madness and folly of shooting when you are cornered, or you will certainly hang. There is some excuse for you now, but there will be none if you turn your gun on the police.'"

Dr. Fell was already climbing the stairs. He moved slowly and steadily, his cane rapping sharply on every tread; *bump— rap, bump—rap*; and a great shadow of him crouched ahead on the wall.

"I do not intend to look for this person," he said over his shoulder. "You and I, my boy, will go to the study and sit down. Now I am going to turn on the lights in the upstairs hall, here."

A silence. Hugh felt his heart rise in his throat as the switch clicked; the bare, desolate hallway was empty. He thought, however, that he heard a board creak and a door close.

"*Tap-tap, tap-tap* . . . Dr. Fell's cane moved along the uncarpeted floor. His boots squeaked loudly.

In desperation Hugh tried to think of something that would help him. The doctor spoke with quiet steadiness. He was trying to draw the murderer out into the light, delicately, with gloved hands, as you might handle a nest of wasps. And the house was listening again. If the murderer were here, he must have heard in desperation each hope of escape taken from under him; and each tap of the cane must have sounded like another nail . . .

Hugh expected a bullet. He did not believe the sniper would submit without a fight. Nevertheless, he played up to the doctor's lead.

"I suppose you can prove your case?" he asked. "Would it be any good for the murderer to deny guilt?"

"None whatever." Dr. Fell leaned inside the study door. He stood there a moment, looking into darkness, silhouetted against the light if there were anybody inside. Then he pressed the electric switch. The study was as neat as it had been that day, and the body of Depping had been removed. The bright hanging lamp over the desk left most of the room in shadow, but they could see that the chairs still stood as before, and the covered dinner tray on its side-table with the bowl of withered roses.

Dr. Fell glanced round. The door to the balcony, with its chequered red-and-white glass panel, was closed.

For a time he stood motionless, as though musing. Then he walked to one window.

"They're here," he said. "Murch and his searching party. You see the flash lights, down there in the trees? Somebody seems to have a very powerful motorcycle lamp. Yes, they've covered that end of the grounds, and the murderer isn't there. They're coming this way . . ."

Hugh could not keep it back. He turned round, his voice was almost a yell: "For God's sake, you've got to tell me! *Who is it?* Who—"

A beam of white light struck up past the windows. Simultaneously, somebody cried out from below. The number of voices rose to a shouting; feet stamped and rustled in the underbrush, and more beams were directed on the balcony.

Dr. Fell moved over and touched the glass of the door with his stick.

"You'd better come in, you know," he said gently. "It's all up now. They've seen you."

The knob began to turn, and hesitated. There was a clink of glass as the muzzle of a firearm was jabbed towards them against the panel; but Dr. Fell did not move. He remained blinking affably at it, and at the silhouette they could see moving behind the door in the broadening white glare of the flashlights. . . .

"I shouldn't try it, if I were you," he advised. "After all, you know, you've got a chance. Ever since the Edith Thompson case it's been tacitly agreed that they will not hang a woman."

The steel muzzle slid down raspingly, as though the hand that held it had gone weak. A sort of shudder went through the person on the other side of the door; the door wavered, and then was knocked open.

She was pale, so pale that even her lips looked blue. Once those wide-set blue eyes had been determined, and not glazed over with despair. The fine face seemed as old as a hag's; the chin wabbled; only the weariness remained.

"All right. You win," said Betty Depping.

The Mauser pistol rolled over a hand weirdly encased in a yellow rubber glove, and fell on the floor. Dr. Fell caught the girl as she slid down in a dead faint.

CHAPTER XIX

A Highly Probable Story

THE STORY, it is to be feared, has already been told too many times. It has been featured in the public prints, made the subject for leading articles, controversies in women's magazines, homilies, sermons, and the tearful "humanists" of the family pages. Betty Depping—whose name was not Betty Depping, and was no relation to the man she murdered—told the story herself a week before she poisoned herself at Horfield Gaol in Bristol. And that is why Dr. Fell insists to this day that the case was not one of his successes.

"That was the key fact of the whole business," he will say. "The girl wasn't his daughter. She had been his mistress for two years during the time he lived in America. And this was the explanation I had only begun to guess at the end. From the evidence on hand, it was easy to fix on *her* as the killer; that was fairly obvious from the beginning. But her motive puzzled me.

"Now we have the answer, which would appear to lie in Depping's character as well as her own. You see, she was the one woman who had ever succeeded in holding Depping's fancy. When he grew tired of making cutthroat money in the States, and decided to chuck it up and create another character for himself in England (I do not, at this juncture, make any comparisons), he took her along with him. She, by the way, was the 'high-class dame with the Park-Avenue manner' of whom Spinelli spoke to us.

"I think we can read between the lines of her confession. *She* maintains that his original intention was to present her as his wife when he assumed his new character, but that chance prevented it. She says that Depping, in his desire for terrific respectability, overdid it. When he was just completing arrangements to buy a share in the publishing firm, without having said anything of his domestic arrangements, quite by accident J. R. Burke encountered him and the girl unexpectedly in a London hotel. (You may remember that she told us a rather similar story, while pretending she really was his daughter?) Depping, playing his part clumsily, and flustered at being discovered with a young and pretty girl without a wedding ring, imagined that it might hurt his chances for social respectability; and at a somewhat crucial time. So he blurted out that she was his daughter, and was afterwards obliged to stick to his story. Hence, if scandal were to be averted, the girl must live abroad. If she lived in the same house, he might forget himself and become too loverlike where others—such as servants—could observe it. The scandal attendant on a supposed 'father' making love to his daughter would make the other affair seem innocuous by comparison.

"This, as I say, is her version. You may accept it if you like, but I should have thought Depping to have been too careful and far-seeing a plotter to have been forced, by an unexpected encounter, into such an awkward stratagem. I think he maneuvered the girl into this position so as to be quit of her—except on such occasions as he could forget his rôle of country gentleman and pay her amorous visits at not-too-frequent intervals. Hence the flat in Paris, the supposed 'lady companion' (who did not exist), and the whole fiction manufactured about her past life. Depping, you see, really believed that he could *will* himself into his new character. He saw no necessity for putting her out of his life. His arrangement, he thought, was ideal. He had a genuine love of scholarship and his new pursuits; and, if he placed her in this position, no mistress could make awkward demands on his time. He could see her when he wished; at other times, she would be kept a convenient distance away. A good deal of Depping's character is in that proceeding.

"But, as was inevitable, he grew tired of his new life. A good deal, I suspect, because his circle had made it pretty uncomfortable for him. They didn't like him, or 'admit him,' or give him the sense of power to which he had been used. They made it clear that he was being put up with only because of his value to business. Hence his outbursts and his fits of drinking.

"At length he determined to chuck it up and go away; to start a new life among new people. He should keep a certain 'respectability,' and take the girl along either as wife or mistress. And at that juncture, two complications appeared, grew, and wrecked everything. Spinelli appeared, and the girl had fallen in love— genuinely, she declared—with Morley Standish.

"I recommend that you read her confession. It is a curious document: a combination of sincerity, cynicism, school-girl naïvete, matured wisdom, lies, and astonishing flights of cheap rhetoric. Make what you can of it. 'Patsy Mulholland' she signs herself. During all her association with Depping she seems at once to have hated considerably, loved a little, despised a little, and admired a good deal. She had a sort of instinctive gentility and poise; small education, but the wit to conceal that; and a good taste that Depping would never have.

"Inevitably, he had to bring her to England at intervals. At The Grange they liked her, and Morley Standish fell in love with her. She fell in love with him, she says. I remember one passage in her evidence. 'He was comfortable,' she said. 'The sort I wanted. One hates (sic!) one hates existence with a combination ice box and tiger.' When I think of that girl, cool to the last, sitting before the magistrates and talking in this fashion . . .

"Whatever the truth of the matter, it was a dazzling opportunity. She must play it coolly. To Depping she must laugh at his infatuation, and Depping will even assist and encourage it; *because, he thinks, it will bring about his revenge on the people who have slighted him.*

"Depping, you see, was already perfecting his plans for departure with her, and she was agreeing to them. 'Encourage him!' says Depping. 'Get engaged to him; flaunt it in their faces.' It inspired him with a triumphant delight. Then, when the news of the engagement was published, he himself would announce the real state of affairs, bow ironically, and sail away with the bride. If you can readily conceive any better way to make a laughingstock of people you hate, I should be interested to hear it.

"In fact, it was a bit too perfect. Betty (let's call her that) had no intention of permitting it. The issue was clear-cut. She was going to become Mrs. Morley Standish. The only way she could become Mrs. Morley Standish, and put the past entirely behind her, was to kill Depping.

"It was not merely a case of cold resolve, though that was the beginning of it. The girl seems to have indulged in a sort of self-hypnosis; of convincing herself that she had been bitterly and unfairly treated; of working up the state of her wrongs in her own mind until she genuinely believed in them. In her confession, a hysterical outburst against Depping precedes a statement wherein she prides herself on the workmanlike way she set about to plan his murder.

"For Spinelli had already appeared. And Spinelli was a serious threat to both of them. That Spinelli, when he accidently came across Depping in England, knew Depping's former mistress was still with him in the pose of his daughter, I am inclined to doubt. But Depping decided he must be put out of the way. To begin with, he might spoil Depping's last 'joke'—engaging his supposed daughter to Morley Standish—before Depping was ready to reveal it. But most of all because he would now be a blackmailing leech on Depping wherever he went, and in whatever character he chose to assume. In brief, he was not so much a menace as a nuisance. And Depping had a curt way of dealing with nuisances.

"Betty Depping encouraged his design while she was formulating one of her own. Spinelli could be a very deadly danger to *her*. She corresponded with Depping about means for putting Spinelli out of the way: monstrously indiscreet letters. Depping wisely destroyed all she sent him, but a packet of his letters was found in her flat in Paris. One, dated two nights before the murder, informs her that he had procured 'the necessities,' and 'arranged a meeting with S. in a suitably lonely spot for Friday night.'

"The details I dare say she did not know. The interesting thing is that by this time she had worked herself into a bitter, wild, virtuous, crusading rage against Depping, mixed with a certain music-hall theatricality. 'I felt,' she says—and almost seems to mean it—'that I would be ridding the world of a monster.' Did anybody ever really talk like that? Oh, yes. Talk. But her actions show the intrinsic falsity of the emotion. I don't wish to do the woman an injustice; and I thoroughly agree that the world was well rid of Depping. I am only pointing out that she slightly overdid her emotion when she painted that little card of the eight swords . . ."

This is what Dr. Fell will say before you ask him to explain his means of determining the guilty person.

Hugh Donovan, in the ensuing months, heard the details many times. It has always been a favorite topic of conversation at The Grange, where he has been a frequent visitor, due to asking Patricia Standish to marry him, and being accepted, and also learning firmly to utter a certain vigorous phrase to his prospective mother-in-law. Maw Standish maintains (between listening to the wireless, and assuring the colonel that his mind, for the head of a great publishing house, is in a deplorable state and needs improving), Maw maintains she knew of Betty Depping's perfidy all the time; and also that the trip around the world is doing Morley good. These endings are eminently commonplace and probable, you will perceive, and serve fittingly to conclude a probable story.

But, as regards explanations, Hugh remembers best a conversation in J. R. Burke's office, one wet and murky October afternoon in the same year, when several of the characters were sitting round a fire, and Dr. Fell talked.

Dr. Fell was smoking J. R.'s cigars, which were kept rather for effect than for use, and leaning back amicably in a leather chair. Outside the rain was pattering in Paternoster Row, and the dingy tangle of window fronts that straggle under the shadow of Paul's dome. The fire was bright, the cigars good; and J. R., having locked the door of the book-lined room against his secretary, had produced whisky. Henry Morgan was there, having just brought up to London the completed manuscript of his new book, *Aconite in the Admiralty*. Hugh was there also, but not the bishop. And Dr. Fell had been talking in the fashion indicated, when J. R. interrupted him.

"Get on to the point," he grunted. "Tell us why you thought the girl was guilty. We don't want these characterizations. Not in a detective story, anyhow. The public will only glance at this chapter, to make sure it hasn't been cheated by having evidence withheld. If you've got any reasons, let's hear 'em. Otherwise—"

"Exactly," agreed Morgan. "After all, this is only a detective story. It only concerns the little emotions that go into the act of murdering somebody."

"Shut up." said J. R. austerely.

Dr. Fell blinked at his cigar. "But that's quite right, nevertheless. It wouldn't be true to life. It wouldn't be true to life, for instance, if a modern novelist devoted to motives for murder the same profound and detailed analysis he devotes to little Bertie's early life among the dandelions, or the sinister Freudian motives behind his desire to kiss the housemaid. Humph. When an inhibition bites a man, it's a fine novel. When a man up and bites an inhibition, it's only a detective story."

"The Russians—" said J. R.

'I knew it," said Dr. Fell querulously. "I was afraid of that. I decline to discuss the Russians. After long and thoughtful reflection, I have come to the conclusion that the only adequate answer to one who begins rhapsodizing about the Russians is a swift uppercut to the jaw. Besides, I find it absolutely impossible to become passionately interested in the agonies and misfortunes of any character whose name ends in 'ski' or 'vitch.' This may be insularity. It may also be a disturbing sense that, from what I read, these people are not human beings at all. Ah, God," said Dr. Fell musingly, "if only somebody would make a bad pun! If only Popoff would say to Whiskervitch, "Who was that lady I seen you with last night?" Try to imagine a conversation, in the after life, between Mark Twain or Anatole France and any of the leading Russians, and you will have some vague glimmering of what I mean."

J. R. snorted. "You don't know what you're talking about. And, besides, *get back to the subject*. This is the last chapter, and we want to get it over with."

Dr. Fell mused a while.

"The extraordinary feature about the Depping murder," he rumbled, after refreshing himself with whisky, "is that the thing explained itself, if you only bothered to inquire what the facts meant.

"I had a strong inkling of who the murderer was long before I had met her. The first fact that established itself beyond any question was that the murderer was definitely NOT one of the little community at or around The Grange. And the murderer was not only an outsider, but an outsider who had known Depping in his past (and, at that time) unknown life."

"Why?"

"Let us begin with the attempted murder of Spinelli by Depping, at the point in our previous deductions where we had decided that it was Depping who left the house in disguise and came back to it through the front door. The problem was this: Was Depping working with a confederate whom he had planted in that room as an alibi? Or was he working alone, and X somebody who had come unexpectedly to that room with the intent to kill—only helping him in his deception when X saw the opportunity of an alibi for him (or her)self? In either case, were there any indications as to X's identity?

"Very well. Now, all the weight of evidence lay *against* Depping's having a confederate. To begin with, why did he NEED a confederate at all? It's a very poor alibi, you know, merely to put somebody in a room; somebody who can't show himself, or act for you, or prove you are there. If Depping had genuinely wanted an alibi for his presence in that room, he would have had a confederate *do* something that could have testified to his presence . . . running the typewriter, for example. Or even moving about or making conspicuous sounds of any sort. But it didn't happen. And what's the good of an alibi that doesn't alibi, but merely puts you into the power of your confederate? Why share a secret that you don't have to share at all?

"Which brings us to the second and most powerful objection. Depping was acting a part before that community. The last thing in the world he would think of doing would be to reveal himself: to tell what he was—"

"Hold on!" interrupted J. R. "I made that objection myself. He couldn't tell anybody what he'd been, or that he intended to go out and murder Spinelli; he didn't know or trust anybody well enough for that. But somebody"—he sighted over his eyeglasses at Morgan—"invented a long yarn about an 'innocent victim,' who had been persuaded by Depping to stay there on the grounds that he was playing a practical joke on somebody, and afterwards the accomplice couldn't reveal the plot without incriminating himself."

Dr. Fell followed the direction of his glance at Morgan, and chuckled.

"Consider it," he said. "Can any of you conceive of a person from whom an excuse of that sort would come with less plausibility than from *Depping*? Could any of your community, Morgan, imagine Depping in the role of light and graceful practical joker? If he had come to you with a proposition of that sort, would you have believed him or assisted him? . . . I doubt it. But the real objection lies in the eight of swords. If you believe in an innocent confederate, what becomes of that symbol and trademark of the murderer? How did it come there? Why did an innocent confederate bring it there to begin with?

"We will consider that card next. For the moment, we establish in theory that Depping had no confederate (a) because he didn't need one, and (b) because he would not have dared to reveal himself: which thesis I can prove in another way. As actual evidence of this, we have your evidence, J. R. . . ."

"Hated to give it," said the other. "Thought it might give you ideas." He snorted.

"When you called on Depping, he was startled to hear a knock even when he couldn't see you. That's not the behavior of a man expecting an accomplice. Furthermore, he first took the key out of his pocket to unlock the door, and later you saw him through the glass putting it back in his pocket when he'd locked the door after you.

"In brief, he was going out alone, and he was going to lock the door and take the key when he went to kill Spinelli."

Dr. Fell tapped his finger on the chair arm.

"In deciding where to look for Depping's murderer—the person who had come into that house unseen, and was waiting for him when he returned—there were several suggestions. One of them is so obvious that it's comic."

"Well?"

"The murderer," said Dr. Fell, "*ate Depping's dinner.*"

There was a silence. Then the doctor shook his head.

"Reflect, if you please, on the monstrous, the solemn, the glaring give-away of that fact. Look at it from all angles, if you would try to convince me that the murderer was somebody *from that community*. Study the fantastic picture of Colonel Standish, of Mrs. Standish, of Morley Standish, of Morgan, of yourself . . . of anybody you like to name, going up to kill Depping, finding him not at home, and then whiling away the time by sitting down and eating a hearty meal off the tray of the man you shortly expect to kill! Of, if you prefer, imagine any one of those people paying an ordinary social visit, unexpectedly, and eating the dinner they happen to find conveniently on a tray! It's not only absurd; it's unthinkable.

"That's why I remarked that the case explained itself. There is only one explanation that can account for it. When I was meditating over this astonishing behavior of X, I said, 'Why did he eat Depping's dinner?' Morley Standish triumphantly replied, 'Because he was hungry.' But it didn't seem to occur to anybody that X was hungry because X *had come from some distance away, and in a hurry.* It did not seem plain that people who eat normal dinners in the neighborhood of The Grange are not apt to behave in this fashion.

"The corollary to this not-very-complicated deduction is that X not only came from some distance away, but was so thoroughly intimate with Depping that he (or she) could sit down and eat a dinner like that without ever thinking twice about it. It's the sort of thing you might do with a close relative, but few other people. You have only to ask yourself, 'How many people *were* close enough to Depping to fit into this picture?' And on top of that you will inquire about the key. How many people would have a key which fitted Depping's balcony door? Depping locked it when he went out, and X had to get in."

"Yes, but X might have come in the front door—" Morgan was beginning, when he saw the flaw and stopped. "I see. It would be the same whichever door was used. X couldn't ring and be let in by the valet."

"Certainly not for the purpose in mind," said Dr. Fell; "that is, murdering Depping. Now, to the combination of these two things, a person with keys to the house yet living a great distance away, is added another significant circumstance . . . After his attempted murder of Spinelli, Depping returned. It was then he discovered that somewhere on the way he had lost his key to the balcony door. He went up, looked through the window, and saw X in possession. Would he have revealed himself so readily to some member of the neighborhood; gone into conversation; agreed to the scheme for walking in the front door; unless the person inside had been . . . who? And the answer that occurred to me in my innocence was: a daughter, who, being a daughter, he thought would not betray him. The fact that she was his mistress I didn't know, but the rule still works.

"Now we come to that mysterious eight of swords. The curious part there was that not only was there nobody there who knew what it meant, but that nobody had ever heard of Depping's interest in the occult. He never mentioned it, he never played with fortune-telling packs, though his bookshelves were stuffed with works on the subject . . . I filed away the idea, still wondering, when—as soon as Spinelli appeared on the scene— *he* recognized it. It was definitely a part of Depping's dark past. The murderer, then, was somebody who had known Depping in America; or, at least, known something of Depping that nobody else did.

"With my growing suspicion of the daughter in my mind, I tried to couple it with this fact. It was corroboration, even though it had never entered my head to suspect the daughter of being anything else than she pretended *until* Spinelli and Langdon were on the scene.

"I noticed how all references to the daughter were scrupulously kept out of their talk. What Langdon did was to hint at a 'mysterious woman' with whom Depping was going to run away: Why did he do that? Then Spinelli made a slip and revealed that he knew the amount of Depping's estate. Whatever you deduce from this, you will admit that these two—between them—knew something about Depping's past life out of which they both believed they could make capital.

"Spinelli I could understand, because I believed he knew who the killer was. But what could both of them have known, which would be of profit? What had Langdon found out? And the first faint suggestion began to come to me, though I didn't believe it. This daughter, who didn't live with her father, although—*vide* Morley Standish—he was 'always worrying about her, and what she was doing'; this card of the taroc that Depping only used in America, and whose painting in water color suggested a woman; this queer attitude of the lawyer . . .

"For, you see, if Betty Depping were not really his daughter, it would be an excellent thing for Langdon. I mean blackmail. 'Split half the estate with me, or you get none.' And it would fit in exactly . . ."

Dr. Fell waved his hand.

"What happened was simply this. We know it from the girl's confession. She came over from Paris that Friday night with the intention of killing Depping. She didn't know where Depping would be, except that he would be out on Spinelli's trail, and she wanted him to do that piece of work for them both before she shot him. She was prepared with a pistol—the same one she later used on Spinelli and Langdon.

"She came up on the balcony and let herself in through the door. Depping had already gone. But she saw . . . you understand?"

Morgan nodded, abstractedly. "His disguise preparations, his own clothes left behind, and all the traces of that masquerade."

"Exactly. She knew he was out after Spinelli in disguise. As yet the brilliant idea had not occurred to her. She could not have known Depping had lost his key. But it did occur—she says with some pride—when she heard Depping fumble at the door, and say he was locked out. You know what happened. She short-circuited the lights with her rubber glove, and the comedy was played.

"Meantime, Spinelli had followed Depping back from the river. He saw everything, and heard everything at the window. The woman got Depping back into his ordinary clothes, her stage set; and then she did not have to use her own pistol at all. She picked up Depping's own gun from the desk—not wearing her gloves, of course—sat on the arm of his chair, and shot him. Afterwards she wiped off the gun, blew out the candles, and left . . . to meet Spinelli on the lawn below.

"He was careful. He took away the handbag in which she carried the other pistol; got it out of her grasp first, and removed the bullets, before he talked business. He had her cornered. She couldn't give him all he demanded; she protested that Depping hadn't been as rich as Spinelli thought. But let her get away from the place, she swore, and she would arrange something, and agreed to meet him on that spot the following night to discuss terms.

"*Eheu!* Naturally she never went back to Paris at all. She caught the last bus to Bristol, where she had a hotel room under another name. She then took a morning train to London; put through a trunk call to Paris, to the maid at her flat (who had been well coached from the beginning) and found that the telegram informing her of her father's death had arrived. So, allowing a reasonable time, she called on Langdon in Gray's Inn Square, and asked him to accompany her down to The Grange . . . But Langdon, you see, knew she was not really Depping's daughter. On the way down, he informed her of it. Depping had been indiscreet, and told him the whole story.

"He wanted half, to which she agreed. Meanwhile, Langdon was wondering how he could connect up this murder with the phone call he had had from Spinelli, saying that he (Spinelli) was on the point of being arrested for murder and asking for advice. Langdon jumped to the conclusion— which was true—that Spinelli knew the facts of his own case: *viz.*, that the girl was not Depping's daughter. Langdon hinted as much to her.

"And *she* invented a brilliant scheme for disposing of them both. She said that Spinelli did know, and was asking for his share of hush money. She told him that she was to meet Spinelli at the Guest House that night: Would he, Langdon, be along, and use moral terrors, or legal terrors, or both, in an attempt to intimidate Spinelli?

"It nearly fell through; because, you see, we confronted Spinelli with Langdon, and they had the opportunity to confer in private. You can understand now Langdon's horror and nervousness when I announced that Spinelli was ready to *talk*. He thought I meant talk of what he knew about the girl. But the girl's scheme worked because Langdon's suspicions were aroused at Spinelli's talk, and he wondered whether 'Betty Depping' mightn't have deeper reasons for wishing silence all around than that matter of her identity.

"We shall never know what passed between Spinelli and Langdon at their interview. Langdon realized that Spinelli knew something more; but he kept his own counsel, and determined to be present that night—unseen and unheard—at the rendezvous between Spinelli and the girl."

Dr. Fell threw his cigar into the fire. He leaned back and listened to the rain.

"They were both marked," he said. "You know what happened."

"Moral observations," remarked J. R., after a silence, "are now in order. Somebody will have to talk for a page or two on the futility and sadness of it, and how she would have been safe if only she hadn't left one-little-damning clue behind . . ."

"It won't go, I'm afraid," said Dr. Fell. He chuckled. "The one-little-damning clue was a large and many-caloried dinner, steaming before your noses. You might as well say that the Guiness advertisements plastered over the hoardings are a clue to the theory that somebody is trying to sell stout."

J. R. scowled. "All the same," he said, "I'm glad that the only detective plot in which I ever took part was not full of improbabilities and wild situations, like—well, like Morgan's *Murder on the Woolsack* or *Aconite at the Admiralty*. There are no fiendish under-clerks shooting poisoned darts through keyholes at the First Sea-Lord, or luxurious secret dens of the Master Criminal at Limehouse. What I mean by probability . . ."

Hugh looked round in some surprise to see that Morgan was gurgling with rage.

"And you think," Morgan inquired, "that *this* is a probable story?"

"Isn't it?" asked Hugh. "It's exactly like one of those stories by William Block Tournedos. As Mr. Burke says . . ."

Morgan sank back.

"Oh, well!" he said. "Never mind. Let's have a drink."

THE END

DISCUSSION QUESTIONS

- Were you able to predict any part of the solution to the case?

- After learning the solution, were there any clues you realized you had missed?

- Did any aspects of the plot date the story? If so, which ones?

- Would the story be different if it were set in the present day? If so, how?

- Did the social context of the time play a role in the narrative? If so, how?

- If you were one of the main characters, would you have acted differently at any point in the story?

- Did this novel remind you of any contemporary authors today?

- Did this novel remind you of other titles in the American Mystery Classics series?

- What kind of detective is Dr. Gideon Fell?

- If you've read others of Carr's works, how did this book compare?

MORE

JOHN DICKSON CARR

AVAILABLE FROM

AMERICAN MYSTERY CLASSICS

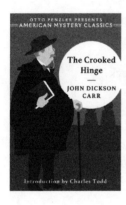  

THE CROOKED HINGE
Introduced by Charles Todd

THE MAD HATTER MYSTERY
Introduced by Otto Penzler

THE PLAGUE COURT MURDERS
Introduced by Michael Dirda

OTTO PENZLER PRESENTS
══ **AMERICAN MYSTERY CLASSICS** ══

All Titles Introduced by Otto Penzler
Unless Otherwise Noted

Charlotte Armstrong, *The Chocolate Cobweb*
Introduced by A. J. Finn
Charlotte Armstrong, *The Unsuspected*

Anthony Boucher, *The Case of the Baker Street Irregulars*
Anthony Boucher, *Rocket to the Morgue*
Introduced by F. Paul Wilson

Fredric Brown, *The Fabulous Clipjoint*
Introduced by Lawrence Block

John Dickson Carr, *The Crooked Hinge*
Introduced by Charles Todd
John Dickson Carr, *The Mad Hatter Mystery*
John Dickson Carr, *The Plague Court Murders*
Introduced by Michael Dirda

Todd Downing, *Vultures in the Sky*
Introduced by James Sallis

Mignon G. Eberhart, *Murder by an Aristocrat*
Introduced by Nancy Pickard

Erle Stanley Gardner, *The Case of the Baited Hook*
Erle Stanley Gardner, *The Case of the Careless Kitten*
Erle Stanley Gardner, *The Case of the Borrowed Brunette*

Frances Noyes Hart, *The Bellamy Trial*
Introduced by Hank Phillippi Ryan

H.F. Heard, *A Taste for Honey*

Dolores Hitchens, *The Cat Saw Murder*
Introduced by Joyce Carol Oates

Dorothy B. Hughes, *Dread Journey*
Introduced by Sarah Weinman
Dorothy B. Hughes, *Ride the Pink Horse*
Introduced by Sara Paretsky
Dorothy B. Hughes, *The So Blue Marble*

W. Bolingbroke Johnson, *The Widening Stain*
Introduced by Nicholas A. Basbanes

Baynard Kendrick, *The Odor of Violets*

Frances and Richard Lockridge, *Death on the Aisle*

John P. Marquand, *Your Turn, Mr. Moto*
Introduced by Lawrence Block

Stuart Palmer, *The Puzzle of the Happy Hooligan*

Otto Penzler, ed., *Golden Age Detective Stories*

Ellery Queen, *The American Gun Mystery*
Ellery Queen, *The Chinese Orange Mystery*
Ellery Queen, *The Dutch Shoe Mystery*
Ellery Queen, *The Egyptian Cross Mystery*
Ellery Queen, *The Siamese Twin Mystery*

Patrick Quentin, *A Puzzle for Fools*
Clayton Rawson, *Death from a Top Hat*

Craig Rice, *Eight Faces at Three*
Introduced by Lisa Lutz
Craig Rice, *Home Sweet Homicide*

Mary Roberts Rinehart, *The Haunted Lady*
Mary Roberts Rinehart, *Miss Pinkerton*
Introduced by Carolyn Hart
Mary Roberts Rinehart, *The Red Lamp*
Mary Roberts Rinehart, *The Wall*

Joel Townsley Rogers, *The Red Right Hand*
Introduced by Joe R. Lansdale

Vincent Starrett, *The Great Hotel Murder*
Introduced by Lyndsay Faye

Cornell Woolrich, *The Bride Wore Black*
Introduced by Eddie Muller
Cornell Woolrich, *Waltz into Darkness*
Introduced by Wallace Stroby